R0200829299

01/2020

D0368897

PRAISE FOR *THE COMPANION*

"A vivid and sensuous domestic drama, *The Companion* is also an atmospheric crime story."

—Emma Donoghue, bestselling author of *Room*

"Sarah Waters fans, welcome to your next obsession. *The Companion* is an elegantly written tale of beautiful lies and ugly secrets, a reminder that love's transforming power makes not just angels, but monsters. Telling one from the other will keep you guessing until the end."

—Greer Macallister, bestselling author of *The Magician's Lie* and *Woman 99*

"As her date with the gallows approaches, Lucy Blunt is struggling to understand why she is at odds with society. In a literary tradition stretching from *Jane Eyre* to *Alias Grace*, her intoxicating account took me to another time and place, a confession with the illicit excitement of a thriller. *The Companion* offers everything I like about modern historical fiction; a resonant voice that brings women's lives out of the shadows."

—Jo Furniss, bestselling author of *All the Little Children* and *The Trailing Spouse*

"*The Companion* is a brilliant study of all that makes us human—our terrors, regrets, passions, and the lies that shape our worlds. Kim Taylor Blakemore's novel is both astonishing and captivating, and will leave readers spellbound."

—Lydia Kang, bestselling author of *A Beautiful Poison* and *The Impossible Girl*

"A vividly-rendered and chilling tale of murder, desire and obsession."
—Sophia Tobin, bestselling author of *The Vanishing*

"With exquisitely vivid and lyrical writing and a subtly layered narrative, *The Companion* is a fascinating and beautiful novel. If you enjoy Sarah Waters, you'll love Kim Taylor Blakemore's latest."
—Lily Hammond, author of *The Way Home*, *Alice & Jean* and *Violet*

"*The Companion* is a totally absorbing read - beautifully written, atmospheric and intriguing. Kim Taylor Blakemore's characterization is both convincing and compelling as she evokes the gritty reality of nineteenth-century life to great effect. I loved this book."
—Lindsay Jayne Ashford, bestselling author of *The Woman on the Orient Express*

"The narrator is riveting. The prose, gorgeous."
—Ron Hansen, National Book Award Nominated author of *Atticus*, *The Assassination of Jesse James by the Coward Robert Ford*, and *Mariette in Ecstasy*

"Reading *The Companion*, I felt myself pulled authentically into a distant time and tale reminiscent of Charlotte Bronte and Henry James. Blakemore's mastery of language and character lend credence to her absorbing narrative of guilt or innocence as a young woman of mysterious identity awaits hanging. There is a body count, right from the opening of the novel. From there, the reader follows Blakemore through almost effortless shifts of time and circumstance, rendered in magnificent language, to an unexpected finality. This is a haunting tale that will remain in the reader's consciousness for a long time."
—Diane C. McPhail, author of *The Abolitionist's Daughter*

The
COMPANION

ALSO BY KIM TAYLOR BLAKEMORE

Bowery Girl

Cissy Funk

The
COMPANION
A NOVEL

KIM TAYLOR BLAKEMORE

LAKE UNION
PUBLISHING

Text copyright © 2020 by Kim Taylor Blakemore

Published by Lake Union Publishing, Seattle

www.apub.com

Amazon, the Amazon logo, and Lake Union Publishing are trademarks of Amazon.com, Inc., or its affiliates.

ISBN-13: 9781542009669 (hardcover)
ISBN-10: 1542009669 (hardcover)
ISBN-13: 9781542006392 (paperback)
ISBN-10: 1542006392 (paperback)

Cover design by Shasti O'Leary Soudant

Cover photography by Richard Jenkins Photography

Printed in the United States of America

First Edition

For Dana, always

Chapter One

New Hampshire State Prison

1855

Count the bodies.

One. Two.

Three if we count Mary Dawson.

Four if we count my Ned, who breathed and suckled three days and nights before succumbing to the ague.

All blamed on me.

It is cold here. The last of winter. Wednesday, I think. Matron has brought another blanket but not lit the stove. Fingers of cold claw my collar; the mist cuts my lungs. Knives of ice.

Mary Dawson died in winter. Maybe Mary should be blamed. She was found facedown in a frozen brook, on her way home from the Burtons' after finishing the laundry and washing up. The men chipped her out of the ice, carried her like a board on their shoulders, her overcoat and skirts frozen in the patterns of the water's ripples and flows.

It was to be her last day at the great house. She had been promised to Thomas Rogers in Peterboro. He was a cooper, though that has no bearing on her unhappy death. I've heard she was of fine character. She gave her wages to her family and was deemed good-natured. People called her "sweet" and "helpful" and "cheerful." Drop those words in a pot and stir and they might congeal into the word "thick."

Cook called me rude when I said that, though she did not deny it.

Mary Dawson was nothing to me then but a story. She was dead and the Burtons required a maid.

It was deep winter. The snow banked against the trunks and limbs of bare trees. It cracked under my boots, clicked and rattled in my hair. It rested in the seams of brick on the great house before me. The oil lamps flanking the wide stone staircase hissed and fluttered. They lit nothing, their glow meek in the purpling afternoon light. The curtains were closed on the tall windows, and the only sign of life came orange and warm through the thin slits of fabric.

I was not meant to call there. I was meant for the back entrance. I weaved around the carriages waiting in the drive between the stable and the house. Steam lifted from the feed bags twined round the horses' nostrils. I pressed into the shoulder and neck of a chestnut mare, thankful for the warmth, wondering if I would make the last steps.

The door to Josiah Burton's kitchen was thick. I could not coax the glove from my frozen fingers, my knock a dull thump against the wood. There was a squeal of metal, a lock tumbled, a door opening. The fat hand of the woman holding the handle connected to a round shoulder. Her jowl swung in disapproval, and her skin was gray from winter, red from kitchen heat. Colorless eyes ticked. I could tell she didn't like my features. Steam floated off her, as her stove-warmed body met the February air.

"Yes?"

My lips felt clumsy, heavy as lead. "Lucy Blunt, mum."

"And?"

"I've come in place of Mary, mum."

She said nothing. Her eyelids fluttered and then lowered, her lips moving as if sending a silent prayer.

"Mr. Beede hired me. This morning."

"Did he?"

"I've got excellent references," I lied. Who's to know? I had letters in my pocket, letters of reference extolling my virtues. I had made sure to find three different types of paper, used three different pens and ink.

"Give them over."

I took them from my satchel.

She did not read them. Just pocketed them in her apron instead.

"You're old for a washer-up."

"Twenty-two."

"The mistress is particular."

"So am I." I felt the wind against my neck. I wanted nothing more at that moment than to shove my way in and throw myself directly against the stove. "I have strong hands. She won't find anything wrong with my work."

The air in the room waved with heat. It was so close—a step away.

"Please, mum."

The woman's sigh filled with pity, rumbly and moist. "Then get in the door before my fingers are frozen to it."

I slid past her. The door was shut, a key lifted and pressed, the lock turned.

"Clean those pots," she said. "The master's having a party and you'd better know what you're doing. I've got chicken coming out and potatoes to fry, and I need that pot for a stock. Water for cleaning's on the left range near you. And I'll need you to clean the serving platters, and I mean with a gleam."

"Where do I put my satchel, ma'am?"

"Give it here. And it's not ma'am. Nor mum. Cook will do." She tossed my bag into the low-ceiling pot room. "Have you lodging tonight?"

"Not yet."

"You'll sleep here, then." She stared at me, as if assessing my worth. "If you're good, you'll stay on."

There it was: the great cast-iron stove, all filled with food. Boiling, frying, baking. Sputtering and warm and lovely. Close by sat the pump and sink, and Lord, already too many pots. A thick pine table ran down the middle of the room. The white shelves along the inner wall were filled with plates and glasses, dainty and fine.

"What are you staring at?"

"Nothing, Cook."

"Exactly, stupid. The serving trays are in the cabinet below the shelves. The towels are on the rungs. I need five oval servers set on the table—in a line so I can dish this all out."

Then or never. I slung off my coat, threw it on a chair. Wiped the serving plates and lined them up. Watched Cook fill each with mound upon mound of chicken and leeks and mutton and rice and muffins. She was quicker than she should have been with the heft of her. Not even a second to sneak something in my pocket.

Behind me came a clatter on the stairs. Black polished boots first, then the man. He was thin with very long fingers that wrapped round the rail. Long legs like a heron's. His vest was tufted and padded, but the effect only emphasized his spindliness. He stopped at the bottom, peering at me with faded gray eyes. "Ah. Miss Blunt. You are sent."

It was Mr. Beede, the man who had hired me that morning at the intelligence office.

"It's our new Mary," he said to Cook.

"Where's Jacob?" Cook's voice echoed in the open stove as she pulled out the last of the roast.

The door at the top of the stairs swung wider. A boy barely in facial hair took the step above Mr. Beede. He wore black polished boots and white stockings and some silly blue frock like a toy soldier.

"Jacob!"

"Here here here, Cook." He cut his eyes toward me. "Who are you?"

"This is the new washer-up. And there's no time for this. Food upstairs. Now."

The old man stepped down to the table. He set his hands on his hips, bent over a plate and sniffed. "Good." He side-stepped to the next and the next, each with a bend and a sniff and a "Good."

"No fish tonight?" he asked.

"It's off."

"Well, I suppose the Bostoners would look down on our river fish anyway." He nodded to the boy. "Ready?"

"Yes, Mr. Beede." Jacob grabbed a tray of leeks near me. "You're not as pretty as Mary," he whispered.

Mr. Beede ascended the stairs, holding the door for Jacob. A flurry of laughter and men's voices tumbled down. "Adieu." He clicked the latch shut behind him.

We stood in the sudden silence—Cook at the stove, me at the sink to continue my work.

"Go to it, girl."

The night played the same for hours. Dishes cooked and platters taken, and sounds from above. Ale and brandy and wine replenished. All the while, I stood at the sink and scrubbed. Content for the pump in the kitchen and an ever-warm pot of water nearby. Big tin tub under the sink to empty the dirty water. I washed and dried and followed Cook's pointed finger to the correct spots in the pot room where the things should hang.

I'm fast at learning. I refused to be sent away.

Through the window came the jingle of harnesses as the horses and sleigh transports were called back to service. Each time the door opened to the upstairs, the voices grew less until there was finally no sound at all.

"They don't stay?"

"Thank God, no one stays," Cook said. "I'd need three of myself and two of you, to boot."

Jacob threw himself akimbo in a chair. "Jesus, Mary, and Creation. You should have seen them, Cook. Bet if one of them cuts himself, it'll be brandy he bleeds." He stared at the stove. "That's a good smell."

"There's plenty for all. I've made a nice stew."

The boy rubbed his face. He was as thin as Mr. Beede, but not sunken. A blond-thatched sapling growing every which way. He crossed a leg and removed a boot.

"Don't take those off in here. You can offend the floors of your own room later. Take this plate to Mr. Friday and empty the dirty tub water. It's practically overflowing and it's hard enough to clean the floor." Cook turned and stared. Empty sink and not a pot in sight. "It seems our new Mary has worked a house or two." She handed Jacob a towel-covered pot.

He turned to the door and waited. "Key, missus."

Cook reached for the ring of keys on her waistband, found the right one, and turned the lock. Closed and relocked the door after him. She dabbed a towel to her forehead to mop the sweat.

"The stew, missus."

"What?"

I pointed to the pot and the froth that bubbled and threatened to spill out.

"The stew." She picked up a ladle and stirred. Shifted the pot to a cooler place.

There came a knock on the door. Cook stared at it. She glared at the stew, her lower lip pushed out. Then she handed me the ladle and attended to the door—Jacob.

"Mr. Friday sends his thanks," he said.

Plates, food, fuel. Four of us around the table. Cook in the seat nearest the stove, Jacob across from me, Mr. Beede at the other end. No one spoke; the only sound was the slide of metal forks against plates. I hadn't eaten so well in days.

"Divine. To a divine stew, Mrs. Cook." Mr. Beede rose from his chair and lifted his wine glass. "And to a startling good claret. Or what's left of it." He sipped as daintily as a child would sniff a flower, then tilted his head. His eyes were watery, as if he were perpetually on the verge of tears. But I knew it most likely meant he was a habitual imbiber. The fine threads of red on his nose and cheeks confirmed it; my father's looked the same. He took a pipe and bag of tobacco from his coat. "A bit of claret, Cook?"

"Don't mind if I do, Mr. Beede."

"And for our new Mary?"

"Lucy. I'm Lucy. I don't take spirits."

"Good of you not to," he said. "Sinful thing." He uncorked the bottle sitting hard by him and filled a small glass. "The master's got the contract for the new timber." Mr. Beede sighed and rubbed his nose. "They're speaking of building a rail line to the mills."

"Lord, no, they're the worst sort of men."

"Progress, Mrs. Cook. Business and progress hand-in-hand. The master knows his plan. The navvies would be temporary. And would stay in their own camps. You shouldn't worry yourself over them. Just think, though, our little spot in the world grows. Harrowboro, New Hampshire—manufacturing capital of the world."

Jacob glared at me, his elbows resting wide on the table. "Mary drowned."

"Did she?" I swallowed and gave a slow nod. The hiring agent only stated the girl deceased. An "unfortunate passing."

"God rest the girl. It's Lucy's turn now." Cook lifted the spoon and bowl from in front of me and set them in the sink.

"Are there only the three of you, then? For this large a house?" I didn't say how queer it was to find such a place in the middle of wilderness and villages and sheep. I couldn't imagine Cook on her knees sweeping ash from a fireplace, though I could see her gathering and throwing out the piss and shit from the chamber pots. She had the arms for it. "Are there children?"

"None." Mr. Beede lifted an eyebrow, then let it rest again. Said nothing more, though plenty of thoughts traveled his forehead.

"Who does the maiding?"

Cook pressed against the table and slid the claret bottle closer. "That would be yourself. Jacob will help. And Rebecca dusts when the fancy takes her."

"Rebecca?"

"The mistress's companion." Mr. Beede reached for the claret, tipping it to his glass, waiting for the last splash to land. "I suppose if one counts Rebecca above and John Friday in the stalls, there are five of us. Six with you."

"But it's such a big house. How in the world—"

"We know our ways." Mr. Beede sucked in the last bit of wine. "How many does one need?"

Later, I lay on my pallet, a nub of candle casting light on the irons and coppers, my satchel tight between me and the wall. Oh! Not much to be watchful of, really. Nothing but an extra shift, an apron, a tortoiseshell comb. And my secret treasure, folded into a square of paper: a lock of hair white as the summer sun and smoother than silk. My baby's. Ned. All I had left of him.

The house slumbered. Master and mistress dreamt in one room. Down the hall past the larder, heavy snores. Could be Mr. Beede's or Cook's. A sleepy cry and then silence from Jacob's. I snuffed the candle, curled under the blanket. I was to be the new maid in a new house with a new life. I'm good with lies. Lucky me.

Chapter Two

I'd never slept well in unfamiliar surroundings. With the worsted blanket pulled tight to my chin, I watched the black night through the kitchen windows. Three small squares of glass set high in the wall, the whorls and bubbles catching threads of ice, splintering the shafts of gray light as early morning crept close.

Here, as always in the split between night and morn, came the terrible vision of my Ned, blue and still on the cot beside me, his body warmed only by my heat. I was given a week with my babe. He was then to be taken by a family. Given a different name and different life. Mrs. Framingham promised she'd find him the best home. Only the best home, she said, and took the last of my coins. Mrs. Framingham kept the coins and God took the baby. Who is to know if he'd have had a better life?

The metal lock on the kitchen door squealed. I sat up with a start but stayed far in the shadows. The door swung open, blocking my view of whoever visited so early. There was only a dull thud on the table, a shuffle of boots, then the door shut and the lock turned again. The frigid breath of air warmed and dissipated.

Then came the toss of shadows as Cook's oil lamp sputtered round the kitchen. She seemed a great shadow herself, floating in and out of the lamp's thin glow, her thick skirts and stiff petticoats a whoosh and whisper. I heard her grunt and sniff, then the squeal of the stove door and the flash of red as she shifted old wood and placed new wood to join the heat.

"What time is it?" I asked.

"Four forty-five, and it's the last time you'll sleep so long."

There was a pop and bubble of new boiling water in the kettle. Cook's hand and arm appeared in the lamplight; I caught the glint of a knife as she set it on the table. She held up a burlap bag—the thud from earlier—and her great fist and fingers pulled apart the twine that bound the opening.

"John Friday's brought rabbits."

She stuffed her hand in the bag, lifting one out by its hind legs. She turned her wrist this way and that to look at the animal. Its fur was brown and matted. Melted ice clung to the edges of its ears. The front legs dangled stiffly, frozen and lifeless from fear and the weather.

"Lean winter for this one." She laid the rabbit on the table, patted its side once, then reached back in the bag. "You've skinned rabbits before?"

Out came another, clutched tight in Cook's hand, this one white with a ragged circle of gray on its shoulder.

"I haven't." I moved into the room. "Mrs. Temple, at my last house, wasn't fond of it."

"Who's not fond of rabbit?" She hesitated, the rabbit clutched tight, then narrowed her eyes. "What sort of person is not fond of rabbit?"

"She liked . . . ham. And cod. I know how to fillet a fish."

"Well, New Mary, we're fond of rabbits in this house. I'll show you how it's done. There's six good rabbits here; you'll be an expert by the fifth."

Out came the rabbits. She laid them side by side, nestled stomach to back, then rolled the burlap and set it on a narrow shelf behind her.

"Come around here so you can watch and learn."

I moved next to her, my back to the sink and windows. To my right was the larder and entrance to the hallway with her room and

Mr. Beede's and Jacob's. Directly across, three stairs led to the floors above. The door at the top was painted black and disappeared in the dimness.

I felt like a rabbit, down a deep hole under heavy stone and earth. As if Cook and I were all that breathed and moved, save the slow shift of the continents above.

The rattle of keys shook me from my thought. "Pay attention." She used the toe of her boot to shift the offal bucket between us.

I took a breath. I had been charged with learning to skin a rabbit.

Cook was bound and determined to be patient. She kept her frustrations to long sighs and a few twitches of her eyelid. A vein pulsed under the skin of her jaw. Sometimes she reached for the knife. Sometimes she darted her hand back.

"Drain the urine, you daft girl. That was instruction number one."

Rabbit by rabbit I made mistakes—too deep a puncture in the belly, too shallow an incision on the back, guts spilled on the floor. They slipped through my fingers, the slick fattiness causing me to wrestle them into the bucket. On the fifth rabbit, by which time I was meant to be an expert, I struggled to pull the fur and skin off in one piece.

"Give me the knife." In nearly the blink of an eye, she skinned the rabbit, snapped the pelvis, dropped the head in the bucket. She laid the knife beside me. "Continue."

The room went from gray to lavender as the weak sun struggled for morning.

A door banged. Jacob hopped down the hallway, pulling on a boot and tucking in his shirt. "Rabbit!"

"Not for you. Egg and toast when you return." Cook trundled around the table, her hip upsetting a chair. It wobbled, then mended itself upright. At the steps to the main floor, she grasped the rail and lifted one foot and then the other to the next riser. Her breath came out a wheeze, but up the few steps she went, fingering the heavy keys on the ring at her waist. Lifting the right key to shift the lock.

"Do you lock us in, or them out?" I asked.

She stopped, her hand hovering above the handle, and looked down at me. "What's your meaning?"

"Nothing."

Jacob shoved a cold corn cake in his mouth, catching the crumbs with his tongue. "It's to keep Mrs. Burton from wandering and getting lost."

"Jacob." Cook smacked the keys on her leg.

He flicked me a look as sharp as a cat's, then bounded up the steps toward Cook. She spit in her palm and smoothed his hair flat.

"Maybe a bit of rabbit," she whispered to him. She pushed the door—and if I'd been paying attention to the rabbits at that moment, I'd have missed the flit of movement on the other side. A young woman with wide green eyes blinked at me in surprise. "Oh." Then she disappeared in a swirl of dull blond hair, leaving only an empty space for Jacob to sidle through.

"Who was that?"

"Rebecca, already pressing for the morning tray. Every day, she prods and pushes . . ." Cook plodded down the steps, waving me away from the meat. "You know how to do toast?" She grabbed her hip and sucked in a breath. "Bring me a chair, will you? And stop the driveling questions."

After settling into the chair I proffered, she blew a breath, her cheeks puffing wide and deflating. "My bones are not fond of winter." She untied the key ring from her apron, holding out a small key while the others shifted and jangled. "Bread's in the larder. I'll be watching you."

I grew used to being watched at the house. I grew used to watching. Watching and waiting for the slips of attention, the temporary diversions. There Cook too concerned with the spilled flour, and there Mr. Beede pacing and awaiting Mr. Burton's return from the mill. Jacob helping John Friday with the foaling in the spring. Mr. Burton focused on his ledgers and plats, devising plans for more money and more land. It was easy to slip by them all.

Except for Rebecca.

I'm hanging because of her.

"What day is it?"

Mr. LeRocque fidgets on the low wood stool. He's not doing well, my newspaperman—not by the soil on his collar and the fray of his trouser bottoms. Still, he shined his boots. Too bad for the mud on the way to my cell. There he sits, fingering the collar of his black coat. The elbows shine with too much use. The cheap wax and wick of the candle at his side give little light, just a grim umber glow.

"It's Wednesday."

"Already Wednesday? Well."

He twists round to open his leather satchel, pulling from it a small package wrapped in faded chintz. He leans forward on the stool, just enough so his hand and the package cross the boundary of the bars between us.

"Lemon tart. From my wife."

"Give it to one of the guards on the way out."

"It's one of her specialties." His long mustache curls in and out as he speaks.

"It's one of your bribes."

"All I want is the truth."

"You seem to have done well without it." I lean back against the stone of my cell. "I'm quite interested in what you wrote last month. I was twisted by my 'desperate surroundings'? Oppressed by the 'unending death-wielding hours of work'? Oppressed by the room I slept in as a maid? I slept in more than one at that house, but it's simpler for readers your way, isn't it?"

He knits his brows and looks at me like I'm being a petulant child.

"Have you seen my hands?" I splay my palms up, show off the sloughing skin and the swollen fingers. "They've put me on the men's washing. At least I won't be doing that much longer."

"Miss Blunt—"

"I know you're trying to gain me sympathy. You've written before that it's sinful to hang a woman. But how many women have your stories saved? I think none."

"Letitia Blaisdell. We saved Letitia."

"And now she serves tea to the warden and his family. I don't envy them that worry." I shrug. "How did she get out from the rope?"

"She showed remorse." He sets the tart on the ground between us. "You show none."

In the passing days, the only sign there was life above our kitchen came from the infrequent pull of the bells, the food carried up (a plate of cold meats and broth for Mrs. Burton and her companion; a variety of substantials for Mr. Burton come back late from the mill), the chamber pots carried down.

I even wondered if there were a master and mistress. Perhaps Rebecca took the trays up the narrow stairs, then sat straight down at a table and gobbled everything up.

There were no children, no pups yapping, no cats mewling. I never heard a piano or harp or viol. No guests came to the door after that first night, no other maids knocked for a visit at ours. It was as if Josiah Burton's house was an island or some strange ephemera created by my mind. Even Mr. Beede and Cook seemed transitory, the only permanence to them their bristly chatter. Rebecca, who remained on the floors above, was nothing more to me than a name, a wan silhouette I'd seen that first morning.

I kept my mouth shut and woke early. I was in charge of eggs and making the toast. I bedded late. In between was full with washing pots and pans, with wringing chickens' necks, with scrubbing the stones and floors and breaking the ice sheets from the well. No time to think, and I thanked God for that, for it was hard enough in the few minutes that were mine at the end of the night.

On the fourth morning, I dropped the water bucket by the well and hefted the iron, letting the weight shatter the ice. My hands and face were already numb. I wrapped my scarf up round my cheeks and felt the rough crystals of tears. My shadow was dark; the sharp early sun cleaved the image, freeing it from my toil. Now it could meander, for the cold wouldn't bother it. It would see the bones of the trees at the edge of the property, and down the hill the workers ambling along a road from the township to the mill. The town itself was nothing more than clapboard and brick, the boarding houses and businesses built right against the steep rock walls. In the middle of the valley—if one could call the narrow junction between those walls something so vast sounding—sat a simple white church at the end of a triangular commons. It was all owned by Mr. Burton, whose ice I chipped in the yard.

I think Mary Dawson tipped herself into the creek just to escape this chore. I would have, save I was too damn cold to go a step farther from the house.

I grabbed the handles, turned, and saw the mistress. She stood in the middle of the wide swath of yard, her face tilted to the sun. Her dark hair tumbled loose and tangled down her back. Her gown was too delicate for any but summer weather. A sapphire cloak pooled in the snow at her feet.

I stepped forward then, off the path, wanting to see her properly, to see if she truly existed or was just an image as unreal as my wandering shadow.

She had heard me. She lifted the cloak to her shoulders, then stumbled and half crawled to the house. But she did not enter the front door; instead, she reached her fingers out, as if she were searching for something in the night, finding then the bare branches of the shrubs that girded the stone. She pushed her shoulder into the limbs to make room for her body, then crouched. Her hands pressed the frame of a low window and she slid feet first inside.

The window was one in a line of four others. Mr. Beede's, Cook's, Jacob's, and mine.

I tightened my hold on the bucket, loped along the path, and pounded my elbow to the kitchen door. I'd certainly see her now. Face-to-face. What would she do? Tell Cook to ignore her, she was only out for a stroll?

Such long minutes until Cook opened the door. I barreled past, the bucket slamming my shin as I ran past the larder and turned the corner, boots sliding to a stop at my room. I set the bucket aside and tried the door handle. Locked. As were all the other doors. I pulled the key from my waist pocket, but I knew, once I had egress, there would be no one there. I had been too slow in returning. I should have followed right on her heels. The room was as I left it, the quilt folded at the end of the bed, my comb on the dresser, my shift hanging on a wall knob next to an extra apron. And a trail of melting snow splattered in the middle of the plank floor.

Chapter Three

Mary was a little lamb,
Her soul as white as snow.
And everywhere that Mary went
Death was sure to go.

He tracked her to the brook one day,
Which was against the rule.
He tempted her quite far astray
And made the lamb a fool.

She tried, she tried to turn him out
But still he lingered near
And waited patiently about
Till Mary did not fear.

What made the lamb trust him so
Most any would descry?
O! he loved Mary, too, you know.
Tis pity she must die.

The ground was too solid to bury Mary Dawson; she was draped in
shrouds, her body strewn with winter-dried lilac and marjoram, the
coffin awaiting its shift to the receiving vault until the arrival of spring

daffodils and more forgiving earth. She would share the stone vault with the Messrs. Whitworth and Michaels, the widow Daughtry, and two newborns. All quite natural—if not quite expected—deaths.

The entire house had been invited to the viewing and the funeral. Mr. Burton sent over the finest grosgrain ribbon woven by the mill and a spool of strong thread. Cook and I sewed black cockades and badges for each of us. I pierced my thumb more than once—I had never been one for needles—so Cook moved me to pressing the men's shirts and the mistress's fine petticoats. She prayed quite loud that I wouldn't burn down the house with the iron.

I will admit my concentration was not keen and my temper impatient. I didn't want to attend the funeral—I truly did not know the girl, no matter the hiss and whispers later printed in the papers. I had hoped for the day alone, to find the path the mistress had taken from my room to the floors above. I was certain there was a set of hidden stairs along our hallway or tucked in the linen room. I'd seen such before and spied those who stole up and down them.

I would have had the time to explore had not that black-clad invitation ruined my plans and my afternoon off.

We stood at the bottom of the front steps that morning, watching John Friday draw the new-waxed bobsleigh around. He sat ramrod straight, white-gloved hands on the oiled harnesses, staring forward to a spot directly between the two chestnut geldings, his dark skin beaded with iced sweat. Then he lifted an arm and tapped a metal bell to call us on our mournful journey.

Cook murmured penances, eyes heavy lidded, fingers picking and pulling at the corners of the prayer book she held tight like a lover to her bosom. Mr. Beede straightened Jacob's jacket, then stepped forward to wipe the curve of a runner with his handkerchief. He opened the half door and reached in to fluff the blankets that would cover the Burtons on the ride.

The front door swung open. Mr. Burton emerged on the landing, his suit coat and beaver hat darker still than the band twined round his arm. His lean features were humorless and sharp cut. The face of an ascetic—or a king.

He stood in front of us, the space between empty but for the mingling of our frozen breaths. He did not move, his visage still, his eyes blank.

"You're the new maid."

A sharp poke in the shoulder from Cook startled me back into focus. "Yes, sir."

"The new Mary."

"Yes, sir."

"Ah."

He turned back to the open door, his gloved fingers finding the arm of his wife, guiding her by the wrist and waist, a whisper in her ear warning of each granite step. As if this was the first time she'd encountered them, or she was a porcelain doll that might shatter with the slightest misstep.

As if she were blind.

I caught a breath, feeling the burn of the air's teeth and realizing that indeed this was true. I recalled how she stumbled across the lawn and how her hands searched the bushes and pressed against the wall until she'd contacted the frame of my window.

The mistress was blind.

But while this was a shock, it did not perturb me as did Mr. Burton's cloying kindness as he guided her down the steps, and Rebecca, now solid rather than the drift of light hair and green eyes that had passed by the first morning, trailed obsequiously behind. How meek the mistress looked. The drop of her shoulders, the bend of her neck, those wild tresses braided tight to her head. So tamed and timid, her small hand fluttering above his arm, taking his lead as he moved to the carriage. Sitting like a pliable lump as her husband shifted the wool blankets round her skirts before holding a hand to Rebecca to assist her to the seat beside.

Rebecca plucked the blanket smooth and straightened the tails of the cockade on the mistress's shoulder. Mrs. Burton batted Rebecca's hand away, twisting her mouth in defiance before ruffling the blankets about and lifting her chin.

"We are met, Mr. Friday." The sleigh dipped and swayed as Mr. Burton dropped next to him.

John Friday flicked the reins and gave a soft burring sound to the horses, then the sleigh pulled forward for the trip down the hill to the Dawson family cottage and all the tears inside.

We walked behind. Mr. Beede murmured and his voice lingered. He stopped and waited for a nod from Cook before continuing on.

Jacob slowed his stride and dropped to my side. He shrugged his shoulders and pulled at the tight collar of his shirt but took care to keep his boots in the hard ruts of the road and away from the dirtied snow that clung to each side.

"I'm to help with the foaling this spring," he said.

"Are you?"

"Ayuh." Ice pellets dropped from the tree limbs with a rat-a-tat. Jacob pulled his cap lower and balled his hands in his pockets. His eyes were tinged red from the cold or crying.

"Did you know Mary well?" I asked.

"Ayuh."

"My sympathies."

"Nothing to do." Jacob sniffed, then turned and peered at me before quickening to walk with Mr. Beede and Cook.

The Burtons' sleigh was the only transport near the Dawson cottage. The other mourners walked from the mill housing or the neighboring streets. The path along the picket fence and up to the black-wreathed entrance had been shoveled clean, and mourners shuffled forward to give their regards to the newly dead.

"Go to the back door and help in the kitchen, child." Cook tapped my shoulder. "You know not a soul here." She pressed a roll of cloth in my hands: our aprons.

I turned away from the line and moved toward the kitchen. Mr. Burton alighted from the sleigh and assisted Rebecca to the ground. He strode up the walkway, slight tips of his head to those waiting, and moved into the front hall. Rebecca's eyes followed him, then caught mine. Her lips curled at the edges, then she adjusted her muff and trudged toward me, her shoes sinking in the snow banked near the house.

"You'll leave the mistress?" I asked.

"She has blankets."

The kitchen was full of women and a table of small cakes and cordials. The trays were of different patterns, as were the manners of baking. Rebecca took my elbow and walked us closer to the stove. We were greeted with gazes both curious and hard, but nods of greeting were given, as was a space near the warmth.

Rebecca sneaked a cake, lifting it to her lips and raising her eyebrows at me in challenge as she took a bite.

She was no more than my age and close in height, with a sharp nose and curious, wide-set eyes. Her gaze flickered over my features and cloak. "It was an odd place for Mary to be, wasn't it? Down Windall Hill and quite away from the path to the house?"

"I wouldn't know."

"No. You wouldn't." She offered me the other half of the cake, to which I demurred, then popped it in her mouth. "What's your name?"

"Lucy Blunt."

"Not from here."

"No."

She leaned against the wall, wiping the cake crumbs from her palms, the muff swinging from her wrist.

"So, the mistress is left in the cold?" I asked.

A shrug. "She's not one for company."

"Should you take her a tea?"

She straightened. "Of course. It's what I came for."

"Did you not know Mary? To give condolences?"

"I've shared more words with you today than I ever did with her. Saw her come and go, of course. She was a maid; I am Mr. Burton's cousin." She picked up a teacup from the counter and poured from the large pot. "What good graces you must have to gain a room and a full position." She leaned close. "Not so lucky for Mary, though."

I rubbed my arms against sudden pricks of cold, and before I could ask her meaning, she turned to bring the tea to the mistress, leaving me to the stove and strangers who ignored me.

Cook finally came and waved from the doorway. I snuck a maple cake still warm from its pan and gave it to her on the walk to the house.

Good graces are earned, are they not?

Here, for example. I've spoiled the matron with compliments. On the cut of her dress and the braid of her hair and the lilt of her voice— though I gritted my teeth when I did. I've called her over and cooed in her ear that indeed John Currier would soon ask for her hand even though I know nothing of him but her talk. He walks the men's cells. I've seen him once or twice when I was summoned to the warden's office on some offense.

He looks much like a man who steals other people's suppers. He's fond of his mustache, much like you, Mr. LeRocque.

Down the corridor a new girl's been brought in and mewls on her cot.

"That's Laura Reed. They won't have her in the warden's attic right now. She likes to scream."

LeRocque turns on his stool. He runs his finger along his mustache and blinks in time with the whimpers and sniffles.

"Are you listening?" I ask.

Still, he looks down the way. I kick at the door and it hurts. I do it again and again, until he rises from the stool and raises his hands and pleads for me to stop.

The girl sobs now, piteous and fake.

My foot throbs.

My hands curl round the bars of the cell door, the iron rough and sharp, cutting and stretching my waterlogged skin, peeling it back to the stinging pink underneath.

I bite the inside of my mouth, swallow the sharp blood. "Have you seen someone who's drowned, Mr. LeRocque? The skin slurries and grays, like my fingers from the laundry, can you see?"

"I see."

"It's an interesting place, the laundry. You've no idea the trinkets and treasures hidden in hems and pockets. Last week I found a match-stick with an entire seascape carved upon it. And—listen to me."

"I'm listening, Lucy."

"They covered Mary's face with lace to keep the women from fainting."

"How would you know that?"

"I saw it for myself."

"You were in the kitchen."

"Not the whole time."

The women in the kitchen regained their shawls, making for the procession to the graveyard and the temporary interment in the vault.

Jacob came through from the front, pressing a finger to his lips and then gesturing me into the heart of the house. I grappled for the ker-chief in my sleeve, though I knew it would be useless against the smell of the dead. We moved past mirrors covered in cloth, into the front room, where the clocks had been stilled and the mantel draped in black crepe. A woman leaned heavily on the arm of another, her mourning clothes fresh pressed. She held a handkerchief tight to her mouth, her breath ragged and thin as she slowed in front of her daughter's casket, then continued to the door.

Jacob and I crept in; the pallbearers stood by, hands piously clasped and waiting for the last string of visitors to depart. The casket was plain pine, the interior lined with a soft white linen. Mary's body was clothed in what looked like her Sunday best, her hands gloved, her pale hair curled and fanned on the pillow. And indeed, her face was hidden behind an intricate square of lace. Jacob glanced over his shoulder, then reached in and lifted the corner.

Enough. Just enough to see the damage the water had done, the stitch that held her mouth shut, the pennies against her sunken lids.

I grabbed a hand to my chest, no breath moved in nor out, and stumbled back, upsetting a chair as I careened away to the kitchen. I bent over, my fingers digging into my knees, and cursed Jacob for showing me. I could hear the furniture being pulled aside and low voices as the men lifted that simple pine case from the table. Her father, a brother perhaps, or cousins. Strong shoulders to carry her to her final fate.

No one to carry my Ned.

No one but me to mourn.

And there was Cook then, standing in the doorway, holding the rolled apron I'd forgotten like an accusation of my sloth.

"Let's to home and get the meal started. Mr. Beede and the boy will give the respects."

I lifted my head and stared at her.

"Are you deaf?"

"No."

"Come then before Peter Savage freezes my bones."

"Peter—"

"Give the weather a name and invite it round like a guest. Keeps it from getting the better of you."

She didn't wait for me. Turned and hobbled toward the road, her broad hand flat against her hip. She stopped at the gate and watched the mourners plod to the cemetery. When I joined her, she stared hard at me. "How does someone drown in a half-froze brook?" Then shook her head and bound her scarf round her nose and mouth. "Stupid girl." We turned away from the cottage and trudged toward the house, our feet following the path the Burtons' sleigh had carved earlier that day.

Chapter Four

It snowed for ten days.

The flakes swirled and knitted round the house. Jacob dug a path to the privy and the barn, then met John Friday to bed and feed the livestock. Mr. Burton and Mr. Beede left for the mill on Monday and remained in town, for the path was impassable. The temperature was a steady bit of hell, and the woodstoves were greedy for fuel. Our diets narrowed to salted pork and potatoes and puckered apples, though Cook surprised us with Indian pudding one night.

Still the sheets and underclothes and linens dropped down the chute to the laundry, and still I boiled the water and swilled it all in lye soap and breathed the thick humid air as the woodstove steamed the hanging fabrics.

Still Jacob attended to the slop buckets and filled the great fireplace and the stoves.

All the stoves.

The mistress insisted, or so Rebecca told him.

And one does exactly as the hand that feeds you dictates.

Three raps at the door to upstairs. Three raps as usual to state the breakfast trays were empty and ready to be washed. Three raps from Rebecca waiting near the door.

Rap rap rap.

Cook, sitting to my side as I kneaded and punched the bread dough, grunted but did not stop peeling the last of the winter potatoes.

"Keys, Cook."

She stared at me. "What for?"

"Rebecca knocked. Didn't you hear it?"

"It's too early for the trays." The paring knife rested in her hand, a half-blacked potato tight in the other fist. Peelings curled in the folds of her apron.

"Three raps," I said. "There. She did it again. She has the trays."

"She doesn't have the trays."

I twisted the dough tight. "Didn't you hear it?"

"Jacob's still above. It's too early."

She was right; the trays had only just gone up. And yet, it was three raps, I was sure of that. It wasn't two for the linens or four to summon Mr. Beede.

"It's not the trays." But Cook pressed the knife to the table and dropped the potato in a bowl. She lumbered to the railing, grabbed and pulled herself up to the door. Her hand shook as she searched for the key. She yanked the door wide.

Rebecca held a tray with a single silver egg cup that bounced and skittered on the surface. She looked past Cook, her eyes finding me, and gave a half smile. "You're still here."

"What do you want?"

"Mrs. Burton doesn't like the egg."

She pushed the tray at Cook. "And she threw the hash at the cat." She raised her hand in front of her, as if she were setting up to block an imminent blow. "I found both to be of perfect consistency."

"She doesn't like the egg."

Rebecca shook her head.

Cook's mouth, so often tight with murmured prayers or curses, loosened and slacked. She turned her head to the small windows, her eyes glazing as she stared at the sharp edges of frost and fingers of ice that trapped us inside this kitchen. She quivered. Then a bellow from her gut, hurling past her lips. She slammed the tray to the floor then knocked her fists against her skull, twisting round with wild eyes.

My hands slowed, and I stepped away from the yielding bread, away from Cook, whose body shook with anger as she cut a zigzagging path through the kitchen, her elbow knocking a plate to the floor. She grabbed the heavy dough and hurled it at the larder. Her white hair unfurled from its pins, and her hands flailed, grabbing wood spoons and strainers and pans and throwing them on the ground. No words passed her lips, just the wheezing keens and growls of a great horrible witch.

Rebecca retreated to the stairwell. "Jacob!"

Cook lurched to the stove. I grabbed her arm with both hands, trying to pull her from the boiling water and the iron heat, my heels skidding and catching on the seams in the floor.

"It's just an egg, Cook."

But it wasn't just an egg, and I should not have belittled its rejection.

I cut a glance to Rebecca, frozen with her hands clawed to the iron banister. Jacob shouldered past her, hesitating at the sight of Cook. Then he grabbed her hand and pulled her to the door.

"It's just Peter Savage," he said.

She blinked at Jacob. "Peter Savage."

"Peter's come to call, Cook. Just Peter Savage."

He took both her hands in his and coaxed her out the door. I yanked a thick shawl from the hook nearby and followed them, wrapping it round Cook's shoulders.

We all squinted against the white. The air was sharp and smelled of cold and the smoke from the chimneys, not stale like the inside.

"I make perfect eggs, Jacob."

"Yes, Cook, you do. I've never had one better."

"Is that true?"

"Ayuh."

"You wouldn't lie to an old woman?"

"I don't see one of those here." Jacob released her hands and stepped back, his eyes widening as he spread his arms and fell straight back in the snow. He laughed, arms and legs sweeping round as he created an angel in a drift.

"You're too old for that, lad."

"Never too old, Cook. Never ever."

Cook ducked her chin and gave a quick shake of her head. And with a great swoop she landed beside him.

I shrugged and joined them. Why not?

Our arms and legs flailed with glee, kicking and throwing the snow. Cook laughed and laughed, looking like the little girl she no doubt forgot she'd ever been. Above us, the crystalline tree limbs burst scarlet—a flock of bandit-eyed cardinals gazed down at our lunatic selves.

"Look." I pointed.

Cook's chest heaved and slowed. "Will you look at that."

Jacob shook the snow from his hair and sat up, clasping his hands round his knees. "Don't see that often."

"Get them a handful of millet, child." She patted my knee.

I rose carefully, not wanting to startle the birds or the angel I'd made. Rebecca waited at the door and followed me inside. The ceiling seemed even lower than usual, pressing my shoulders, competing with the sudden clutch of heat.

"What about Mrs. Burton?" she asked.

"Let her go hungry." I shifted the lid of a bin and scooped the millet.

"I'll tell her you said that."

"She's a spoiled thing, isn't she?"

Rebecca's gaze flickered round the room, then settled on me, her eyes edged with a ring of something frantic, like a feral cat caught in a dark cellar. She spread her fingers then curled her hands into fists over and over, and I kenned that she, like us below, was confined by the snow, the never-ending white—and the whims of Mrs. Burton.

"Will toast with molasses do," I asked, "or should I bring down a deer for her?"

"A bottle of tincture and spirits would please her best. But molasses and toast will do fine."

So. Mrs. Burton was fond of her laudanum. I didn't blame her. Think of the house, Mr. LeRocque, and all the locks to keep her in. Nothing but the low gong of the clock and the rattle of the wind to occupy her mind.

Later that night, as John Friday played the viol, the notes rolling both warm and melancholy round the table, my thoughts skimmed past Cook and her pile of mending, and Jacob's boot blacking, and slipped instead up the stairs. I laid my sampler on the table and tapped the wood in time with the tune.

"I'm to bed," I said. I lit a nub of candle in its plain glazed holder and stood.

Cook glanced up, a slight hesitation as she caught my gaze, perhaps a tint of embarrassment from her earlier behavior. But she pressed her lips in a line and gave a quick nod to allow my freedom.

I unlocked my door and opened it, then waited a brief moment before pulling it shut again and turning the key. I snuck a look back at the turn in the hall—Mr. Friday now played a piece that set Cook's foot thumping. My fingers trailed the hallway walls, nails dipping in and out of the crevices between boards. Pressing against the wood and pausing for the telltale give that would provide me access to the floors above.

And there, five paces beyond the linen room, the hidden door swung open at the lightest touch.

The steep narrow stairs were bathed in the black of night; I was glad for the scrim of candlelight, though its reach was frugal at best. I edged into the space, clicking the latch behind me and shifting my foot until my toes found the first riser. The walls were rough to the touch of my palms, and I knew in the daylight would be but whitewashed wood that belonged neither upstairs nor down. Though the kitchen stairs were a short flight, the yard at the front of the house curved down toward the town and river, and thus I found myself on a square landing that turned to a second flight of stairs.

I heard movement on the steps above me and froze, my hand thrown flat against the sudden erratic beat of my heart.

"Who's there?" I whispered, lifting the flame toward the sound.

I was met by a pair of eyes, dark black and shiny as a doll's. It was Mrs. Burton, sitting on the top step, wrapped in a simple gray cloak, her hair unadorned and tied back with a thin ribbon. I caught her staring at me, her expression both curious and awaiting, though of what I knew not. I had to remind myself she was blind. Her forehead was smooth, her cheeks high and tapering to a narrow cleft chin. Fine lines etched the corners of her eyes, sharp shadows of laughter and life. Her skin was pallid, and as my eyes settled into the low light, I saw the cracked dry flesh of her lips and the pulse of the vein along her throat. Her mouth quivered and she pulled in a quick breath.

"Hello, Lucy." She reached out her hand, and her fingers twitched slightly as she waited for my hand to meet hers.

"How do you know it is me?"

"My jailer's asleep in her rooms, and your Cook is enjoying a reel." She let go my hand, then closed her eyes and rested her head against the wall. "He plays so beautifully."

My ears tuned to the muffle of music that came from under the door. "Why don't you go down and listen to it properly?"

"Why don't you sit down and listen from here? Though I don't think that was your intention."

"My intention?"

"You came to steal a bauble or ogle at the mad wife."

"I was only—"

"Curiosity killed the cat, you know." She tilted her head and looked in my direction. "Do you play whist?"

"Whist?"

"Rebecca hates it."

"And Mr. Burton?"

Her lip curled and she let out a cheerless laugh. "He's not inclined toward cards." She gathered her skirts close to her legs and pointed to the landing. "Sit and play a game with me." From the purse at her waist, she pulled a deck of cards and fanned them out before me. Each was punched with a sequence of raised dots. She touched her fingers lightly to the corners before scooping them into a stack and pressing them into a shuffle. "German whist? Thirteen-card start."

I placed the candle at my side and arranged the cards.

"So, which was it?" she asked. "To steal or to ogle?"

"Maybe a bit of both."

"And do you cheat at cards?"

"On occasion."

"But not tonight. Not with me." She touched the three of hearts that sat atop the kitty. "What's your bid?"

I don't know how many hands we played. She was ferocious, and my attention to the game began to wane with each loss.

"You were in my room," I said.

She frowned and picked the corner of a card with her thumb. "Is that your room?"

"Yes."

"Mm. It's technically mine. Isn't it?"

"Technically, it is."

She flicked her hand, then reached forward to gather the deck, tapping the edges straight, reaching once more in a circle for an errant jack or ace. "Tell me more of you, Lucy Blunt."

"There's not much to tell."

"I have few visitors." She shifted, straightening her legs and bouncing her knees. "Humor me."

I flipped through my tales, tossing aside those that would beg further questions. "I'm the girl in the moon."

"Are you?"

"I slipped right off and landed in a field. Outside Newburyport."

"Ah! We were neighbors," she said. "I'm from Portsmouth, originally. And your family? Still there?"

"I have no family."

"But everyone—"

"I don't."

It was then I heard the absence of John Friday's music, followed by the quick rap on Jacob's door and then Cook's nightly "God rest" before she retired to her bed.

We waited, still and quiet, until the greatest sounds were the hiss of the candle and the slide of the cards back into her pocket.

"It's late," I said.

She leaned toward me. "You wouldn't happen to have a sleeping draught I could . . . Never mind." She rose, smoothing her hair and skirts. "Good night, Lucy Blunt."

Chapter Five

I will hang next Thursday. I've been given the time: 10:15 a.m. Not just "sometime in the morning," but this specific time that falls neatly between the men's constitutionals and their lunches. I've been excused from the laundry that day.

Matron is attending; she told me it is required of her, but I noticed she is not indifferent to the duty. As she read the missive, her cheeks drooped and she turned a greenish blue. She averred it was man's sin to hang another. I told her it was man's sin to kill another, and there was nothing to wipe that stain from me.

10:15 a.m., Mr. LeRocque.

What does the Almanack bode for the weather? How many spectators will pack the yard? Ten? One hundred? Will they wipe sweat from their brows or huddle under black umbrellas? Will Matron guide me through the crowd? Will people hiss *murderer*? Will the man who puts the noose around my neck really wear a hood? Or will his face be naked? Is he handsome, this man, this face that will be the last I see? Will he look at me at all? Or will he mask me in black wool too?

10:15 a.m. At least there's no clock here to bludgeon me. Maybe I should stay ignorant—not ask the day, not ask the time. But it will be there, anyway, tapping the backs of my eyelids when I close them and chittering in my ear when awake.

I don't know how to beg for mercy, and there is no chance I will receive it. I am as detached from atonement as the Devil. All I can do is endure the days and outlast the nights. Wish they would end and plead they do not.

It's near spring now. Look at my window: the icicles no longer bare their teeth. And the sky is blue, like Cook's gingham spring dress. The ground to the laundry is more mud than dirt, and spears of flecked grass push toward the promise of thaw.

"The linen room will flood. And the wall behind the glasses and plates will bloom with mold. Who's there to clean it?"

Mr. LeRocque stares at me. He swallows, the lump of his Adam's apple gliding under the skin of his throat. The directive flutters at the tips of his fingers, as if the formal decree of execution will scorch.

I drop my head against the chill of the wall. "Tell whoever's at the house now that a mix of lye and chamomile does the trick. And not too hard with the brush; gentler strokes save the paint." I grip my legs tighter to my chest and dig a bare heel into the floor. "What have you brought today?"

"Rum cake."

I glance at this gift left just inside the bars, at the deep brown of it and the sugared orange peels curled atop. I envision Mrs. LeRocque lifting the last piece out of the baking tin. Perhaps her mouth is tight with disapproval of her husband's request for cake or pudding or pie. I have so far been most impressed with the lemon tart.

"I like rum cake."

LeRocque beams and relaxes back in his chair, his hands slapping his knees, the paper flittering from his grip. He reaches out, grasping, the chair tilting awry and resettling as he captures the note. Lays it on his knee, smoothing it as best he can. Then he lurches up, legs splayed like a sailor as he stumbles and walks the corridor, breathing in and out.

He fumbles in his coat, pulling a long handkerchief from his pocket and wiping his mouth. He holds himself up against the wall with one hand, wheezing, not looking at me. Eyes screwed shut, lips flapping like a fish.

"You'll need a stronger stomach than that, Mr. LeRocque, if you're to visit on Thursday."

He turns suddenly, face sheened with sweat and the handkerchief balled tight. Crouches down and reaches a rough hand through the bar. I do not want his comfort.

"Go away."

I want my bed. It's four steps away, but my legs are heavy as lead. The best I can do is crawl to the mattress. Pull the sheet up over my head and press myself to the wall.

"I'm sorry," he says.

I know this cell as well as I knew my room at the great house. Eyes open or closed I see the high walls, crude and rippled. The paint peels in the north corner, and the east has turned a shade of salmon. The floor lists to the door and picks up a slant near the slop bucket. There is light only as God or the whim of the matron provides it. Laura Reed's gone back with the other four women. At least for now, she is quiet and tamed. The cells are empty of people but stuffed with stores: saws and glue and a broken barber's chair, an old pump, a warped shaft, a cracked pulley. Matron told me yesterday there is a new wing at the asylum for the women. That the warden would get his wish soon and all the women would go. That it wouldn't do to move me with them. Too much trouble.

Lucy Blunt was good.
Lucy Blunt was bad.
Lucy Blunt will be hanged.
On Thursday.

Cook would appreciate the candied peels. A little sweet and a little tough, same as what follows us breath to breath, she'd say.

I'll give the slice to Matron. She's got a sweet tooth and hasn't once denied my gifts. Mrs. LeRocque's gifts.

I roll over, avoiding the corner of the mattress that's damp and chill from water that collects in the corner. If I press my eyes tight enough, I can hear the mistress's laugh, bright and loose like the drips along the window ledge. I can taste the cake she offers me, a thanks for some task or other: the sugar coat of rum on my tongue, the tang of salt in the crumbles, and her self-satisfied smile.

Never mind how the gift was procured or the consequences of her generosity.

The snow had abated, though not the freeze. With each small step to the well, my boots punched through the icy shell of it.

No amount of salt could melt the paths. John Friday had taken to spreading the straw he'd mucked from the stalls along the trackways and footpaths to the woodlot. The dull echo of ax against trunk was a regular beat as he and Jacob cut the timber that the house consumed without repent.

In the deep night, I sneaked through the hall to the hidden door, but found no one waiting on the other side.

Then came the return of Misters Burton and Beede. Jacob first noticed the bob of lanterns and jumped from his seat at the table. He pressed his hands to the windowpanes. "They've got Rebecca."

"Why is she outside?" I asked.

Cook and I started, making our way to the glass. The lanterns grew brighter, met by another as John Friday trudged from the stable to take the horses' reins. Mr. Burton dismounted and reached up to the figure nestled behind Mr. Beede. His arm circled Rebecca's waist and he lowered her down, hands under her arms to steady her and shift her from the horse's nervous hooves. Mr. Beede slung a heavy leather bag to the ground and alit.

Cook slapped a towel on her shoulder. "They'll need something hot." She snapped her fingers at me, but I was setting out cups and bowls before she could follow with a command.

Then the kitchen was full of the smells of horse and camphene oil and wet wool. Jacob took hold of Rebecca's arm as she swayed forward. Jackets were shed and valises dropped and Rebecca was maneuvered to the long bench at the table. Her lips were a deathly blue, her skin bright red at the nose and gray on the cheeks. A thin moan tumbled from her lips and then she tensed and cried out in delirium.

Mr. Burton filled the room, wide shoulders, deep voice, tall enough to touch the ceiling without reaching. His gaze caught mine across the table. "Who locked her out?"

I won't deny my hands trembled as his attention pierced. Cook's mouth dropped open and snapped shut, and her neck mottled pink.

"Is there no one upstairs, then?"

How were we to know what went on upstairs? Or how Rebecca could decline all of a sudden, when not more than an hour or two prior she'd rapped the door and collected the trays for dinner?

Mr. Burton leapt the steps to the manse proper, shouldering past Mr. Beede, who trailed behind in a scuttling echo of boots.

"We'll move her to your room, Lucy. Jacob—" The two lifted Rebecca, and her arms swung loose. Her eyes were glassy and rolled round in a chaotic pattern.

I led the way, unlocking the door, then rolling the ribbon that held the key from my wrist, and setting it atop the chest of drawers before striking a match to a candle that fluttered and flamed to life. The ewer was empty; I lifted it and returned to the kitchen as Cook and Jacob took to settling her.

Mr. Beede stopped my hand as I raised the ladle from the water urn. "Come. You're to help Mrs. Burton now."

He lifted the leather satchel, forgotten in the fright. And after holding the door had me follow up the stairs.

The sitting room had a high ceiling, the walls a wash of blue that could not leaven the weight of the deep plum curtains closed tight against the night nor abate the heat of the fire. Portraits hung along each wall: powdered wigs and dead pheasants and voluminous skirts and half-cocked hunting rifles the main features of each. The only painting that varied from the Burton family lineage occupied the space above the fireplace: a larger-than-life study of the woman who shifted in the chair below. The cheeks in the oil above had an apple glow, and the bare shoulders a becoming roundness. Mrs. Burton, though, had neither. Her eyes were puffy, and her dress plain, buttoned hastily and undone at the throat.

At our entrance, Mr. Burton turned from the window. "You've brought the girl."

"Yes." Mr. Beede gave a half bow and pulled me by the wrist until I stood directly in front of Mrs. Burton. "I've brought Lucy to assist you with your . . ."

Mrs. Burton twisted to her husband. "Rebecca didn't tell me she was sick."

"We'll not fret." He touched the top of Mrs. Burton's hand and continued to the hall.

Mr. Beede swallowed and moved to follow him. But then he turned back, lifting the leather bag from his shoulder and setting it on the rug near my skirts. He moved to the doors, then turned to us. "We'll fetch the doctor in the morning."

Mrs. Burton grasped the edge of the round table. "For Rebecca?"

"For Rebecca."

And then we were alone.

"Why would she be outside?" I asked.

Mrs. Burton picked at her collar. Her thumb poked at the lace until it rent a hole that she then patted flat. "They'll say I sent her out. I didn't. But they'll say I did. She'll say I did." She stood from the chair and paced between a settee of gray velvet and a marble-topped card table. "She had a headache at dinner. I remember she said she had a headache and was feeling out of sorts and would eat in her room. I'm sure the tray is still there if you want to . . . no—she brought it down. It's with mine."

She veered away from the table, toward the double doors, and stumbled over the bag Mr. Beede had left. I reached to catch her, but she swung away. She clenched her skirts in her fists and her breath went shallow. Then she dropped to her knees and searched the floor until her hands grappled the buckles on the bag.

She gripped a small, blue glass vial of clear liquid. In one motion, she untwisted the cork and took a sip. "There." She crouched back on her heels, let out a sigh, and then pressed the cork tight with the flat of her palm. Then she smoothed her skirts and stood, shifting the bottle to a skirt pocket.

There was a tinkle of a bell and a flicker of movement to my left. A large orange cat dragged itself from under the settee and lumbered across the floor to disappear behind a hutch.

We both followed the sound of the bell.

"That's Mr. Quimby."

"Is he a good mouser?"

"Does he look it?"

I shook my head. "No."

She swallowed a sob, then bent forward, dropping her head in her hands. Her hair, now loose from the comb, fell forward and hid her expression.

The bell again, harsher this time. Spoon on metal pot. There's no steam from it; Matron has carried it across the yard, and the drizzle will have congealed whatever makes up the stew.

The decree that states my time of death is folded, the words are out of sight, though she's left it neat by my bowl and spoon.

She's taken the rum cake.

As I knew she would.

Chapter Six

Her name was Eugenie Charlotte, but I did not know that until later. Later still, I would call her Gene, and perhaps then I should have been more careful. But that night, as Rebecca lay a floor below in semiconsciousness, I knew only her fear.

"Oh God." The mistress—Eugenie—dropped her head in her hands. Then she turned in a rush, stopping just at the boundary to the hall to gesture me to follow. "Come."

I gripped the valise and moved toward her. There was only the rustle of her skirt as she hastened along the wood floor. Her fingers trailed the walls and tapestries and the edges of tables as we sped along, taking the opposite path to the foyer and well away from Mr. Burton's study. She clambered the wide stairs, feet silent on risers carpeted in swirls of calla lilies and vines. Her figure was quickly swallowed by the shadows. It was an advantage, wasn't it? To be familiar with the dark's quirks and moods?

She thrust open a door at the end of the gray-tinted hall. The room was frigid, the long windows open, air pawing at the curtains. The fire had burnt to ash, only a low red glow left. Enough for me to see her fling her body into a tufted chair of robin's-egg blue. She clasped and unclasped the bead and embroidery pocket at her waist.

Then, in a start, she rose to shut the door and light a lamp on a curio table nearby.

I set the valise near the wall, crossing to the windows, reaching past the curtains to pull the windows shut. My foot caught on the curved shard of a porcelain teacup. I bent to it, finding other shattered bits, here a portion of a violet petal, there the lift and bend of green and yellow grass. I dropped the mismatched bits in my apron pocket.

The mistress perched on the edge of the chair, her fists now pressed against her stomach. She frowned and stared at the door. Her eyes glistened with a tumble of tears. "Will she live?"

"That's for God to determine," I said.

"Then she has no hope."

"Perhaps the doctor, then," I said.

"He'll give her arsenic and call it a salve."

I looked away, at the bed with its turned posts and thick covers, at the writing desk that contained both pen and paper and an odd wood frame coursed with wire, at the half-open door to the dressing room and the vestibule with drawers full of the linens I scrubbed and ironed twice a week. Against the wall near the small woodstove stood a lacquered cabinet inset with yellow herons and a gilt sun. Above it hung a watercolor of cattails prattling to each other on the edge of a brown pond. Her room alone, this woman who sneered at God.

My own diffidence of the Almighty was deep. Father proclaimed God a dullard's crutch, and I could not disagree. But those troubled relationships were not for public dissemination.

I lingered nearby, unsure what my duties should be, or if I should give her comfort. Mr. Beede had pulled me up the steps, leaving me with no explanation, though it was clear I was meant to replace Rebecca. A word of instruction would have been appreciated. Instead, I was dropped in the middle of the sitting room with as much attention paid to me as the leather bag I lugged up the stairs.

I chose to stoke the fire. I chose to roll the pieces of teacup onto a dinner tray and let the bits float in what was left of the beef soup.

What did Rebecca do for her? What was done for me, once upon a time, when my name was good and God not a bitter flavor? What had I done later for others, when my family was lost to me, for a penny or a bed? Remove the jewelry and the tortoiseshell combs. Lay out a nightgown. Hang the skirt and give it a quick brush. Fold a shawl over the end of a bed that will be carelessly picked up in the morning with no thought of the girl who'd put it there.

"Now, now," I said, my voice stilted. "There, there."

"I won't be blamed." She trembled as if she had caught a chill, her teeth chattering.

I laid my hand to rest on her back until her breath slowed. "Let me brush your hair."

I found the brush atop a dresser in the alcove to the dressing room. It sat by a matching sterling-silver mirror that swirled with filigree and the initials *eBc*, and a set of keys. I lifted the brush, wondering what the *e* and the *c* stood for. She looked so small, and brittle, her unseeing eyes resting on me and waiting like a small child for the familiar stroke of the brush.

"It's not my fault," she whispered. She winced as the brush caught a tangle. "How could she—why—she's made herself sick. It wasn't—" A drop of scarlet bloomed on her lower lip; she had bit hard enough to break the skin.

"You're bleeding," I said.

"Am I?"

I set the brush down and gave her my handkerchief. She dabbed at her lip.

She shook her shoulders, straightening in the chair, her neck and jaw tense. "She told me yesterday she wasn't feeling well. I should have listened. I should have given her the day to rest. But she said nothing today. If I'm not told one way or another, then I won't think of it one way or another. Why should I?"

"Are those Rebecca's keys?"

"What are you talking about?"

"On the dressing table."

"You think I locked her out."

"No, I . . . I don't think that." But I did wonder; who else would lock the upstairs doors? Mr. Burton and Mr. Beede could not have, for they were in town. And I'd not seen Cook set a foot to the upstairs.

Mrs. Burton reached out. "Give them over." How swift the cloak of scorn dropped on her shoulders. How ugly the look that followed it. "I'd like a glass of water."

The ewer was empty. But perhaps she knew it.

She worried the strings of her purse and removed the blue vial from the pouch. "Did you hear me?"

I lifted the ewer from its bowl. "Of course."

She flicked her hand in dismissal. On my exit, I found the door shut behind me with a thud and locked.

"She'll lock the servants' door too." Jacob snipped the wick on a candle, then lifted a match to it.

"Were you listening?"

"Why would I care what a madwoman says?" Down the hall he sauntered, snipping the wicks and setting the second floor ablaze in light.

I gripped the ewer to my chest and followed. "She feeds and clothes you, so you might think to care a bit."

He smirked. "Care didn't do much good for Rebecca, did it?"

How Rebecca writhed and gasped that night. The poultice Cook applied aided her naught, nor the towel-wrapped ice pressed to her forehead and chest. Cook shushed and hummed hymns, brushing Rebecca's sweat-matted hair from her forehead, leaning away from her flailing fists.

The air in the room—my room—was stale and putrid sweet. I pressed my palm to my nose and mouth, as my kerchief remained upstairs with the mistress, and waited on orders from Cook. I'd ferried broth and tea, swung the mallet to gather thick shards of ice from the well.

Once, Cook reached out to me, clasped my hand until the bones pressed and ground, sure she'd been that Rebecca was meeting Death in the cold of night. But Rebecca, whose breath had quivered and stilled, arched her chest of a sudden. She coughed and rasped before collapsing back to the fever-soaked mattress.

"That's the spirit." Cook released her grip on me and rubbed Rebecca's arms. "We'll need no doctor here." She glanced at me, and there was a desperate look in her eye. The same look I'd seen from the mistress just hours before.

I, too, had no faith in doctors. When I was eleven, I watched my brother and mother die within hours of one another from whooping cough. John succumbed at 6:48 a.m. and Mother at 8:32 a.m., the broth the maid brought still steaming in its cup as she gasped her last. Doctor Ainsworth, who left the hair to grow from his ears and whose breath smelled of peppermints he never shared, draped the sheet over my mother and patted me on the head as he strode by. "You were a good girl, Lucy. You took all the medicine I prescribed. And here you stand."

John and Mother took the medicine, too, and there they lie.

My father fixed his gaze on me, alive and breathing. I spread my arms as he stepped forward. I wanted him to wrap me up, to carry me as he did once when my tooth ached and he spent the night walking a circle and reading *A Midsummer Night's Dream* with all the voices. But he pressed his palms to the sides of my face and squeezed until my ears rung and my skin burned. "She's dead," he said. "She's dead."

For many days following, he cried out in grief, keening in his room at the God he once dismissed, blaming him for Mother's death, for John's, and not the dose of bitter brown liquid my mother spooned religiously into our mouths. He was a man of rational thought; medicine was meant to heal.

I blamed them all.

Years later, when I'd quickened with Ned and returned to the house in shame, another doctor, whose name was never mentioned, gave me a bottle of tonic to stir into my morning oatmeal. He followed the gift with directions to remain in my room with ample cloth and water and not be too startled by the bleeding. I buried the extract in the garden.

It wasn't my growing belly I worried about. I had more of a bond with my neighbor's dog than I did with the child. But I was selfish in wanting to keep my own life.

I had no certainty the poison was meant only for the child.

The only time Cook moved from Rebecca's side was to make breakfast for the Burtons upstairs. She sang:

> *See gentle patience smiles on pain*
> *Then dying hope revives again . . .*

Her voice was like a bird's in late May, sweet and full of life, each note meant to coax a soul from the lip of death. I took up the stool, the cool cloth, the psalm.

> *The promise guides her ardent flight,*
> *And joys, unknown to sense, invite,*
> *Those blissful regions to explore*
> *Where pleasure blooms—*

But the psalm was too well known to me, meant for a dying child, one I'd sung before, and I could not continue it. And the question of those keys in the mistress's room and Rebecca's rescue at the edge of the woods gripped me.

I pressed the cloth to her febrile forehead. "Did she lock you out?" Was the mistress that heedless, or did Rebecca deserve it? Although to be put out in the snow—

Her head lolled on the pillow, eyes bright with fever, and her brow creased in a deep frown. She wanted something, but her mouth formed only a thin whisper. She twitched her finger for me to come closer. I leaned over, my ear near enough her lips to feel the scratch of chapped skin against my own. "Has she asked for me?"

"No."

Her hand snaked in my hair, fingertips sunk into my skin, and her teeth clamped to my earlobe.

"Jesus." I rolled my shoulder into hers to alleviate the pain as her teeth clenched on cartilage and lobe.

My arms flailed as I looked for purchase, then found it. I pressed my palms to her face, thumbs digging into the soft ridges under her cheeks to force her to let go. Then I nearly tumbled from the stool.

I swiped at my ear, sure my hand would come away with blood. I swiped again in disbelief that her bite had not broken skin.

I didn't know I'd raised my arm to hit her until it was stopped by Cook's grasp. She stared down at me, mouth in a narrow line and lips lost in the fold. "Turn the other cheek, child."

There was a commotion then at the door, and the appearance of a doctor with grand sideburns and a solemn glare. His girth was contained by a satin vest checked red and black. He set his bag on the floor, shucking off his long coat and holding it out to me.

He waved me out of the way. "I'll see Mrs. Burton next."

"What do you want?" The mistress's voice was muffled by the door—still locked. The water ewer sat where I'd left it earlier.

"I've your breakfast."

"I don't want it."

I blew out a breath and rolled my eyes. My skin and muscles ached from tiredness, my ear thrummed, and I shook badly. The tray with its simple meal of oats and corn pone was heavy in my hands.

"Then I'll leave it for the cat."

"Leave me be."

"Are you afraid of her?" I whispered.

There was silence, then a loud bang of something hard hitting the door. I prayed she'd not tossed the chamber pot.

I remembered then, as Rebecca released me, the way she glared. Her eyes so full of venom. Yet our paths had rarely crossed. The venom was not meant for me.

"Are you there?" Mrs. Burton's voice was low.

"Yes."

"Is she alive?"

I set the tray on my hip. "Yes."

"The doctor—"

"Is coming up straight after seeing her. Let me help you."

We met the physician in the sitting room.

"I am so sorry to hear about Rebecca." Mrs. Burton kept her hands crossed in her lap, her shoulders square, chin lifted. As composed and beautiful as the portrait that hung behind her. "Please let me know all we can do. Of course, there will be a donation to your clinic. For the paupers."

Chapter Seven

The doctor proclaimed it typhus. Rebecca was ordered to remain in confinement and not be moved from the bed. He left me instructions of what to give her, which I shared with Cook.

"Two drams of this." I swirled the small vial of brown liquid. "Harlan's Coca Extract upon waking. Stiff dose of brandy for the late afternoon. A tepid elixir of larkspur and crushed nettles for the main meal."

"Nettle?"

"It goes on." I held the paper to the lamp. "Eye of newt and the wing of a Belgian firefly are to be given at the first signs of decomposition—but only when accompanied by a long chant to Hecate and the waxing moon."

Cook snatched the paper from my hand and gave me a smack on the back of the head. "Your imagination does not become you." She pored over the directions twice before tearing the paper in half, opening the oven, and flicking them into the flame. "No drams or extracts needed here. I trust my own medicinals. Give me the bottle."

I held it out to her, the murky liquid sloshing the bottle's interior and leaving a ring of oily dregs, and watched as she poured the contents into the slop bin. I felt a pang of sorrow for the potato grindings and apple cores.

She lifted a jug of vinegar from the larder and set it with a thud on the table.

"Everyone's getting a bath," she said.

All around me hung day dresses in plaids and various patterns, and evening ones that shimmered in peaches and blues. They were all out of date, the shoulders too narrow, the lace too articulated, too fancy.

The mistress allowed me only to remove her dress, petticoats, and crinoline, before asking me for the corset hook. She sighed and waited for me to turn my back.

I pivoted round in the dressing room so I faced the tall built-in drawers painted a flat light blue.

"Are you turned?" she asked.

"Quite around."

I counted the drawers that went from the floor to just above my waist. Six in all, quite thin. The top drawer for everyday brooches and trifles. The next down for gloves and handkerchiefs. The lower drawers contained pantalets and bloomers, a partition for the stockings, and the bottom two drawers reserved for the daily change of her chemise.

Behind me came the shirring of the hook on the corset, the soft slide of it to her feet, and a long intake of breath.

I knew the cut and weight of all of them. She was fond of pink ribbon ties. Each chemise was identical to the other, wide necked and short sleeved, all of a fine Egyptian cotton. Each was embroidered on the collar with a raised letter to designate the day of the week. Only one chemise remained untouched by the needle. It was plain lace and worn only on Sundays.

There was a curl of movement, the air stirring as her underthings dropped and she shrugged on her robe.

"Where did you set the tub?"

"Near the fire."

"You can turn around now."

I glanced at her over my shoulder. Her hands clutched the robe tight. A thin white light cast itself in from the window, leaving her face half in shadow and half lit. The muscle in her jaw twitched.

There was a tinkle of a bell as the cat ambled through the bedroom and into the closet. With a purr and a shake of his head, he made a figure eight around Mrs. Burton's legs, detaching himself and wandering on before she could pet his fur.

"Would you like a vinegar bath, too, Mr. Quimby?"

He leapt to the window ledge, his attention on the sway of the bare trees beyond.

"Have you had him a long time?"

"Mr. Quimby?"

"Yes."

"Since I was fifteen. I could still see. That makes him—oh, that makes him seventeen. Does he look seventeen?"

"Besides the cane and the false teeth, he's looking particularly well."

She laughed, then her eyebrows dropped and she gave me a quizzical look. "That makes me thirty-two. Do I look ancient too?"

"No, you look . . ."

She shook her head. I stepped aside as she moved past me and out to the bedroom. "Show me the tub so I don't fall in it."

I took her elbow, thinking how thin it was, and how I felt her pulse between my fingers. "I've put the cloth and soap on a chair next to it."

Her hand reached out.

"To the right," I said.

Her fingers traveled the fabric and soap, explored the seat of the chair, found the lip of the metal tub. She hesitated, then dipped her hand to the water, and her nose crinkled at the sting of vinegar in the steam.

She stood. "I can bathe myself."

"I'll wait outside, then."

She nodded and hesitated before speaking. "Do you read?"

As she bathed, I perched on the edge of the settee in the dressing room, reading aloud a letter from a Mrs. Aurora Kepple of Concord.

Dearest Gene,
I so wish you and my brother had the means and time to visit
from your wilderness. You would find Tad and Theo more
than a handful, but loveable nonetheless. We are putting on
a production of As You Like It for no one but the staff and
dear Otto's pater and mater. How much better it would be
were you to play Rosalind instead of me. I am much more
convincing as a Celia, but alas Otto's cousin Mar—

But here something had spilled on the ink, and the blotches and single letters were unreadable.

"There's nothing more to read. It's been sent like this."

"Rosalind suits her."

I wondered why Aurora Kepple had not chosen to rewrite the letter. I ran my eyes over the address and then across the date in the right-hand corner.

A half year prior.

"Is this the latest letter from her?"

There was a lap of water. "She is much in demand for her speeches."

"Too busy to rewrite a letter to her sister-in-law."

The water sloshed and Mrs. Burton rapped the metal. "Where did you put the towel?"

I set the letter on the dresser and rose from the settee. "It's folded on the chair. Can I help you?"

She did not answer. There was a dull thud; the soap just missed the chair and landed on the floor.

"Mrs. Burton?"

"Yes. I would like your help." The words were clipped.

Mr. Burton was attentive to Rebecca. Each morning, before he departed for the mill, he pulled a chair to her bed and sat vigil. Sometimes he smoothed the blankets, others he tied the bow on her nightdress. Little kindnesses. I had never seen such offered to Mrs. Burton, though he was not cold to her. Just formal, as if they had agreed to a partnership and were fulfilling the terms. Cook said the mistress's marriage to him brought with it enough money for the establishment of the mill. And, she said, I should mind my own soup pot, for that money and the mill gave each of us a room and ample board.

I slowed on my way from the linen room, my arms heated by just-ironed sheets. There he sat and peered at her, as he did the other mornings.

"Would you like a tea, Mr. Burton?"

He turned with a start. "How is she?"

"I think she's past the worst."

"Mm." He looked me up and down, not with diffidence, but curiosity, I suppose. In another man I would find it insolent. I don't know why this was not the case with him, save the fact I had witnessed the care he paid Rebecca. "Are you fitting in?"

"I suppose I am."

"Cook speaks well of you."

"Does she?"

"She is a fine judge of character."

My chest and face grew hot. "If you say, then it must be so."

He gave a short laugh. "Then I say so."

"Well."

"Well." He pressed his hands to his knees and stood. "I'm keeping you from your work."

"No. I mean, yes, I have work to do."

"You'll let me know if she turns for the worse?"

"Of course."

"Thank you . . . ah?"

"Lucy."

"Lucy. Yes. I remember."

Laundry at the prison is not so much different than the Burtons'. Oh, the vats are larger, the lye stronger, the water colder, the brush more beard than bristle. But the rhythm does not change. The chilblains and aching back remain cloying companions.

Tuesdays were washdays at the Burtons' house; here the wash runs in an infinite loop of stink and ripped hems and the general malingering odor of rough men too tight held.

It's Gert's day for the vat and mine to wring. I like Gert. She's broad like a block, and her shoulders are made for the weight of the woolens on the pole she pulls from the vat and swings toward me. She's patient as I remove the water-laden trousers and shirts and move them with a *whumpf* to the wringing table. The water drips through the slatted top, travels a trough to the yard outside, fingering its way round a barred opening.

"Jimmy Sprag's been sent up," she says. She gives a quick lift of her chin at the end of the phrase, an odd quirk of hers. It's a guess whether it is a challenge to contradict or merely nod. "Four years." Her voice is deep as a man's, and her words catch on the gap in her front teeth. She pulls her lips back in a smile and gives me a wink under her wild ginger eyebrows. We're not supposed to be talking. The rule is silence. But Gert is not a prisoner so she abides by her own rule. She oversees the laundry, an employee of this fine establishment, with her own cottage just on the other side of the gates. "Embezzlement," she says. "Thought his talent for twisting numbers was better than the bank manager. And who do ya think was sweetening up the manager's wife? Called into court and she broke down on the way to the stand. 'I been inveigled and ruined,' she said. Broke her nose when she landed in a faint. Oof—wish I'd been there ta see that."

Gert's got an appetite for the penny papers and doesn't let a good crime story pass by. She's a walking encyclopedia of the inmates' sins and swindles.

She twists round and dumps a mound of black-striped shirts in front of me. I yank at the lot, separating them into piles to wring, holding them up to check for holes and tears longer than two inches. Those will be sent to the seamsters, who are allowed a needle and thread. Jimmy Sprag will no doubt end up one of them; it's a nice, quiet room for those of the professional class.

A bright flash of red catches my eye: a small square of red ribbon stitched along a bottom hem. A message next to it embroidered in small block letters, neat stitches, and mismatched thread.

Mary me Lucy. Im a gud man. J. Trindill

A marriage proposal.

I press the wet shirt to my breast, pull the arms of it round my back. How much planning and bribing and threatening went into gaining that piece of ribbon? Was the needle whittled from wood purloined from the yard? Reached for without a guard noticing the misstep in line? Did this J. Trindill sweat over the cross-stitch and curse the French knot? I don't know who he is, only that he's clever with his plans. I want to roll the shirt tight, shift it and its sentiment under my skirts. Sneak it to my cell and wrap it round me like a lover. Rough written words on rough fabric.

"I've been proposed to, Gert." I drop my hip and turn to her, the shirt still against my shift and apron.

Gert drops a scrub brush and lumbers over, waving her calloused ham of a hand at me. "What are you on about?"

She pushes aside a line of limp laundry and I step back, hugging the shirt tighter. But Gert picks it up by the shoulder seams and brays a laugh once she's gained possession. Holds it up to the flat steamy light so the message furls and flutters.

"Where'd he get the ribbon?" She smiles at the mystery of it, and snorts and presses her hands to the back of hips. "Trindill? John Trindill?" She leans back, hands still on her hips and one rolled sleeve falling. "John Trindill what burned out the tannery in Jaffrey and took the old widow's house and life right with it?"

"You know of him?"

"I wouldn't answer it. He's as bad a man as any here." She clutches her sleeve and works it back up her arm. "You'll have plenty to choose from, mark me." She whistles, shakes her head, slips back to the vat. "You'll be rolling in sentiments come your meeting day."

So the word has spread already. I should have known. The other prisoners who work the laundry—Almira and silent Margaret Terrence—stared at me this morning. It's been their habit to look away. They're afraid of me. Gert says they've asked the warden to transfer me somewhere else.

"Where the hell else do they think you can go?" Gert slapped my back. "Keep 'em aquiver."

But today they stared.

I've left John Trindill's shirt for last. I've nothing to answer him with. No etui to respond in threads of gold and peacock blue. Had I a pen I could dip the nib in ink and give an answer across the inside collar.

Dear kind sir—I would say this because it might be true. The fire might have been an accident; he might not be the J. Trindill who set the boards alight. Just as Sprag's wife might not have broken her pretty nose upon falling in the courtroom, and her manager husband might have been the real embezzler, as Gert would assert.

Dear kind sir, I would say, *thank you for your pity. I must, with great regret, turn down your generous offer. I have thought long on the matter . . .*

But that is an equivocation. If there's one thing I know, an equivocation casts a flurry of shallow stings and leaves the recipient bewildered, muddled, and terribly, terribly angry.

J. Trindill, late of arson and the fiery death of an old woman, deserved better.

The Companion

Dear kind sir,
You may be a good man, but I am not a good woman.

The ribbon is easy to pick out of the ragged fabric. It shines still, the weft heavy, more silk than wool. Nearly the mix of the ribbons that rolled from the Burton Millworks. Smooth as a whisper, those were. Soft as a passing caress.

Perhaps this ribbon came from there.

My stomach twists. It's not from the quince pie Gert shared.

Eugenie gave me ribbons. Blue satin, and red grosgrain, and canary yellow that suited my hair. How smug she was, legs crossed under her skirts, an empress in the midst of the comforters and bolsters. Ribbons wound round her fist, loose ends dangling and teasing. Such color in the midst of that winter and cold spring. Sinuous and tempting and so rich I could taste the brightness on my tongue.

Her fingers pressed and smoothed them, one by one: slick satin of blue with the curled edges, uniform bumps and eddies in the grosgrain, the whorls and nubs in the yellow. All the textures mapped by her skin.

The ribbons, and later the garnet earrings that were but baubles to Eugenie—for she would never see the deep red-umber hue of them—and the bracelet I wore under cover of night were all gifts.

But gifts have consequences.

They become evidence.

Gert flips another load of wash before me. "There was a sawmill burned in Fitzwilliam in '51. I'd set that on John Trindill's head. And what misused girl did he connive that ribbon from?" Her chin jerks twice. "Wonder at that, why don't ya."

I drop the bit of fabric between the slats. It tumbles and rolls past the bars to settle and sink in the mud.

Chapter Eight

Dear Ned,

Just a short bit of quiet now—you wouldn't believe the riot here—the whole house stripped for a flea! Cook dunked Mr. Quimby in the vinegar mix and we're still not sure who had it worse.

She picked up a thick brush and scrubbed him the same as she did the laundry. Mr. Quimby hissed and spit, but Cook was faster than his claws, swinging him one way or the other depending on his choice of attack.

Would you have liked a cat? Not one like Mr. Quimby. He's a grumpy mean-puss to everyone except Mrs. Burton. The world turns on its axis when she pays him attention. No—I think you would much prefer a great roly-poly puppy with breath as sweet as yours. And a rocking horse in gilt with a shiny leather saddle and silk reins. I saw one today, in the nursery, and I thought—I thought of you.

How much I'd give to you!

Do you know tomorrow is your birthday? You would be two years old. How proud I'd be of you. I'll kiss you a good night—wait for it!

With All My Love—

Linens and curtains were subjected to two bouts of boiling water, vinegar, and lye. Jacob and I followed Mr. Beede room to room, pulling curtains, rolling rugs, yanking dust sheets from unused furniture in neglected rooms, exposing it all to a tumble of dust-kissed light.

We were in a room now bare of curtains and flooded with light. The glare of it caused me to blink. The walls bore signs of paintings removed, the wires hanging listlessly from the cornices. Dust motes clung to the corners and feathered up the joins. The cheeriness of the yellow paint tattered at the edges. A room willfully ignored rather than forgotten.

My neck flushed with sweat. Too much like another room, a room in my family's home. That home willfully stripped of spoons and butter presses and Mother's etui and all the books: items traded by Father for drink. Bedframes and spoons. The butter press and pewter. Linens marked neat in the corner, to be handed to me on my wedding and passed by me to a daughter of my own in someone else's hands and the name unstitched for another. Two plates, a pot, a few greens and grains left. All the money I'd sent to Father from the mill disappeared down his throat. The stench of this room the same as that: fust and mildew and disquiet.

That last day, Father on the stairs, his ankle awobble on the first riser. "You're nothing to me."

I remained at the parlor door, belly swelled with a child knocking at the world, my nails gripped tight to the wood frame, and knees locked fast to keep me upright.

His foot slipped slow and clumsy to the landing, his boot catching and jumbling the carpet. He grabbed the railing and pulled himself up, taking in a rasp of air and releasing the bloated stink of whiskey. Each foot carefully set upon each stair. Halfway up, another stumble, his body swinging wide, a sodden bounce from off the rail, an "umph" and shake of the head before he righted himself and continued the climb.

My blood buzzed and sawed through my veins, a hiss of ice under the skin. "Was I ever something?"

He slowed, but my words did not carry to the top of the stairs, and so he continued on. No words to stop him. My grief and gathering hate followed to the second floor, then slid along behind him and careened off the walls. My thoughts snapped to the month prior, to that bottle of solution the doctor left for my "misery." I had buried it under the honeysuckle in the far corner of the yard. The poison leached over the weeks, and as Ned grew and pressed inside me, the honeysuckle browned and withered to hollow stalks.

Father's door shut with a thud. I licked my lip of blood. I should have kept that bottle close by, killed the child inside, or myself, or him. Instead, I killed the honeysuckle, which was one of the only things Father could not sell or trade for his mourner's measure of whiskey and the last of the garden Mother had raised to health.

My teeth clicked and chattered, echoing in the empty rooms. Not even a curtain rod remained, just mud grouted in the divots of the pine planks, gouges from furniture dragged away, and the carpet too bare and torn for even the rag man's fancy.

I managed my way to the front door, my hands turning the brass knob. The sun was midday bright, and I blinked against the glare. A woman with a peach parasol walked past. It was Mrs. Hofsted. One of the ribs was awry, once broken and rough repaired. Mrs. Hofsted, two doors down with the dog that yapped all day. So solicitous when Mother died, sending pea porridge soup and meringues. Holding Father's hand between hers. Fingers short, inflated like balloons, dry hot against my cheek. There in the house for days on end, then not there anymore. I missed the meringues. Father said they'd rot my teeth and that she was rotting him.

She glanced at me, then away, eyes drilled forward again to the walk. The umbrella bobbed above her head. I waited until she was at the corner, had crossed the street, the parasol—once my mother's—shrinking to a spot of color under the elms.

A sharp kick behind the ribs. Ned reminding me of his presence. My breath caught. I pressed my palm to my belly, moved it in circles. "There, there."

How impudent he was. As annoying as Mrs. Hofsted's dog and its unrelenting need for attention.

The lock squealed behind me, then a clunk as the bolt turned. With a jerk, I grabbed the handle and twisted. "What are you doing?" But the lock held tight. I gathered my skirts and hopped from the step, moving around the side of the house to the rear yard. The crisp grass crackled. I wrenched open the back screen, twisting the knob to the kitchen door. "You can't turn me out."

He was right behind the door, his breath a wheeze. "I can," he said.

I lay under the honeysuckle that night, back pressed against the fence, and watched the yellow candle as he moved from room to room. He passed out in the dining room. The candle burnt itself out, and the glass became a gape of dark. I was gone before light.

"Lucy." Mr. Beede tapped my shoulder.

"What?"

"The pillows." Mr. Beede held his list aloft, his thumb marking our progress through the house.

I lifted a square pillow from the end of a brocade settee. It was simple, embroidered in a star pattern of tulips interspersed with angular green stems that each held a single leaf. It was child's work, though there were no children here. It was hidden beneath a silk pillow bilious with smug angels who seemed too fat for their fluttering wings. Both were forgotten on this settee draped in sheets in a room that should have been filled with the memory of guests and conversations past. Perhaps it was, and the Burtons were once a warmer couple with hopes of children still bright. I dropped the pillows in the basket I'd hauled in.

There was a crack of wood against wood behind me, followed by a reverberation of piano strings. Jacob stood at the pianoforte, staring at the keys. The sharp sun reflected off the surfaces, coaxing a honey tone from the deep brown of the wood. The fabric that clothed it lay crumpled at his feet. He pressed a heavy thumb to the high F, then followed with E below C and pounded the lowest notes until the piano groaned. It was quite out of tune, and a few keys were absent of string.

I had not played in too many years to remember. It was not a talent of mine; that was given to my mother. I'd spent many hours half ignoring the drone of Mr. Wiley, my piano teacher, half intrigued by his untoward height and anticipating the moment he'd forget to duck while entering our parlor. But Mother loved our simple upright, and it sung for her.

The instrument pulled me to it. I ran my fingers along the curved edge of the cover. Who owns Mother's piano now? It has surely passed hands. Sits in another parlor with a different set of watercolor portraits atop its frame. Perhaps someone else plays "Annie Laurie" and sighs with the last note.

"Who's here?"

We all turned. Mrs. Burton stood in the doorway, a hand to her throat as if to tamp down more words. Her other arm was tight round her waist. Her body quivered and her face was pale.

Mr. Beede stepped forward. "Mrs. Burton?"

"The furniture's all been moved." She pressed her fists to her skirts. "You need to move the furniture back."

Jacob dropped the piano lid. Mr. Beede jumped. He gave Jacob a quick hard look before turning to Mrs. Burton. "I apologize for the—"

"I don't care about your apologies. I want the furniture put back where it belongs."

"We're in the process of gathering the carpets for beating. All will be returned to normalcy by evening."

"Does one flea really require all this?"

"Typhus requires this." Mr. Beede rocked on his shoes and rolled his list in his fist. "Best to return upstairs, Mrs. Burton."

"It's all a mess up there too." Her voice had grown tremulous. She clutched and unclutched her skirt. "Why this room?"

Jacob shook his head and whistled as he rolled the rug, giving a swat for me to move aside.

Mr. Beede sniffed. "Lucy, could you take—"

"I'm perfectly capable of returning to my room."

She would not admit she was lost. We had moved everything haphazardly, left sofas in hallways, bureaus on opposite walls, books and vases on mantelpieces, baskets of bed linens near the stairs, carpets rolled and waiting for their walk to the yard and a good beating.

Not once had we thought about her.

I wondered if we would ignore her as we stripped her bedroom, if Jacob would lift her and move her to the side with the writing desk, if Mr. Beede's list included returning her clothing and brushes and shawls to their original spots. If the chemises so neatly sewn with the days of the week would be folded and ordered from Monday through Sunday.

I wondered if Rebecca would merely have locked Mrs. Burton in her closet and got on with the work.

"You'll be in charge of your own room." I crossed to the mistress. "And I'd be more than thankful if you could take a handle of this basket."

Upstairs, we tossed the sheets and stamped the dust from the chair seats. Trundled the runners and rugs to the hall. I held out her dresses and gave her the job of brushing them out. She was fastidious—flicks of the brush followed by the touch of her fingers, a quick frown if the nap was not to her pleasing, a repeat of the same pattern of movement from one dress to another.

Mr. Quimby remained wrapped around her slippers in a corner, giving a low growl if I came too close.

"How many poor souls has he mauled?" I returned a skirt of plum-and-brown plaid to its hanger.

"Only those who deserved it."

"Really?"

"Are you worried?" She paused, then let out a laugh. "Shall we do the drawers?"

"Will you help scrub the floor?"

"Will you play a hand of cards?"

I took the chemises from her and tossed them in the basket. "Your cards are marked."

"How else will I know what's what?" She pulled open the bottom drawer, scooping out the pantalets. "How else could I possibly win?"

I tapped the handle of the basket and watched her heft the fabric. "Good aim."

She curtsied, her hand moving in a grand gesture.

"You're not at all what I expected," I said.

"Neither are you." She straightened, shaking her head. Her fingers found the silver watch hung from a short chain at her waist. She clicked open the glass and touched the hands on the dial. "It's already half past one." The corner of her mouth lifted in a smile. "Let's see to the floors."

But Mr. Beede refused her the chance. He escorted her to the conservatory to sit among the ferns and the hard-pruned roses. I brought her tea and nearly spilled it at the sight of her—how she rocked and glared. A fingernail tap tap tapping the glass of her watch.

I set the cup and saucer on the small table.

She did not acknowledge me. Just rocked and glared.

I turned to leave but was stopped by the rake of her chair.

"I am not useless," she said.

"No. You're not."

In the foyer, Mr. Beede roughed my neck and pushed his face close to mine. "What are you thinking?" He gave me a quick shove. "Get to the carpets."

LeRocque did not come today. Matron brought me breakfast and did not stay to talk about her beau. It rained most of the morning, fat drops against the high window and a deafening drum on the roof. Now a stillness. One hour after another. Hours upon hours to drive me mad. "Who's here?" No answer but the rhythm of my breath.

Mrs. Burton set much by her watch. Egg and toast at 6:30 a.m., with hair and clothing to be completed no later than 8:00 a.m., the conservatory at 9:30 to attend the meager plants. Embroidery at 11:00, and a plate of cakes at noontime sent by Cook. The hourly pass of the grandfather clock to match the time on its great hands with those of her own.

Afternoon hours were given over to correspondence. Not received. No, there were no letters for her to open or missives to read her, though she waited daily for the mail. But still she wrote. How careful she was, the nib of the pen placed in the wire grid, as letter by single letter the pen scratched and inked the paper. Then came the powder tipped and sifted, and a forty-five-second wait for the ink to dry. The envelope addressed to this cousin or that dear friend.

"Take these."

And that first afternoon, my eyes dim from the nap I'd stolen while she wrote, my arms stiff from all the cleaning, I took the stack from her, yawned, and descended to the first floor to drop the correspondence on the silver tray by the door.

I ambled down the stairs and set the letters on the tray. My stomach rumbled, and I thought it was as good a time as any to sneak a treat from the kitchen. But I stopped and lifted the top envelope. The address was illegible, each dispatch a chaos of block letters that smeared into pools of black.

I ripped at the wax seal to withdraw pages thick with blotted ink. My breath stuck in my throat and burned. I grabbed the others, shoved them all in my apron pocket and bolted down to the kitchen and to my room.

"What is this?" I leaned over Rebecca, the envelopes crumpled in my fist. "You broke her writing template, didn't you?"

She blinked and stared from her pillow. Then she gave a disdainful sigh.

"How long have you done this? Do you just throw them away? Why?"

"Are you going to hit me?" Her voice was rough from disuse, but her gaze was hard as glass.

"Look at this." I pulled a paper taut and held it to her nose. "Can you read this?" I tossed it behind me, holding up another. "What about this?"

My hands trembled. How I wanted to lift her by the shoulders and shake her. And yes, I wanted to hit her hard enough to remove the smirk from her face. "I'll tell Mr. Beede what you've done."

She gave a quick laugh, then pushed herself up on her elbows. "And he'll listen to you? You're nothing to this house."

My heart thumped and wavered. "And you are?"

"Mr. Burton is my cousin. I think I might mean something."

"What right do you—"

"Mrs. Burton is better off without pining for a past. How she used to cry. It gave me a constant headache. And she doesn't care to mix with the women here. The way they look at her, as if she's . . ." She shook her head. "So, you see, it's kinder this way. Isn't it, Lucy?" She raised her hands to her hair, lifting the dingy tresses and feathering them round her shoulders. "Besides, it's not your responsibility. So tell your little tale and I'll make sure you're out of this job and blacklisted at the mills." She narrowed her eyes to slits. "Or has that already been your fate?"

The blacklist. I had heard it whispered through the burling lines at Amoskeag, the girls turning their heads to follow another as she was sent out the door to face the streets of Manchester in shame.

It was easy to join the list and impossible to leave. It traveled town to town—Manchester to Goffstown to Peterboro to here—carried on gossip and confirmed in formal letters.

Small infractions added up—too many late days, sick days, early days, broken threads, bungled dyes. The shift manager and the boarding house landlady both keen eyed and suspicious.

If you were obeisant and quiet, went to church on Sunday and to the lyceum on Thursday evenings, quilted on odd Wednesdays, well, you were assured your place at the mill and a snug little room with a draft.

I, on the other hand, had caught the eye of Albert Drake. He had wavy hair and a thick dark beard and walked me partway home at night before turning from the tenements toward the brick houses with tidy lace curtains.

And wives.

And children.

But who thought of that? Better to think of the man whose clever eyes are only for you.

Think of the man who takes you to see the traveling players and fancy magicians and steals a rabbit from a hat to give to you.

It was late summer and the moon was overfull and atilt. I had followed that moon earlier, bowing out of the quilting bee, scuttling the tenement alleys until I'd met Albert at the edge of a wide field and entered the players' tent. A woman with flame hair strode the wooden stage, smoking a cheroot, and not giving a damn that people threw fruit at her. And that was when she played Juliet the first half of the evening. By the end of the night she caught the bottles tossed and never missed a word in her speech on women's plights and rights.

I was half in love with her and half terrified, but Albert was certain my sighs were meant for him.

A magician roamed the tent, pulling coins from behind the ears of pretty girls. Earlier in the night he had drawn rabbits and cockatoos, and once a tall lamp from his brown derby hat. He stopped in front of me, and he might have been a mesmerist, for I could not look away from his violet eyes.

"Can I show you another trick?" He tilted his head, and the garnet on his houndstooth coat glittered.

Albert tightened his arm around my waist.

The magician winked and pointed at Albert's coat. "May I?"

He reached forward, his index finger and thumb slipping into Albert's chest pocket.

"Now, wait a minute, sir."

But the magician lowered his lids, and his lips played a smile. "I'll keep all your secrets. Nothing to . . . What's this?"

He drew out a velvet ribbon as purple as the night. His eyebrow arched. Then he turned to me and tied it round my throat. His hand lingered on my shoulder before he slipped into the crowd.

The muscle in Albert's jaw tensed and jumped. His eyes danced in jags around the tent.

"Wasn't much of a trick," he said.

"I thought he'd pull out a rabbit."

"Disappointed?"

"No."

But I was disappointed the night was ending. The people thinned, exposing empty bottles and crumpled playbills and flattened grass. A lanky man in a smock bent to take apart the boards of the stage. There was a throaty laugh from around back, and curls of yellowed cigar smoke from behind the tent.

Albert peered down at me. He touched the ribbon, then curled it round his thumb until the edges bit my skin. He pushed his lips against mine, his mustache tickling the corner of my mouth. It was the first time he'd kissed me.

He stole a white rabbit speckled with gray. I carried it under my arm and followed him to the river.

How bright the moon was. How dark his eyes. I still see both sometimes when I'm on the verge of sleep.

I found out about the blacklist when I confessed to the child. Albert sent me to live with my father, then sent the doctor who brought the potion I buried in the yard.

Rebecca stared at me through half-drawn lids. Her mouth hung slightly open, and every so often she ran her tongue on her bottom lip.

"Blacklisted, then," she whispered.

She blinked and closed her eyes. Her chest rose and fell; her sickness still held sway, and the exhaustion showed in the dull pallor of her cheek. I pressed a wet cloth to her forehead.

"Has she asked after me?"

I held her wrist, rubbing the towel along one arm and then the other. The rash had abated, leaving scabs and divots. I rested her hands one upon the other when I determined she was truly asleep. But it reminded me too much of Mary Dawson in her casket. I pulled the blanket up to her neck to erase the image and glanced to the empty hall, waiting for Cook to set me free.

It's dark now. The watchman has come and gone.

Lucy . . .

"Who's here?"

Chapter Nine

Lucy . . .

Just a whisper at the last edge of sleep.

Lucy . . .

Like a quiver of air, like a sigh.

Lucy . . .

I scramble to wake, my limbs thick with night, too heavy to throw off the murmur of my name. *Lucy.*

I lurch up, pressing my palms to my face, gulping the crystal air, rubbing my thumbs against tears that will never stop falling.

Hoarfrost covers my cell window. The walls are layered with an intricate web of ice. My breath shimmers white. Winter has not fully ceded its battle to spring.

She calls my name more frequently now. It terrifies me.

"Time for prayers." Cook took a bite of biscuit, then set the morsel that was left on the saucer by her bed. It was dark, just a round light of candle between the two of us. She roughed her pillow and gave a long-winded sigh before settling her psalm book on the hill of her stomach. She smoothed the quilt around her, resettled her frill of a nightcap, glanced at the ceiling to mumble something under her breath.

It was her ritual, one I'd become accustomed to, as I shared her room at night. I lay on a thin mattress under pegs that held her apron and frocks. It gave us quick access to succor Rebecca and a few hours each to sleep. I hoped Rebecca would soon take to her own room, though I feared she exaggerated her illness to take advantage of Cook's ministrations and my own half-hearted attention.

Did I say that I was not fond of Rebecca?

If someone bit your ear, you might feel the same.

And indeed, her knowledge of my past hung heavy over me. It had no doubt been passed sour lip to sour lip that day in the kitchen, as Mary Dawson lay still and silent in the front room.

Cook had two aprons so stiffly starched they seemed in a constant billow from the wall. Her Sunday skirt and top hung from a separate peg, both a somber but fine gray wool. I noticed the same rich material in Mr. Beede's vests and coats, and Jacob's too. I had not yet been afforded a new skirt; perhaps a probationary period had to be met. Maybe I was perceived as a temporary acquisition and wouldn't receive one at all.

"I think Psalm 139 tonight, Lucy."

"As you wish."

"It's a comfort to share this with you." She turned her head and peered at me. "A nod of the head to God is good for the soul."

"Does he ever nod back?"

But no, I didn't say that aloud—instead, I muttered "Amen" and yawned.

She licked her pinky, pressing the tip to the corner of the book and shuffling the pages. Her lips pursed and then pulled into a smile. "Here we are."

> *O Lord, thou hast searched me, and known me*
> *Thou knowest my downsitting and mine uprising,*
> *Thou understandest my thought afar off.*
> *Thou compassest my path and my lying down*

From the next room came a sharp screech, and Cook and I both sat up. We waited for another sound, but there was only a mumbling and then quiet.

"What's that in your hair?"

"It's nothing," I said. "Just a bit of lace. Do you like it?"

"Did Mrs. Burton give it to you?" Cook's eyes narrowed. She lifted her teacup, the psalm book tumbling to the edge of the bed. She slurped, peering at me over the cup's lip.

"I repaired her writing board. It's a thank-you."

"Mmf." The cup clicked down. She lifted the biscuit and chewed. Cook shook her head and kept her eyes on the crumbs by her plate. "Can she write more than jibber jabber now?"

I tensed, my hands curling around the edge of the kitchen bench. "The wires just needed tightening and—"

"I don't like the pattern of it."

"What?"

"That lace. Doesn't suit you."

"Well, I like it."

"I'm sure you do. As I'm sure you've grown fond of working up there too." She took another sip of tea, then drained the cup. "But it's Rebecca's place."

It wasn't Rebecca's place anymore. It was mine, and I admit it was a step or two better than scalding pots and skinning rabbits, though I was still required for that service as well.

I admit also to jealousy.

Jealousy. Envy. A bitter sin. It burns the stomach and clenches the heart and runs tendrils of fire under the skin.

It's not a trait I'm proud to call my own, yet it likes to perch on my shoulder and whisper all manner of things in my ear.

Albert Drake had a wife and three children, and lived up from the mill on a street lined with elms. That lush summer had ticked over to a brittle fall. The leaves were browning at the edges, curling into themselves, chattering in the wind. The sky was a bright morning blue with high trailing clouds. The thinning light sharpened the corners of the neat brick houses, all painted a uniform white. I knew Albert would be at the mill, high above the lint that floated like flakes of snow, buoyed by the constant movement of spindles and thread. He wouldn't be on the street with the elms. But his wife would.

I felt the curtains shifting each side of me, wives' heads shaking in wonder. I didn't care. My father had turned me out; I had nowhere to go. I stopped at No. 23, with its gloss black door and jonquils in a pot.

Mrs. Albert Drake answered the door after the second knock. She smiled, then frowned, her blue eyes questioning. A tow-headed boy peeked from behind her skirts. I watched her stroke his hair, no conscious thought to the movement. Her gaze cut past me to the street, then back.

My throat felt thick. I was here, I had come to confront her. To prove I existed. To damn Albert in her eyes.

But nothing came out of my mouth. Not one word. I stood, the wind whipping a strand of hair across my face and the sun too bright against that white painted brick. I watched her smile fade, her mouth grow tight, her eyes widen and then blink in painful acknowledgment.

There we stood, her hand smoothing the boy's head.

Her lips quivered. "You're not the first." She stepped back into the shadow of the house and pressed the door shut.

My hands tightened to fists, nails cutting the skin. "You can't ignore me." I pounded the door, slammed the knocker until the brass vibrated. Pounded until the gardener came and dragged me from the steps.

"Wait."

I turned. The door was held but slight ajar, only enough for the woman to reach her arm out. A small felt bag hung and swayed in her fingers. She let it drop, a clink of coins. Payment for my silence.

The next afternoon, Mrs. Burton shook the powder from her letter, then held it up and blew against the paper to dry the ink. I had told her of the broken wires on the template, that perhaps it would do well to check it from time to time. I did not tell her about Rebecca's deception.

"Will you read it back to me?"

"Of course." I took the paper and smoothed it on the writing table. The printing was exact, large block letters spaced out as evenly as a girl's embroidery alphabet. Even her name was laid out as such.

"Dearest Aurora," I began. "Josiah and I send fond wishes and pray the winter has been kind. We are well here. Are the boys grown big and strong? I am thinking of adding an orange tree to the conservatory this—"

"No." She slapped her hand on the letter, crumpled it, then shifted a blank piece of paper in her writing utensil. She stopped her pen above the inkwell and looked toward me. "Rebecca doesn't watch."

"I'm not watching." I pressed my back against the chair and threaded my fingers in my lap. "How do you know I'm watching?"

She gave a muffled snort and set the pen in its holder. "Letters are personal."

"You asked me to read it."

"I've changed my mind." She picked at a wire above her paper.

"I've just fixed that."

"You can write the addresses. If you wish." Then she pushed up her sleeve and pressed her index finger on the top wire, using it as a guide for the nib of the pen.

"I do. I'll write the addresses. I'll take the letters to town too. Make sure they're delivered."

"You'll make Rebecca jealous."

"So what?" I relaxed, my head lolling to look out the window at gray branches of maples and birches. A few pines brushed dark strokes through the forest. The sky hung like a sodden blanket, threatening an icy drizzle.

"Why did you lock Rebecca out?" I asked.

Her pen stilled. There was a quirk at the side of her mouth, but she did not raise her head. "Is that what she said?"

I shrugged.

"I can't see your response."

"I didn't have one."

"You did."

I shifted in my seat. "I just assumed you'd—"

"Have you ever been doted upon and pestered to the point of screaming? You would wish for a break too." Her finger lifted and dropped again to its place next to the pen. "She locked herself out. She was delirious, if you recall."

"But you had her keys."

"I only knew they were there when you pointed them out."

"Why don't you have your own?"

The pen clattered to the table. "All the questions! Is that how you lost your last spot?"

"I didn't lose it."

She leaned an elbow on the desk, resting her chin against her palm. "Were you always a washer-upper?"

"No, I—"

"Where was your last position?"

"Concord."

"Did you like it?"

"It was—"

"Don't tell me you liked it. You left it, if you weren't fired. My guess is the latter."

"I wasn't fired."

"And I didn't lock Rebecca out." She faced her desk. "I'm not allowed keys."

"Why?"

"To keep me safe."

"But don't you wish—"

"I wish for a lot." Her breath hissed through her lips. "You're pestering me now. Go away."

The cat's bell tinkled as he leapt onto the desk. Mrs. Burton leaned forward to pet him and cooed as she rubbed her nose and cheek on his head. "Open the window as you go."

Frog song.

Sweet and tenuous and the first sign of spring.

I closed my eyes and leaned over the lintel, not minding the drizzle and scalding bits of ice.

"Do you hear it, Mrs. Burton? Frogs."

A laugh bubbled in my throat. I yanked open the other windows and pulled her from her chair.

Her wrists slipped from my grasp and she gripped the window frame, turning her head to listen. She spun round with a clap and stepped toward me, her palms finding my cheeks. Touching and then dropping away.

"Frogs," she said.

We hugged the edge of the house, well away from the kitchen, more furtive than required, for there was no one to spy on us as we followed the song. The ground cracked under us, ice and mud mixing and slipping. I wore one of Mrs. Burton's capes, bunching it carefully to not drag the ground, for she was taller than I. The silk inside smelled of the dried lavender that hung in her closets, and as the hood warmed, the scent of hair oil and verbena comingled.

Mrs. Burton's fingers dug into my arm as we moved. Her step faltered and she reached her foot out often to mind the way. Her elbow bumped my back when I stopped abruptly near the orchard fence.

The limbs of the cherry trees were riddled with brown buds, and just near the gate, a daffodil burst yellow against the post.

I took her hand and crouched down to the flower. "It's the first daffodil. My mother always said finding the first one meant luck and love."

"Did she?" Her fingers explored the stem and bell and stamen. She leaned in to smell it, the drizzle beading on the hood of her cape and freezing in the weft.

A shift bell pierced the air. The frogs ceased their calls. Just the drips of thaw from branch to ground remained.

I pressed my hand in the cape pocket and felt the jags of metal teeth, and the ring that held Rebecca's keys. Our secret escape.

"Lucy." Cook smacked a wood spoon against the table.

"I'm listening." I straightened and stared at her.

"And I'm the archangel Michael." She pointed to the mutton. "What herbs go to tender the meat?"

Five small wood cups were lined in front of me, each containing a different herb that I was meant to identify and choose for the tough old meat. I lifted the first cup and closed my eyes. "Tarragon."

"Well done."

The second: mint.

The third: rosemary.

And I thought then of lavender, and misnamed the fourth herb.

The lock on the kitchen door clicked, and Jacob entered, dropping onto the bench. Steam curled from him and his lips were bright red.

"Where's your manners with your coat?"

"Sorry, Cook." He pulled at his coat and flung it on a knob. He held up a finger, then scuffled around in the coat pockets before pulling out a glass jar. "First of the maple syrup." He set it next to the mutton. His knee bounced below the table as he kept his gaze on Cook. Adam's apple moving up and down, peach fuzz inking his chin—a boy still, awaiting his mother's approbation.

Not that Cook was his mother. God help anyone with that.

"Theo Flieger's already at the sap."

Cook picked up the jar and held it to the light. "He's kind to send it over."

Jacob glanced at me from the corner of his eye. "Enjoy the orchard?"

"It's basil." I set the cup down, too sharp, but it caught Cook's attention.

"Good girl."

"Mrs. Burton wandered again." Jacob smiled at me. "If it weren't for Lucy finding her, who knows what would happen."

"She didn't wander. We went for a walk."

Jacob blinked and kept staring. He pulled at his bottom lip, stretching it out and letting it pop back in place.

"In this drizzle-bit?" Cook asked. "We don't need another down with an ague."

"She's perfectly fine. I left her by her fire—which I lit."

"I was helping the Fliegers," Jacob said.

"I'm sure you were." I picked up the last cup. "Bitters."

The chaplain waits outside my cell, his bible held against his chest. His eyes are gray and do not leave my face. He stands in silence, like an overchiseled statue.

I remain on my cot, knees pulled to my chest, ankles crossed under my dress.

"Will you make your peace with God today?" He has the right voice for the pulpit but it echoes too loud.

"I am still damned," I say. "Whether you attend to me or not."

"Child—"

"Don't call me that."

He lifts a hand to placate, then places it back on the hard cover of his Good Book. "You must speak to him. He will forgive."

Would he? He is already half turned away.

Chapter Ten

I dreamt of Mary Dawson last night—here in my cell, my cot a raft afloat in water bubbled black. She's still here, splayed just under the water's skin, just beyond my reach.

Simple Mary. Trusting Mary.

The skin's sloughed off her legs. Green-white, thick, curled slabs of skin. Algae growing in all the crevices. Eyes poked and eaten, the lids rotted away. Nothing left of her ears, fingers stripped of flesh.

Her body twists and contorts, buoyed and sunk in the rings of an eddy. Her hair spreads and tangles and knots. Bruises darken the back of her neck and I feel a quickening of pity.

"What's it like to die, Mary?"

But she has no mouth to answer.

The cot isn't as heavy as I expected. The window not as high. The bars are strong enough to hold my weight.

Twist the sheet tight, Lucy.

Jump on the count of three.

Death sits on the stool just outside my door.

I hang and twist, my big toes scraping the floor.

Death shakes his head.

He's smaller than I thought, effete even, legs crossed and high brown boots swinging away, waves of white cotton peeking from his red coat. He smiles and his mouth is soft and round as a woman's.

Don't struggle, he says.

My hands are clenched round the sheet.

Let go. And he flings his arms wide.

Let go. I do.

For one brief moment the world is honeysuckle sweet.

But my body betrays me. Hands claw the sheet, toes press upward, lungs heave and burn.

Death laughs and shakes his shiny curls. His sneer cuts through the gray. Who knew his teeth glowed so white?

Matron grabs me tight and grunts as she struggles to lift me. I can't see anything but the spittle at the corner of her mouth. I didn't think I'd made a sound. Her nails press through my shift and dig under the bone. I grapple to release the noose; she's given me enough slack to free my neck. Then she clasps me tight to her, pulling my head into her shoulder, collapsing our bodies to the stone floor. She smells of garlic and damp. She's the first person who's held me since it all went so wrong.

LeRocque's eyes flick to the scabs on my neck but he doesn't say anything. I'm certain Matron told him about my "episode." Even Gert sent a word from the laundry, though Matron didn't want to pass it on to me. She screwed her eyes tight, as if the taste of the message were tart as vinegar. "Gert says she'd have tried the same."

"I just wanted a choice," I say to LeRocque. That's the extent of my explanation. My voice is rubbed raw.

There's a tic in his cheek when I say this, and he rolls his shoulders in that big coat. He bites his lip.

I know what he wants to say—*they* didn't have a choice, did they? It's a fair criticism. LeRocque does not want me to hang, but his faith has never wavered in my guilt.

He slaps his hands on his knees and pins on a smile. "I'm going west."

I nod. My head is so heavy. I reach behind me to pick at the paint on the stone. "Where?"

"I'm thinking of Independence. Maybe beyond."

"Out to the buffalo you showed me the picture of?"

"Think of the stories. The Shawnee and Apaches and Gringo Joe and . . ."

"And no one reads of me anymore."

Why would they read of me now? I stink of sweat and piss. Remember when I was clean and careful with the slop pail, pulling my skirts up to keep them from the damp? Picking maggots from the meat in my stew. Look at your dainty lass now, Mr. LeRocque. What do you think about this rotting thing you now see? I reek like the river. See me lick the wall for water, because there's no pail. See me scratch the stone walls and hump the bedframe for want. See me curl in the corner, for they've taken the bedding from me.

What a pretty picture you drew of me once. Remember the crowds that came? I had so little time to myself. The Fallen Woman, so capable of terrible deeds. Adored and reviled in turns.

I am too real now. I am too much a monster.

With spring, the house gurgled awake, stretching in sighs and groans. The dog's teeth of ice on the edges of the windows pooled and began their gummy chew of the panes. White paint bubbled, slipping into the veins of the wood, curling at the joins with the floor. The no-see-um flies swarmed and battered the glass, their buzz a constant threat.

Cook wore a battered brim hat that swung with wine corks, though I still spied her swatting her hand at the black flies that found their way through. She took to the kitchen garden, a basket slung on her arm, and she lumbered along each row, stopping every few paces to glare at a seed packet. The corks bobbed and swung as she read the packet print, then stared at the ground near her boot.

How Cook had awaited these seeds! Straight from the Shakers, she said. And though they were the oddest lot of worshippers she'd ever encountered, she took great joy in their seeds.

"I've seen them shake and shiver," she'd told me, her eyes aglint as she tore open the long-awaited seed box. "Think the floor beneath them would give out from the stamping. Such a set of tongues. But I suppose God knows their language as well as ours."

I picked up stones lifted by the frost and tossed them to the pile.

"We'll switch out the garlic this year. Should have had it by the east fence to begin with. I think beets and Brussel sprouts here."

I waited on my knees, trowel to soil, breathing in the thick earth, just turned, that smelled as sweet as a baby's crown. The thought was sharp as a knife; I squeezed my eyes shut, then opened them to the sky. Cook tapped beet seeds in my palm, and I prodded and poked and planted the row.

At the end, I pushed my fingers into the loam and pressed a handful into the fist of my palm. I slipped the trowel in my apron pocket and turned to the house. Cook had left the door wide to air out the kitchen and winter-stale quarters.

"You'll not dillydally and traipse dirt on those floors."

I kicked my boots against the stone step but did not answer. What could I say? I was taking a handful of soil to Mrs. Burton because I thought she would enjoy the smell. Because I wanted her to slip the cage of her rooms, and perhaps entice her to the garden to plant.

Mrs. Burton was in a chair by the sitting room window, looking out as if she could image the taut blue stretch of sky. The clear vial she held in her hand was in danger of tipping into her lap. She turned her head at the sound of my step, but it was in languor, and her expression was muddled by the laudanum she had chosen to drink instead of tea.

"You've been ignoring me."

"Cook needed me for the garden." I looked to the tea and tray I'd dropped off in the morning, both of which were untouched on the round table nearby. I squeezed the dirt in my fist. "Have you sat here all morning?"

"I might sit here all day." She pulled her lips into a frown and brushed the hair from her temple before turning back to the window. Her hand slipped from her lap, letting loose the vial to fall into the folds of her dress, the liquid darkening the fabric.

My jaw tensed as I crossed to her. "Lucky it's only me here." I grabbed the vial and set it on the sill. "Can you stand?"

She gripped the chair arms to push herself further into the seat. "I'm quite content here."

"We need to change your dress."

"I'm not a child." Her face flushed with anger and her back went rigid. But she felt the lap of her dress, her fingers stopping, then curling away from the spill. She hung her head, and her lips moved as if she were scolding herself. Then she reached out and grabbed the side of my skirt. "What do you look like?"

Quick she moved, grasping at my waist and elbows, pulling me down until I kneeled in front of her. Her thumbs pressed the curve of my shoulders and slid down to my wrists, exploring bone and tendon, turning my closed palm up. She hooked her fingers around mine, working them open to touch the dirt I'd held tight.

"I've brought you spring," I said.

She bent to it, the crumbles of earth still left in the creases of my palm, and inhaled.

I was unprepared for the brush of her thumbs on my jaw, and I flinched.

"What do you look like?"

Her hands wavered and waited. Our faces were near to touching, my cheeks warmed by the sun tilting to afternoon. The hall clock sounded the quarter hour, and the pendulum ticked a beat before the watch at her waist. I dropped my hands to her lap. Her index fingers grazed my jaw again, then pressed into my cheeks before tangling in my hair.

"What color is your hair?"

"Brown."

I inhaled at a sharp twist of the roots and the scrape of her nail.

"Dark brown or light?"

"Nearly black."

She pressed her palm to my forehead, thumbs stroking the rim of my brow, then circling to the soft skin of my lids. I could not breathe. I was too rapt in such intricate attention. My heart thumped and jagged in my chest.

How she concentrated, two tight furrows between her eyebrows, mouth pursed and serious. "Your eyes?"

"Also brown."

"Walnut or caramel?"

"Just brown."

The clocks ticked, discordant and overloud. A cool bead of sweat rolled between my shoulder blades.

"I see . . ." Her lips whispered against mine, then hesitated, then pressed. Such softness, such fullness. Her breath sour and sweet with alcohol, cinnamon, and another herb I could not name.

She would not remember this. She would slumber in a dreamless fog and wake without realizing what she'd done.

I would scrub her dress and supply new ink to the well and plait her hair and never mention this moment to her.

There was a creak in the hall—a floorboard, a door, the house settling, it did not matter, save it sent me back to my heels. I pushed at her shoulders, soiling her arm with the dirt I'd forgotten. I pulled my handkerchief from my pocket and swiped at the fabric, then stood.

Mrs. Burton let out a low sigh and gripped the edge of the seat until her knuckles paled. "Rebecca."

I turned my gaze to the door, to Rebecca, wraithlike and wan, still in convalescence, her hand on the frame for support, and a thin smile that wavered and dropped as she stared at me. "I've been calling and calling you."

"What do you want?" I asked.

Rebecca's gaze flicked to the mistress. "I'm almost better, Eugenie."

"I'm so glad."

"I heard you up here. And then I didn't. You know how I worry. Though I'm sure Lucy has—"

"Why are you out of bed?" I asked. I ached to shove her through the door. How much had she seen?

Mrs. Burton rested her elbow on the table and caught herself upright, with only a slight sag of her shoulders. "I've been napping in the sun, you'll need to forgive me. Lucy . . ." She circled a finger in the air, as if she were trying to gather words that now succumbed to the grip of laudanum.

Rebecca gathered her robe and crossed the carpet. She leaned over and wrapped an arm round Mrs. Burton. Her eyes glittered, though not with fever. "Has she been good, our Lucy?"

Has Lucy been good? My scalp thrummed; Mrs. Burton must have pulled out some hair. My lips pricked and shivered. My skin quaked with longing. My heart stuttered, and I understood. I was in love with Mrs. Burton.

Rebecca's smile curled the corners of her mouth. "Of course you have."

Chapter Eleven

My mother taught me needlework. She showed me how to unravel my stuttering attempts at the alphabet and borders stitched with tulips, and reuse the cotton threads until they'd thin and break. When I'd fumbled past pinpricked thumbs and jags of crying boredom, my embroidery hoop became a canvas of tilting houses and pine trees that wilted at the top and chimneys I'd not planned the height of and dogs with three legs and half an ear. Still, she was happy when I'd finish any little piece and sewed the ragged nonsense on throw pillows. She would ooh and aah over them, but my father turned them over when colleagues from his school were invited around.

I am ashamed to admit that I was grateful Mother's death brought with it the end of cross-stitch lessons. I stuffed the hoops and threads into the back of a closet, leaving the plain hemming and cuff repairs to old Zebidah, who came to help Father and me when we found ourselves so suddenly alone.

Zebidah did try for a time to continue Mother's training—oak-gnarled knuckles floating over the soft fat of mine, tongue clucking quick when pleased, and dead silent when my threads grew riotous. Zebidah was fond of platitudes and odd sayings, certain the discipline it took to transfer the words to the hoop in both a pleasing (and readable) manner would translate into a discipline of emotions.

I remember this, and the hours I spent, letter by letter, and this time trusted with silk threads of amber and aubergine. How Zebidah was pleased with the height and spacing of the words, and found particularly fine the pattern of apples and peaches I'd added to each corner. It was to be the family register.

As such:

John	*Sep 17, 1801–*	*&*
Abigail	*Mar 1809–Apr 6, 1842*	
MARRIED	*Jun 12, 1828*	
CHILDREN		
Charlotte	*Mar 3, 1829–Apr 14, 1829*	
Emma	*May 11, 1830–May 12, 1830*	
Lucy	*Feb 27, 1831–*	
John	*Jul 8, 1832–Apr 6, 1842*	

It had been, that family register, the very last needlework my stomach could handle. And soon enough, Father had pissed away his tutor position, his acquaintances, and any money at all for food, let alone Zebidah.

There was not much difference between that register and the one hanging near Mrs. Burton's sitting room door, though it was a world away in talent and design. While mine was the crude hand of an eleven-year-old, hers was delicate and fine, with swaths of white thistle and amethystine primrose, draping green leaves, and climbs of feathered vine.

Josiah and Eugenie Burton were wed the year of our Lord 1845.

By 1850, she had born and lost four babes. They were named *Catherine, Josiah, Theodore,* and *Aurora*. None breathed past their first week.

I had set the bobbins and thread in a row on the table near to Mrs. Burton's reach. Silk threads from palest yellow to darkest black, twelve in all, inventoried twice by her. The mauve was low: I was asked to add it to the spring list. Varied sizes of needles protruded from the pin cushion tied to her wrist. Her hoop was tight, an oval of shimmering silk. The pattern was half complete, the embroidery delicate and tight. Peonies and roses cascading like water from a tall urn.

The room itself was quiet, save for the clock in the hall and the whisper of thread and snip of scissors. Every so often came the click of a tin as Mrs. Burton helped herself to a candied violet and held the container out to me.

I was tasked to read aloud: *The Black Tulip*. There had been a mob, a lynching, a competition to grow the most impossible of flowers. But the words slid over my tongue, completely detached from the thoughts that careened in my head. It is true I was bordering on exhaustion: downstairs and upstairs chores, and sometimes flying from the kitchen to Mrs. Burton I would forget to remove an apron speckled with remnants of biscuit dough or chicken down. I had not slept more than a few moments, tossing and turning with Cook's snores and the pangs of weariness.

Outside, the sun spread across the birch trees, and the open window drew in the aroma of a field fresh turned. A horse whinnied. Mrs. Burton lifted her head to it, then returned to the needle.

My thoughts jangled—so certain I was she remembered nothing of the previous week, the laudanum providing a swift erasure or, if she remembered anything, an easy excuse. My mouth filled with a bitter taste—the resentment sharp of the effects of the tincture, and the fervent wish she had been of her own true mind.

"You're restless," she said.

"It's beautiful out."

"Yes." She switched one threaded needle for another, her canvas of silk like a loose loom, the threads available to take up as she willed. "This is the teal?"

"That's the yellow." The book slid from my lap to the settee's cushion as I arose and crossed to her. "Here." I lifted the teal, touching my thumb to hers as a guide before dropping into the seat across from her.

"Stop swinging your foot."

"I'm not." But of course I was. I chewed my thumbnail and rested my chin in a cupped hand. Picked up and examined each of the bobbins. Watched Mrs. Burton's precise work, knots and loops and twists forming the petal of a rose. A rose of impossible color. "How did you learn that?"

"Much, I suppose, the same as you."

"I didn't take to it, though. You, on the other hand . . ."

"It's a way to while the day. And it gives me pleasure. Something created."

"But how do you know—"

"What it looks like?" She rested her hand on the hoop. "I could say it looks exactly how it looks in my head, and I'd always be right."

"I'd tangle it all up."

"I did at first. But I spent a year at a school in Boston, an institute for the blind. I learned how to write again. And read. And be surrounded with people just like me." She pushed the needle under the thread, over again.

"Everyone was blind?"

"Except Laura Bridgman. And a boy who came and went. They could neither see nor hear. She was a wild girl. Mr. Howe tamed her by making her his living doll. He taught her language. Made her famous. Paraded her—all of us—in front of crowds. His crippled dancing monkeys on display." The teal was abandoned for a length of red. "I was requested home when word of that made the Portsmouth papers. I may have been blind, but I was not meant to be on display. I'll give Father credit for that."

She caught up the gold thread, then the white. Teal rose tipped in red, stem of brilliant gold lit white along the outer edge.

"How did it happen?"

"Scarlet fever. Mother quarantined me to my room, of course. I remember waking up all of a sudden, and seeing just a pinprick of too-bright light. And in the days that followed, I no longer saw that."

"Was it frightening?"

"Of course. I was sixteen—I was meant to be coming out to the world. To dance my first cotillion and charm the men. Not be so alone. Mr. Quimby was quite my savior. He was always there." She ran her finger along the pattern of stitches, brows pulled tight in concentration. "I miss color. And sometimes people's expressions. Though their voices can give them away."

She lifted the corner of her mouth in a smile, unraveling a single strand of red thread along the tip of a peony and replacing it with a blush of pink. "And you, Lucy?"

"Me?"

"You've a habit of speaking your mind. It's not the wont of most serving girls. Who are you really?"

My throat grew dry. I pressed my tongue to the roof of my mouth and swallowed. "I'm the girl in the moon. I told you. I'm searching for a ladder tall enough to reach the stars. Then it's just a hop back to the moon. A simple leap."

"Is it?" She dove the needle through the silk. "I'd miss you."

"You wouldn't really."

"There are so few intimates and allies in this life. I'd like to count you as mine. And me, yours."

"But you have Rebecca."

She gave a quick jerk of her chin. "How is she?"

"She asks for you."

"I'd say 'Poor Rebecca,' but that would imply I like her." She lifted her mouth in a grim smile.

I pushed back the chair, disturbing Mr. Quimby as he passed nearby. He gave a half-hearted hiss and jumped to the arm of Mrs. Burton's chair, his corpulent haunches drooping over the arm's edge as he batted the strings on the hoop, setting the needles to tick against each other.

"Stop it." She pushed him, but he caught a claw in the new embroidered rose, spinning the hoop from her grasp as he leapt to the table. She clenched her hands into fists, half standing as she hammered them against her skirts before dropping to her knees and searching for the hoop.

Mr. Quimby stared down at her, then turned his attention to grooming his back leg, his paw aimed high in the air.

I bent to pick up the embroidery, its threads tattered and stretched along the border. "I have it."

"Give it here." She snatched it from me, cradling it in her skirts and running the tips of her fingers over the whorls and then held it out to me. "Is it ruined?"

"No." I kneeled next to her.

With a sigh she pushed herself from the floor and wandered to the window, setting the ruined embroidery on the sill before pressing her hand to the sun-warmed glass. "I've grown fond of you. What will I do when you find the moon?"

Had she? Grown fond of me? I pressed my hands to my cheeks to calm the sudden heat, then shook my head at my foolishness.

"There you are." Mr. Burton stepped around me—for I had not risen—his black boots heavy on the floor, his stride not broken until he stood next to Mrs. Burton. His hands were clasped behind him as he looked down at her. Then he caressed her cheek and set his palms on her shoulders before stepping back. "How does the sewing go?"

"Well enough."

"Good."

Mrs. Burton turned at the rustle of my skirts. "You don't need to leave, Lucy."

I steadied with a grip on the table, then busied myself reorganizing the bobbins Mr. Quimby had batted to and fro.

"Mrs. Burton speaks well of you."

I paused at Mr. Burton's voice, then switched the lemon yellow and aubergine. It was, to be blunt, disconcerting to find the man so physically present. For most of the winter, he was nothing more than a vague idea, more often absent than in the front of my mind. Oh yes, it was never forgotten that it was he who kept us all in house and home. But his orbit so rarely crossed Mrs. Burton's. A touch of his fingers to her shoulders if he joined her at the morning table. The turn of her cheek for a peck as she passed him in the hall. Any other closeness too sharp a reminder, perhaps, of hope chipped away with each child's death.

But the roads were clearing, the town an easier ride, and with the unfurling of crops that needed management and tenants that needed attending, Mr. Burton became a more regular fixture. His footsteps could be heard now up and down the hall and stairs, and pacing his office, all the while his low voice tumbled round corners in calls to Mr. Beede and grumblings about the state of the house.

Now he stared at me, as if there was a reasonable answer to his comment. *Mrs. Burton speaks well of you.* Why yes, of course she does. I speak quite highly of her in return. Can I also mention she does not speak as such of you? In truth, I have not one time heard her mention you. Though I think the fact you lock her in the house should warrant a grouse or two.

"Mr. Beede will put a bonus with your wages." He tilted his head as he waited for me to—what? Splay myself at his feet with gratitude?

"Thank you." I managed a quick curtsy.

"Rebecca is on the mend?" he asked.

"Near to perfect health," I answered.

"Eugenie will be happy to have her back."

"Will you be happy to have her back, Mrs. Burton?" My jaw was tight as I spoke. I'd grown used to having Mrs. Burton to myself.

She pressed her lips together and spread them in a thin smile. "Of course. Darling Rebecca."

"Good, good," Mr. Burton said. "All-around good, then, eh?"

"Is that what you came here for, husband? To ask about Rebecca?"

"Rebecca? No. I've something for you." He reached in the inner pocket of his coat and pulled out a long envelope. "A letter came for you."

Mrs. Burton's face paled, then flushed. Her hand fluttered to her throat, then reached out, palms awaiting the missive.

My own heart beat hard against my chest and I strode over, intent on reading the name of the sender. "It's from Aurora."

I used to receive letters. Scads of letters, some vitriolic and some requesting my signature or a cut of my prison skirt or a snip of hair. There was a long string of notes from a Hiram Bundworth in Ohio cataloging everything from his "sevn cows & 1 bull" to the "pewter ewer" his mother had bequeathed him and he'd brought on his travels from West Virginia. He seemed, from the framed silhouette he sent, a sturdy and durable type. I assumed the notes were his way of proving he would make a good and solid husband; the last described the "rich soils and elegint sunsets" of his Ohio Valley. But I never received a letter to explain all the ones prior, one asking for my hand, which leads me to believe he'd found a local girl more to his suit and gave up his taste for a murderer like me.

I still wonder the girl's name and if she is making Hiram happy.

But the warden no longer allows me correspondence. He says it muddles up the workings of the prison and makes the other prisoners envious and riled.

Gert brings me a spoonful of blackberry jam. It's the last of it, the final taste of the past season's fruit. Soon, the buds so tight with promise will yield and blossom, grow heavy with sweetness. I won't be here for that.

We sit on a low bench striped with sun, well away from the other laundresses. I watch them, heads together, gossip swallowed with their meal, reputations chewed to bits. Today, the main course is the arrival of a prisoner from Hopkinton. A Cochrane, and Irish, and Catholic. Horrible things he did, though none can state what they are. I can envision the women at night, ears squashed to the floorboards above the warden's dining table, listening to the latest convict news.

Gert narrows her eyes. She shakes her head, then scoops thick jam from the jar. "Come evensong, the poor man will have been accused of bestiality and six counts of bigamy."

She hands me the jam. It's dark as midnight on the spoon. I press it between my tongue and the roof of my mouth, releasing the tart flavor. Gert is good to me.

She rests her chin on her palm, elbow to knee. Opens and closes her mouth with a click and a lift of her chin. "Not too much sugar?"

"Just right." I chase the last bit on the edge of my lip, suck it in, flatten it, roll the seeds.

"I've never been one for the oversweet," Gert says. "You should have met my Archie. Not a tooth in his head by the time it hit the tombstone. How that man loved his sugar. He loved it as much as he loved his babes. And sometimes more, I think."

She runs her thumb over her wild eyebrows, then rests back against the wall. "Can't fault a man for that. On his dying day, he said, 'Gert my girl, I've loved you fine, but it's your cakes I've sinned with.'" She laughs, a deep sound from her belly. "Never wanted another after him."

She takes the spoon, wrapping it in cloth and stuffing it in her apron pocket along with her supper tin. "Let's get back to washing our troubles away. And who knows what proposals await our Lucy today?"

"I'll pass the best on to you."

"Had the best already." Then she peers at me, touching a rough finger to my cheek before tapping her thigh and arising. I know she's wondering if I've had my own Archie. She won't ask, though. It's something I won't tell her. She poked and prodded enough when I was first sent here. But as Archie held tight to his sweets, I held tight to my secret.

Perhaps I should tell her, so she can rest the question in her mind. Yes. I had my own Archie who loved her sweets just as much.

Mrs. Burton took the letter and slipped it into the pocket of her dress. She picked up her embroidery and returned to the table, where she sat and made a little *tsk* sound to call to the cat. She stroked his back until he flopped to his belly, once again scattering the bobbins.

Both Mr. Burton and I chased them as they rolled on the carpet. I took them from his hands to return to their rightful places.

"Shall we pick up where we left off?" she asked me, though I was quite lost as to where that point of departure had been.

"Would that be—?"

"Cornelius van Baerle has come down with tulipmania. Chapter five, I think."

"Yes. Yes, that's right." I scooped the book from the settee, spreading the pages open.

Mr. Burton craned his neck to see the words. "Dumas? *The Three Musketeers* was wonderful—I read it to you, remember?"

"Mm."

"I'll leave you to it." He gave me a nod and exited the room.

I cleared my throat. "*It was the time when the Dutch and the Portuguese, rivaling each other in this branch of horticulture, had begun to worship that flower, and to make more of a cult of it than ever naturalists . . .* Don't you want to read the letter?"

She twisted in her chair to face me, her expression as apprehensive as I had ever seen. But she nodded and came to the settee, pulling the letter from the folds of her dress with a trembling hand.

"It's so thin," she said. She pressed the paper along her thigh. "Maybe she's writing to say she's forgotten me completely—"

I covered her hand with mine. "How about we read it instead of needing to find smelling salts?"

She released the envelope, and I slipped the fine paper from its nesting place.

My Eugenie—
It has been so long since you've written and I have felt as abandoned as if my own children had turned against me. I have encased my heart in tin these months so it will not break when thinking of you.
And now a letter, quite from the blue, from your home that is nearer the moon than me.
Tell Josiah we'll be piling into cart and carriage and to expect us all mid-June. At least expect me—we shall be happy bachelors! Or perhaps it's Mr. Beede you should inform, and Josiah you should send up Monadnock for an extended hunting expedition? It would make him happier than spending too many evenings with me.
You have not forsaken me—
Your Always Bright Aurora

Mrs. Burton dropped her head to her hands and her shoulders shook. She pulled in a breath that rattled, and sat up straight.

"We'll need to tune the piano. And the conservatory—I think I've let the plants all wither and die. I have, haven't I?" She reached for me then, her arms wrapping around and pulling me tight. Her palm drew circles on my back. Her breath was hot on my cheek, her skin flushed and near as warm.

"I can count on you, can't I?"

But I did not know whether she needed me as ally, intimate, or maid.

Chapter Twelve

With a snap of his fingers, Mr. Beede returned me to the downstairs and the confines of the kitchen. Aurora's visit neared; I was needed more downstairs than up. Rebecca resisted leaving my room, though Mr. Beede expected the exchange to be complete by noontime and I was near to shoving her out the door. Instead, she stood, hand mirror raised to reflect her face.

"Is it really this terrible? Or is it only the mirror?" A mewling sound slithered from her throat as she turned this way and that to catch the light. She yanked at the neck of her shirt, trembling fingers unbuttoning the fabric, circling the mirror round her neck and across her bosoms. She pressed her index finger to each lingering scab.

She gestured at her face. Her skin was sallow and sagged at the cheeks and brows. Her eyes, so odd and wide set, floated in sockets deep hewn and shadowed. Her hair, thin to begin with, was thinner now still, dry and dull as straw. The bones poked from her collar.

The mirror slid from her grip, landing with a dull thump on the rag rug. "Am I ruined now?"

"It won't all scar." Perhaps it wasn't the kindest thing to say.

Her shoulders shook. She raised her hands to her face, but the moan slipped through her fingers, followed by blubbering sobs.

I glanced to the hall, wishing Cook was nearby to scold the girl into quiet. There was, alas, only me to provide some form of solace, or at least enough to bring her to her senses and send her packing up the stairs. After settling the mirror (facedown) on the small bedside table, I patted her arm. "Give it time."

"Oh God . . ." She sunk to the bed, awash in tears, wiping her nose with the back of her hand. "This was . . . this is all I have."

My jaw tensed. Yes, there were scars, all of which would heal, as her hair would thicken and her body fill out. I tugged the blankets from under her and rolled them tight for the wash. "I'm sure you have more than that."

"But I don't." She lowered her head, then took my arm to rise. "I don't."

I waited as she brushed and pinned her hair, eyes averted from the small frame of glass on the wall by the door. Waited as she wrapped her shawl round shoulders thin as a rail.

She slowed at the turn to the kitchen. "Has the mistress been brought her meal?"

"Yes."

A snivel, a worry of the lip, a lift of the head. "We're more alike than you think. You and I."

"We're not anything alike."

But I suppose she was right. Both tied by circumstance to that house in the woods: me through misjudgment and sin, she the poor cousin of Mr. Burton with no means but his kindness to buoy her. She was the mistress's companion out of obligation and debt.

Matron has a strange look on her face: glee and wildness. She peers down the short hall, quick glances that go from the door and then alight back on me. She's got something hidden in the folds of her apron, her hands juggling between the skirt and the key to my cell, her hip pushing against the door, her left eyebrow twitching and lifting. Then she creeps inside, leaning against the wall with a satisfied little grin. "I've brought you something nice."

But then her forehead crinkles as she searches for a space to settle that's not too damp and won't stain her dress, and finds her choices are the edge of my mattress or back out the way she came. Down she kneels on the straw and cotton, one leg wobbly as she folds herself with a thump and a wheeze of air. "You won't tell anyone, will you?"

It is a kitten. A squirming tiny thing, already a nick in its ear and a patch of tar on a dove-gray haunch. How wild it is, twisting in her grip, paws spreading and retracting as it seeks to escape its captor.

"Where did you find it?" My voice is nothing more than a breath. I reach to stroke its head, and pull away at the rough lap of tongue.

"The gardener's spring cleaning the cats. I happened to be quick enough to save this one from the bin."

"He's a fine one, isn't he? Listen to him purr."

"It could be a she." Matron dangles the kitten aloft, then rests it back on her breast.

"You'll know in a few months' time when there's either another litter or a howling tom in your kitchen."

She presses her nose to his—for I have deemed him a he, have already thought Aloysius a fine name—and purses her lips, planting kisses that make him sneeze. She's not Matron now. She's soft and gentling and sweet. She's rescued a grimy kitten from the hollow of a prison bin.

Jacob had his kittens too. He'd smuggled two to his room while Cook and Mr. Beede caviled over the weekly order of sugar and lard. He christened the tabby JimJumJummy and the round black-and-white Checkers. I could hear him coo and cluck his tongue at night, and imagined them rolling across the pillows and leaping to the window before careening across his forehead. How else to explain the scratches that glowed pink and red?

"I had a terrible dream, Cook. I think I aimed to tear it directly from my head."

It was near a week before the secret was out. The kittens clawed the doorframe, dropping with incessant thumps and plaintive mewls to the floor. No amount of whistling or pot clanging on my part could mask the sound.

Cook handed him a burlap bag and length of twine. She said to round up any others he could find.

It was on his chore list anyway.

He grabbed the kittens by the scruffs, dropping them in the burlap, twisting the top, his knuckles white as bone. The scratches stood red across his forehead, one disappearing into his pale hair. He stood by the door in silence, eyes boring the floor while Cook took her time with the keys. Out like a shot he was, legs stiff and determined, bag cradled against his chest and alee of the rain.

As he had his chores, I had mine. Rebecca was not fully fit to regain all her duties, which left me to lug the meals up and down the stairs. I lifted the tray Cook made for the mistress and Rebecca and ascended the stairs to serve.

Rebecca sat in the morning room across from Mrs. Burton, chewing through a rash of bacon and sloshing back a third milky coffee. I stood at the window. Rivulets of rain slipped the contours of the glass, parsing and distorting the lines of the carriage house and muddied paths to the paddocks and beyond. I watched Jacob stumble back empty-handed from the wood.

"It is a bleak day," I murmured.

"I fully agree," Rebecca said. "It is a horrible start to spring."

I turned from the window. The sconce candles, lit against the grayness of the morning, caught the typhus scars that still marred her skin. Her tongue darted out, catching a bit of yolk from a pock at the edge of her lip.

Her eyes slipped to slits and darted to me before returning to her breakfast. She forked a third fried egg to her plate.

Mrs. Burton skimmed her fingers across the cloth in search of the sugar bowl. It should have been sitting to the right of her teacup; that was where she expected it. But it was far across the table, tucked between the salt and a curious porcelain figure of a monkey in a tall red hat.

Rebecca puckered her lips: "Are you looking for the sugar?"

I crossed the room to reach for it, but Rebecca curled her hand around the bowl, lifting the spoon and dropping the contents with a splash into the mistress's tea. Then she held the spoon aloft. "Another?" She didn't wait for an answer, just spooned in more sugar and returned to her stack of bacon. "I read in the Almanack we're to have a veritable cornucopia of rain this year."

Mrs. Burton blew a few quick breaths on her tea to cool it, hesitating before bringing it to her lips. "Are we?"

I shifted on my feet, the empty tray pressed against my skirt. "Is that even possible? A cornucopia of rain?"

Rebecca blinked. "Why wouldn't it be?"

"A torrent, perhaps. A deluge, a Noah's Ark event, even. But a cornucopia?"

Mrs. Burton cleared her throat and set her cup in the saucer.

Rebecca stared at me, then at the open door. "Do you need something?"

There was, of course, no reason for me to be up here anymore. I had lingered. All I wanted was a moment between Rebecca's inane droning. Just a moment to say to the mistress how much I appreciated the gift she had presented and the kind words. Just a moment to let her know it was quite a surprise to find the tin of violet candies on my pillow and the note: *You are already missed.*

I glanced at Mrs. Burton, but she let out a breath and turned her attention to her scarce-eaten plate of food.

There was a thump in my chest, hard and insistent. I wanted to shake her shoulder. To tell her I missed her too. That I listened for her steps to the grand clock and imagined her setting her own watch by its beats. That my stomach clenched to see she'd left Rebecca to again choose her outfits—an awful puce this morning—and that the plaids Rebecca seemed to hate were the ones that suited her best. That when the house was drowsed with sleep, I crept across the hall with a clutch of hope she would be waiting on the back stairs for a game of whist. I wanted her to know I was not like Rebecca at all, that my attentions were not of obligations to be met. And yet, to say any such thing would find me turned out to the road yet again.

Mrs. Burton rolled her napkin under her palm. "Tell Cook Mr. Burton will be home for dinner."

"Of course," I said. "Is that all?"

"Should there be something else?"

"I wonder if you'd sent for the piano tuner?"

"You needn't worry yourself," Rebecca said. "It's all to hand, though Cousin and I wonder why there's such a to-do. Over Aurora, no less."

I drummed my fingers on the tray and forced myself to ignore her. "And the conservatory? I saw the orange tree. Through the window. Blossoms already. I hope the poor tree can hold up all the fruit."

"You know about plants?" Rebecca asked. "Our Lucy's full of secrets."

I admit to wondering if arsenic or strychnine had the fastest effect and why typhus was kind to some of its victims.

"Lucy is a marvel with plants." Mrs. Burton slid a look toward me, her eyes bright as a doll's, as she dissembled. "Her grandfather was a master gardener. Mr. Friday is giving us a tour this morning. I think you should come, Lucy. We'll attack your bleakness full force."

Rebecca dropped her fork to her plate. "I'm sure Lucy has quite enough to do without muddling about with us."

"Cook can spare her for an hour, can't she? It's so little to ask, really. Besides, all the sewing scissors have been sent down for the grinder, so with what else shall we pass the time?" She leaned toward Rebecca, reaching out a hand. "You should have a good lie-down, Rebecca. We can't have you overtired." Mrs. Burton clasped tight and stroked her knuckles.

Rebecca hesitated, her skin flushing red. "Perhaps a small nap."

But Cook would have none of it. She glared at me across the cutting table, then pointed to the utensil drawers in the hall. "Get the knives and sort them out for the grinder. He'll be wanting a rest from the rain, and I'll be wanting the knives sharp as my mother's tongue by evening." She clutched her apron and turned to the stove. "A tour of the fancy greenhouse . . ."

"She's only asking for an hour."

"And that's an hour I need you, Lucy."

I should have nodded, gone to the drawers, and sorted the knives— the apple parer, the fish scaler, the meat cleaver, and all the shapes and uses in between. The peddler was coming to grind the knives and axes, to sit and tell Cook the state of the world beyond ourselves. Instead, I lifted my shoulders and pressed a hand to my stomach and said, "No."

"No."

"No." My stomach jittered. "The mistress asked. I said yes."

Cook narrowed her eyes and crossed her arms. "You'll see to the knives."

"I'll see to them after I've seen to her."

She creased her lips and moved them all around, peering hard at me before letting out a breath.

I swallowed. "She asked—"

"Jacob will tell her you're indisposed here."

"But—"

"Don't cross me, Lucy. You've a place here. And you're best to stay away from up there."

But I did not have a place, did I? I had stopping points is all. Miss Lawrence's Academy for Girls was quite a nice one; the barn I gave birth in was a rough one. The loom was a weary one, and Albert's lips a dangerous one. The boarding houses, the alleys, the quick kisses and clutched coins, the damp straw and circle of candlelight as I watched the wonder of Ned's breaths for the short time he lived.

A clanging bell interrupted us.

The peddler had arrived. He stood on his buckboard, rain rolling from the sodden brim of his beaver slouch hat, dripping from the tips of his long beard, and beading on his oilskin coat. He clanged the cowbell that was tied to a precarious leaning pole, and slackened the reins until they settled on the back of the mule that carried him into the yard.

Cook folded her towel and gave a great clap. She grabbed her bonnet from the wall, tying it round her throat, and slinging open the kitchen door. I followed behind, covering my eyes against the insistent drizzle.

A fine mule neared, with a stubborn fierce eye. With a jangle of his traces, he slowed to a stop before us. A tall chest of drawers and a wide wardrobe were lashed tight to the base of the wagon. The round-wheeled grinder hung by ropes over the side. The man dropped the spoon he'd used to clang the bell, and it swung in an arc from its rope cord.

"Would you welcome this peddler to tinker and toil, grind and grouse, sell you wooden nutmeg, pasty jewels, sweet snake oils, maps to purgatory, and not much beyond?"

Cook stepped from the kitchen. "Tom Knapp, get down off your wagon ere you drown."

He pulled the brake, then swooped his hat from his head and bowed. "Mrs. Cook, you are the divinest of sights."

He caught my gaze and bowed even lower. He was the most uniquely ugly man I'd ever seen. His gray eyes glowered under the jutting hang of forehead. His nose, crooked in the middle, flattened against his right cheek. When he smiled, his long beard fluttered and returned to rest on his chest. He wore a tanned leather shirt with thick black tattoos just visible above the collar.

"Who have we here?" he asked.

"Lucy," I said.

"Lucy. Who has taken the place of Mercy after her tragic demise."

"Mary." Cook wrung her hands. "Sweet girl."

"Right. Mary." He clapped on his hat and released the brake with a squeal. "But we're not wanting to intrude or bring bad remembrances. Old Jedd and I will settle ourselves in the barn. I've a clock tells time backward that I'm keen to show John Friday."

"You'll come in for my minced pudding and I'll hear no more."

He pulled his beard, then slapped his hand over his heart. "Mrs. Cook, you are my star." His eyes lingered on me as he pulled away.

The kitten rolls in Matron's lap, pink-and-black paws kneading the air. "Will you hold him?"

I wrap my arms tight around my chest, dig my nails into the skin of my ribs. "I'd better not."

It hurts too much to do so.

Chapter Thirteen

Candlesticks from Laconia, mourning pins from Rochester, butter stamps from Rumney, starched collars and sock garters from Lebanon. Saffron and pear soap and pasty gaudy bracelets. The peddler's cabinet was full of treasures, but we were none allowed its delights. There was no money to speak of, at least outside the confines of Mr. Beede's small safe. We were paid in scrip and lodging. The peddler, Mr. Beede said, had nothing that could not be found in town.

Oh! But Tom Knapp worked to tempt us all; he laid a trestle table near the tack room to spread his wares. Suggested buttons and laces for Cook, a Jew's harp for Mr. Friday, a jackknife for Jacob, a delicate carved bird for me. All the while he sharpened the knives Cook and I had lugged out.

At her bidding, I counted them all prior to their release into his hands. We inventoried them again on their return. In between, we sat on a hay bale in the barn, both forcefully ignoring the spread of wares sat right next to us.

"You'll give us a fair price this season, peddler," Cook called out.

"I've been none but fair to you in the past, Mrs. Cook." He pulled a rag from his leather smock to wipe his hands. Then he reached into the knife box, lifting out a cleaver. He held it to the meager light, pointed it straight out like a swordsman, and squinted down its length. His jaw worked side to side, and he gave a click of his tongue. "I can see it's your favorite, but its life is near complete. I've a better one here."

"You'll sharpen it until there's nothing can be done."

He shrugged. "I'll not put my name to its outcome."

"You don't put your name to any of this," Cook said, "so I don't believe it will make a difference one way or the other."

He narrowed his eyes, then let out a sharp laugh. "What do you think, Lucy? Are my wares so dismal as to deserve Mrs. Cook's scorn?"

I picked up a ribbon of delicate buttons that were meant to be placed along the back of a lady's garment.

"That's fine ivory from Africa," he said. "And I've horn ones from the great llamas of Peru."

"Your ivory looks much like New Hampshire birch," I said.

Cook gave a snort of approval and settled her hands in her lap.

"Never mind the buttons, then," the peddler said. "I have indigo. I have peppermint oil. I have tortoiseshell combs. No? None of the above?" He shrugged, and pumped the grinder's pedal with his boot until the wheel spun and the cleaver's edge threw sparks.

After all were sharpened and laid neat on a cloth for Cook's recount and blessing, she handed him a small envelope. "You'll join us this eve, then."

"I wouldn't miss it."

I wrapped each knife in its linen, and Cook and I lifted the box by its handles. On our way out, we passed John Friday mucking a stall. Strips of hay hung in his hair from the workings of the day. He slid a look in our direction.

"God's day to you, Mr. Friday," Cook said.

"God's day to you, Cook." He returned to raking manure and flipping it to a wheelbarrow outside.

We dashed across the yard, mud sputtering round our shoes and staining our skirts. As we crossed from barn to kitchen, I glanced up at the windows. Rebecca watched from the second story—was her visage bored? Envious? I could not tell. She kept to the window, one hand resting on her waist, the other absentmindedly stroking the curtain. Then she turned away, saying something to Mrs. Burton that was silenced behind the glass.

We were all about the table that night, each with a cup of cider, save Mr. Beede, who had his glass of wine left from the Burtons' dinner. Cook took residence at the head of the table, hands busy with mindless mending. Jacob sat with his elbows splayed and chin resting on his arms. He rolled the cider mug between his fingers and ignored Cook when she spoke to him. Knapp leaned in his chair, his arm encircling the back of mine. He tamped his lips down on an unlit pipe, removing it to the table as he lifted his drink or passed the jug round. My cheeks and nose were numb from the cider; I was not in the habit of it.

"There's unrest around, sure," he said, though I must have missed the preceding words. "Been some blood Kansas way. Over the coloreds. Will it be free soil or not?"

Cook shook her head. "Who's to say?" .

Mr. Beede held up his glass, tipping it toward Cook. "A right many people choose to say. Ruffian or Free-Soiler."

"A right many people do." The peddler half stood to grab the jug, and his hand trailed along my back as he moved it from near my shoulder to now quite near my thigh. I shifted away. But not soon enough to escape Jacob's leer.

Knapp poured the tawny liquid into his cup and then mine. "But news from closer to home. It's raining in Boston, Concord has a new manufacture of brass fittings, Althea Brown finally died in Apthorp at the remarkable age of a hundred and one, the sisters Steppenwald took as husbands the brothers Cod, and John Jacob Miner insists he did not poison his wife."

He swallowed all his cider, Adam's apple sliding up and down his throat before settling in the tufts of hair that curled from his collar.

Cook pulled in a breath. "They say she cooked it into her own tea cakes. He'd mixed it in the flour."

"The poor man says he does not even know where the flour is kept. He was convicted last month nonetheless." Knapp pushed his chair back and moved around the table, mussing Jacob's hair as he passed. He walked with a rolling gait; I'd grown up seeing men with much the same step. Theirs came from years on the sea, while I think his came from driving Jedd, standing at the head of the buckboard like a captain at his prow. He pulled a thin piece of paper from the inside pocket of his stained coat that hung on a hook near the door.

"I know you're fond of the news, Mrs. Cook. I've brought you a gift." He unfolded a penny paper, smoothing it onto the table.

POISON AND PASSION
Tea cakes sweetened with MORPHINE!
Sugar cookies prove the FATAL DOSE!
John Miner blames mistress!

The bulk of the page was taken with a drawing: A fire roaring in a hearth. A candle overturned on a table. A man standing over the prone body of a woman, a contemptuous smirk staining his face. A half-eaten cake, a broken plate, a trail of crumbs artfully splayed round her corpse. Her hair spreads in beautiful waves from her head.

And in the corner of the frame, half hidden in the inked shadows of the dining room door, the corseted figure of the other woman— the mistress—who had, through her charms, pushed poor John Jacob Miner to murder his wife.

Cook and I were last to bed. I held a stub of candle as she turned the lock on the door, then shuttled the coals in the stove one last time. The space contracted without the peddler and his entertaining stories, as if he folded the wide world into his pocket and we'd see nothing more until his return in autumn.

Cook hummed as she ambled to the hall, pausing to shift a chair, to look back to the door. "Did you count the cups?"

"I—"

"Thieving rascal, he is. I'll need two psalms just to settle myself."

I followed her, holding the candle as she unlatched her door. "If he touches you such again, you've my permission to slap him."

110

"Good night to you, Cook."

She set a rough hand to my cheek and gave a pat. "God rest, sweet Lucy."

I turned—too fast, I think, with too much cider in my belly—losing my step and stumbling toward my room. With a press of my shoulder against the wall, I regained enough of my senses to continue.

The key stuck in the lock, and it took a sharp twist for the tumblers to release their hold. I gave a sigh as I entered, for the day had been longer than most, and my limbs were listless. I set the candle on the narrow chest of drawers, following the reflection of its sputtering light in the mirror—then turned with a start to the face cast from the shadows beyond.

"Sweet Lucy," she said, her voice pitched to a low murmur.

"Mrs. Burton."

"Did the peddler make your day less bleak?"

She sat on my bed, hands clasped in her lap. She had changed from the puce attire of the morning, clad now in a purple-and-jade shawl over a wide-hooped dress of fine dove-gray wool. Her hair was plaited tight to her head and held in place with an ivory comb. I would give Rebecca that—I had never mastered such intricate designs and was happy if I'd pinned Mrs. Burton's hair well enough it did not tumble from its moorings by noon.

I felt my heart in my throat, but from the fright or her closeness, I could not ascertain. "Do you require something, Mrs. Burton?"

She gave a quick shake of her head. She crossed to me, stopping close enough our skirts tangled and loosed. There was a tic in her cheek and the glower of a frown. "I waited for you."

My back was to the dresser now. "I couldn't—"

Her breath smelled of violets and the sharp sting of wine. Lemon verbena and the ghost of a cologne more masculine. She reached for my arm, running her fingers down until she'd clasped my hand tight in hers. "I waited."

"I couldn't."

She reached her other hand to my chest, pressing her fingers against the flight of ribs, stroking my neck, then fluttering touches along my jaw and cheek. So close her lips rested on the corner of mine. "You kissed me once before. Will you again?"

"You remember?"

"Yes." She pulled me tight, arm round my waist, our hands still twined. The candle hissed and spit its last bit of light. "Come with me."

I followed her up the narrow staircase where we'd once met and gambled with cards. She held my hand tight. Pointed to the creaky steps. On the second floor, we crept through the serving hall. A slit of light leaked from under a door. The air smelled of pipe tobacco; Mr. Burton would be behind the door. We tiptoed past.

Mrs. Burton did not slow until we had slipped through her closet and into her room. The curtains were drawn tight, muffling the tap of rain on the glass. She released my hand. Let out a long breath. Moved into the darkness.

I could barely breathe. Dizzy, uncertain, unsure of where exactly I stood. "Where are you?"

Behind me then, her lips tingling my neck. The curve of her smile burned across my skin. "You shiver."

I could only nod.

There was a hollow trill—Mr. Quimby's bell as he crossed the floor.

"Take my shawl," she whispered.

Above us, a tread on the floor. Footsteps.

"Rebecca—"

She pressed my hand to the rapid beat of her heart. "Feel."

I undressed her, releasing the ties on the hoop skirt, unhooking the stays of her bodice, lifting the thin linen of her chemise. My hands wandered the fabrics, searching for buttons, fingers against ribs. Lifting her arms and sliding the last bit of soft fabric over her head. "I want to see you."

"You are," she said. She clutched my hips, fingers wrapping in the folds of my skirt, and pulled me to her. I heard a rip where the button held at my waist.

"Please."

She released me long enough to open a curtain. The rain had stopped, clouds slipping to reveal a crescent moon. The watery light draped the room and curved over her shoulders, scattering pellets like pearls in her dark hair. Lustered swirls patterned her stomach and hips as she reclined amid the pillows on the bed. "Come."

LeRocque's late today.

I press my cheek to the bars, peering along the length of whitewashed stone, and I don't mind the bruising if it allows me another inch of view. How heavy the air is. It makes the lungs work for breath. Matron's left the outer door open in the hopes of drawing in a draft for me, though it's just pulling in mist that creeps the walkway and claws my bare feet.

I'll give him another ten minutes.

As if I had a timepiece. As if the time mattered.

But it does matter; it's slipping now. It's hazy like the ground fog, and seeping away into the grates and gullies.

Mrs. Burton untangled her legs from mine, twisting away with a pull of the sheets. I reached to yank them back against the morning chill. "You need to get up."

She rested her hand on my waist, her breast pressed to my shoulder blade. "Darling." Then her fingers curled and poked my skin as she gave a sharp shove.

I yawned and clamored round to face her.

The sky was a dull pewter.

"Oh God."

John Friday would have already delivered rabbits.

"What time is it?" I asked.

Cook would be halfway through the morning routine. She would have checked on me and found the bed quite neat. Untouched.

"Get dressed."

"What am I going to say?"

Mrs. Burton shook her head, pulled the quilt around her and paced.

I dressed quickly, rolling my stockings and stuffing them in my pocket, struggling to get my feet in my boots.

A quick knock at the door stopped us both. "Eugenie?"

"Take up my things. Take up my things like you're going to dress me." She cleared her throat and moved to the door, the quilt sweeping the floor like a gown. Mr. Burton, shaved and neat in his dark suit, flicked his gaze from the paper he held. "I'm off, then . . . What's this?"

"I wanted to go to town. I'd like some trifles for Aurora." Her voice lilted and sparkled. "And I couldn't rouse Rebecca—you know how she can sleep, and I roused and roused—so Lucy . . . well, who else would I ask for? We can have a nice ride together. I see you so little."

"This morning?"

"Why not this morning?" She smiled, though the brittle edges of it gave away her nerves. "I haven't been to town since Mary's . . ." Here she shook her head, closed her eyes against the apparent pain of the memory. "If you'll wait, husband."

"I was going to ride."

"I think the brougham." She rested her hand on his arm. "If you'd mention to Cook I've Lucy here. And we won't need breakfast." She turned to me. "You'll need your coat, though, Lucy."

"I'm coming?"

"Why else would we need the brougham?"

Mr. Burton tapped his newspaper against his leg. "If you insist."

And so I found myself squeezed in a red lacquer brougham with the Burtons, rattling down the hill toward Harrowboro, under the threat of rain and the dour receding image of Cook standing in the drive.

Chapter Fourteen

It is deep night, no moon. The dark rolls oily black down the walls of my cell. It spreads in the cracks like the edge of a whisper and oozes toward my mattress in a murmur and sigh. It is not quiet here. I am not quiet. My breath is sandpaper rough. Blood drums my ears and swooshes back to my chest. Knocks against my ribs. When I shift, the straw bedding cracks like lake ice under my weight. There's a scratch of a creature's nails at the corner near the door and a hiss of movement as it slips through the bars. I hear the plod of the guards' boots along the walkways and the troubled hum of the men's dreams. Two cells to my right, Laura Reed wails. There's an answering keen.

It comes from me.

Mrs. Burton—Eugenie—lived by the intricacy of sound. It sometimes made me pause, this talent of hers. She would slow her voice, cock her head, the garnet bead of her earring swinging. "Ah," she'd say. "There's Mr. Beede. He's opening the wine cabinet." Or "Jacob winds the clock too tight." Or "Cook looks for a turnip in the garden."

Cook, she told me, moved with a humph and a huff. She bent to the stove with a wheeze and stood muttering a psalm.

Mr. Beede was simple, for he constantly cleared his throat, and his set of teeth clicked and clattered, particularly over his esses.

Jacob was like a bull, slam of doors and clomp of boots on the steps. He incessantly snapped his fingers near his thigh when he was restless.

Her husband's gait was determined but light. He was, she said, a very fine dancer, and more than one girl swooned when he led her in a mazurka.

Rebecca? All Mrs. Burton needed to identify her was the turn of a knob.

"And me?" I asked one night when the air was warm through the tall windows of her room and her hands along my back even warmer.

"You take the stairs two at a time, and you hold your skirts, not the railing. Quite self-assured."

"Only when I'm stealing to see you. What else?"

"In the kitchen, you sometimes hum with Cook, and she corrects the words. I think it's when you're kneading bread."

"How would you know that?"

"Well, there's fresh warm bread that night. And the aroma." She buried her nose in my neck, setting my skin to sizzle. "Nearly as good. I could eat you up." She curled next to me, soft thigh over the back of mine. Butterfly kisses. I touched each place her eyelashes met my skin. "Listen."

The breeze shifted, stirring the leaves on the orchard fruit trees. Eugenie raised to her elbow, one hand lazily circling the small of my back. I closed my eyes, and we listened to the susurration of the land.

"I think, husband, it is time to find Rebecca a suitor." Mrs. Burton retied the ribbon of her bonnet and smoothed the front of her dress.

Mr. Burton had indeed ordered the brougham. Cook had given him my coat and asked that I be back by noontime. I dressed Mrs. Burton in a fumble, my heart in a fisted knot. She found a pin to replace the button on my skirt waist. She lifted her gaze toward the ceiling, toward

Rebecca's rooms above, blowing a breath and hurrying me as I plaited her hair.

The weather, which had squalled the previous week and through the morning, broke agreeable and bright as we made our way down the hill. The brougham was quite intimate, and my shoulder protested as I was jostled against the watered silk fabric at each divot in the road. Mrs. Burton sat between me and her husband. Both remained straight of back, peering forward in much the same fashion as the framed silhouette profiles that graced the mantel in the drawing room. Mr. Beede rode his gray mare in pace with the trap, slowing and following as the road narrowed. John Friday handled the horses. The leathers of the reins and fittings squeaked and slapped, and his coos and chucks kept the two horses' skitter of energy in line. He wore a tall beaver hat with a yellow feather at the brim.

The light flicked through the leaves of birch and oak, losing its way in the tangled growth of nettles and whortleberries that choked the forest floor. All round, the air was sweet and heavy with spring—yet I could not settle into the pulse of it.

Not after such a night.

Not with Mrs. Burton lifting her head to catch the warmth of the morning, curling her lips in a smile, letting out a contented sigh. Gripping my fingers with her lace-covered hands.

Certainly not with her husband so straight-backed and earnest, sitting also with a gloved hand in his.

"You must know someone who would do," she said. "What of Tom Harken?"

"He's gone to Lowell. I thought I told you that."

"Did you?"

"This past October."

She bit her lip. "Of course. I remember. Are the leaves unfurled?"

Mr. Burton blinked and gazed out at the trees. "Yes. I suppose they are."

We turned on the post road, which ran by the ponds that fed the turbines that powered Burton Millworks Co. The road grew wider, and a succession of enclosed carts passed to deliver their shipments of muslins and wools to shops and finishers farther abroad. Mr. Beede took the opportunities between to pull near the brougham to address Mr. Burton.

"Temmet Martin is asking about the acreage . . ." and

"Amoskeag has lowered the bolt price of chenille . . ." and

"We've to decide on adding a carder . . ."

We were then upon the millworks itself. Two hulking brick buildings reverberated with the thrum of the turbines and heavy machines, and on each of the four stories the paned glass windows shook.

Mrs. Burton let go my hand. She picked at her collar, pressed her palm to her stomach, flinched at the bark of a rough dog that took to following us. Then she clamped her hands to her ears, shuddering forward against the clang and clamor.

"Are you well?" I asked.

"Turn us round." She rocked forward, the skin of her knuckles taut as she pressed her hands to her ears.

Mr. Burton grasped her wrists and lowered her hands with impatience. "Not here, Eugenie."

She clutched the rounded edges of the seat. "I want to go home." Her voice was thin and tremulous.

"You asked to come."

"Perhaps a turn by the churchyard for a bit of quiet?" Mr. Beede slowed his horse.

John Friday glanced over his shoulder, waiting for an order.

Mr. Beede gave a nod, then continued to the stables. The mare's tail flicked as he maneuvered round a group of mill girls hurrying to beat the shift bells, their lunch pails bumping their skirts as they crossed the street.

Harrowboro was no Manchester. In Manchester, a day could be spent ogling the wares in the shops. No—here was but two blocks of merchants, and we were soon past the wood-and-brick shops and boarding houses.

Mr. Friday brought the brougham to a stop near the graveyard. Large drops of rain slipped from the tree branches and splattered the roof. A thin mist slipped between the trees and around the silent tombs and plain markers.

Mary Dawson would be buried by now, I thought. She would have been carried from the winter vault along with the others to reach her final resting place. I pressed my eyes shut against the sharp vision of her face under the lace, but the sight lingered.

There was a sway and drop of the carriage. Mr. Burton had stepped to the road, pulled at the hoops of Mrs. Burton's skirt until they cleared the narrow door. He grabbed her upper arm, yanking her toward the turn to the church. There he bent to her, speaking words that made her skin blanch.

I hated him then.

I hated how her head bowed and how she took his arm to return, her walk as dull as a somnambulist's.

"Here we are, Mr. Friday." He opened the door on my side. "Miss Blunt."

My heel caught on my skirt hem as I scrambled down; it was John Friday who gave his arm to assist me as I disentangled the fabric. My stomach soured. Was this my dismissal? Had we been careless when passing his door, a tread too heavy, a breath too rasped? Was I to be let go again to make my way to another town with another lie?

"Have your outing." Mr. Burton lifted his hat and strode toward town and his office at the mill.

I nearly stumbled in relief. Not today.

Mrs. Burton turned an overly bright smile my way. "So much noise. I am quite twisted around. Tell me where we are."

Her presence in the town was not common. I saw it in the long glances that followed us as I led her down the street and in the stupefied looks of the clerks. It didn't help that John Friday kept pace with the brougham, even if it meant moving the horses five paces before setting the brake yet again.

At the confectioner's—one of the few stores open so early of a morning—Eugenie grasped my elbow, allowing me to guide her past the few round tables to the glass case that housed a variety of treats. Across the counter a clerk of indeterminate age—but, if one took in his stomach, a fondness for his sweets—waited. His apron was starched white, his hair a bristling cap of ginger and gray.

"What do we have today?" Mrs. Burton asked.

He opened and then clapped shut his mouth, giving a flaccid sweep of his hand as if that would describe all the sweets. He looked at me. "Is there something in particular she's looking for?"

"I'm particularly looking for chocolate." Mrs. Burton's grip pinched.

"Of course."

"White chocolate?"

"Both imported from France and our own local, which I think you'll find—"

"Two cups of cocoa milk, then. And tell me all the choices, Lucy, while we wait."

So I did, starting from the sugar-dusted truffles on the top left corner to the marzipan cakes and sassafras sugar sticks on the farthest shelf. The clerk was tasked with offering samples. Mrs. Burton was fond of the caramels, and rolled one in her mouth and against her cheek as we traversed the case. "A marzipan for Mr. Friday."

"Yes, I think he'd like that."

"Which do you want, Lucy?"

"There's so many. I'm afraid I wouldn't know where to start."

"One of each, then." She reached to touch my cheek, but I shied away. Still she searched, only dropping her hand when I murmured a quick thank-you to the clerk and took up the saucers and cups of cocoa. I set them on the nearest table, then took her hand and guided it to the chair.

"I would give you all of it, if you asked," she said.

"I'd be in bed with dyspepsia for a week." I smiled over the lip of my cup. "And what would you do without me then?"

"Let me spoil you."

"No."

"Yes." She twisted in her chair and raised her voice. "I would like one of each, please. And an extra marzipan."

"Mrs. Burton—" I placed my hand on her arm to quiet her.

"Eugenie. Please."

"Eugenie."

She looked toward the clerk. "Did you hear me?"

The clerk reddened. "One of each, Mrs. Burton."

"Separately wrapped."

"Separately wrapped."

She gave a nod and settled back in the chair. "I will feed them to you," she said, her voice soft again and meant to travel no farther than the width of our table. "One a night. To keep your breath always sweet."

Mr. Friday was not at the carriage when I came out to give him the boxes of candy and the marzipan treat. Instead, a small boy stood in front of the horses, holding each by the ring of its bit.

"Oh! Who are you?" I asked.

The boy shrugged, took an apple from his pocket and fed it to the horses, leaving hunks to fall to the road. He licked the juices from the tops of his hands and stared at us. "Ginger drops are my favorite."

"Where's Mr. Friday?"

"Off and about. He said you'd give me a candy."

But his eyes were crafty, and I knew he'd been promised nothing of the sort. There was no sign of Mr. Friday. I glanced back through the window to Mrs. Burton, who sat with her chin on her hands and the pallor returned to her face.

"Did he say when he'd be back?"

"He said you'd give me candy."

"Well, I won't." I dropped the box to the floor of the brougham, then shook my head. Where could he have gone? It wasn't his place to go anywhere. Now I was confronted with a little boy who would be trampled should the horses balk, and Eugenie sitting forlornly at a table awaiting my assistance.

But there he was, exiting the tobacconist across, shifting a package to his vest pocket.

"Mr. Friday!" I waved, but he did not respond. Instead, he strode along and turned the corner by the milliners. "What is he doing?"

"He said to watch the horses."

"I know he said to watch the horses. But why?" I clenched my teeth. "Never mind."

I spun on my heel and yanked open the door to the confectionary. Mrs. Burton looked up. "You've been gone too long."

"Not really. It's just Mr. Friday . . ." But I would not finish. "Where would you like to go next?"

Mr. Friday was seated on his perch by the time we had regained the street. He kept his gaze forward and followed us as we walked to the milliners and then on to the apothecary. The boy tagged along for a while, eyeing me despondently when I still did not give him a treat. Then he was gone in a flash, chasing the peddler as he clanged the cowbell and lifted his hat to me before urging old Jedd on to a trot.

When we returned to the house, Rebecca jerked from under the portico and down to the drive. "You can give her to me now." She opened the brougham door before John Friday set the brake, lurching forward with the motion of the carriage. Her eyes grew wide with surprise, lips tight, feet staggering under her skirts. "Stop the carriage. Stop the—"

Friday pulled the reins and stopped our motion. The door swung, pushing Rebecca into the body of the vehicle. She set her legs wide and gripped the frame for balance. "You stupid man."

"Rebecca!" Eugenie stamped her heel on the floor.

With a gasp and swallow, and hands braided politely, Rebecca lowered her head. "I apologize, Mr. Friday. I was overcome."

Mr. Friday nodded before descending from his seat and moving to open Mrs. Burton's door. "My apology, Miss White." But I saw the flash of anger cross his features, darkening the raised scars on his cheeks. Saw the clench in his jaw before he lifted his hand to help Mrs. Burton down. "Ma'am?"

Rebecca grabbed for Mrs. Burton's hand. "Why didn't—"

"Help Lucy with the packages."

"Yes. Yes, of course."

Friday walked Mrs. Burton to the front door, leaving Rebecca and me behind.

A rumble of thunder sent us both to gather the packages. We stood, Rebecca and I, on either side of the brougham, the seat and rumpled blankets between us.

"It's not your place," she said.

I did not answer. Merely lifted packages of linen napkins and brocade running mats to my arm.

"She'll tire of you."

The sky turned yellow green, then darkened. Dollops of rain pelted down, splattering the soil and pinging the gravel. I balanced a box of candies on the fabric and sprinted for the front door, shifting aside to let Friday pass back to the brougham.

Rebecca hid her gaze as she passed him by. She pushed her shoulder to the door and we both tumbled into the entry. The hall was empty, the only feeble light coming from the open door to the morning room. Rebecca snatched the box from me and set off down the hallway. She slowed midway, turning partially back. "Don't confuse pity with love."

She continued on with a small clearing of her throat as she neared the door. "It's only me, Eugenie. Now, what have you brought . . ."

The door was shut with a thump and snick of the latch.

My shawl dripped rainwater along the carpet as I made my way to the kitchen stairs.

There were no more words from Eugenie that day or evening. Rebecca came down for the trays, and Jacob retrieved them on his rounds to bank the stoves and fires. Mr. Burton read late in his study and sent Beede down to the kitchen near eleven for a final glass of port.

Cook skillet-fried breasts of grouse, and I scrubbed the burnt leavings until the skillet was raw as my fingers. Only then was she satisfied and left me to finish the rest.

It was hours before I slipped to the servants' hallway. I pressed my hand to Eugenie's door, waiting for her to turn the lock. Hoping she would.

I slid down the wall and pulled my knees to my chest. Leaned my ear to the wood. All I heard was the muted tinkle of Mr. Quimby's bell as he crossed the closet floor. The bell rang and then the sound slipped away as he moved into the bedroom.

How I wanted to whisper *I am waiting*, to murmur *I am wanting*. But I daren't: the waning rain had left too much quiet, and the narrow hall was still.

Chapter Fifteen

The house was a frenzy of activity as the day of Aurora's visit neared. The piano tuner came and went. Mr. Beede and Jacob carried curtains and paintings down from the attic and hung them in the great room. John Friday took to the conservatory, snipping and shaping the roses, and planting calla lilies, gardenias, hanging ferns, and a sapling orange tree too young for the one fruit that bent its trunk. It was the first time I'd seen him with any expression save a scowl. I watched him shuffle the white ceramic pots from one place to another, each day adding something new until the room was awash in a lush green. He festooned the doorway with teal velvet bows and waited for Mrs. Burton to join him on a tour.

I was glad, finally, to chuck the slops to the pigs, glad at least for a break from Cook's incessant instructions. On a return to the kitchen, I spied Mr. Friday and Mrs. Burton through the panes in the conservatory glass. He pointed out each petal and leaf, nodding and answering whatever query she made. She wrinkled her brow as she listened, hands restless to explore. It was the orange tree that delighted her most. She cupped the fruit to her nose, breathing in the scent. She returned again to the tree once Mr. Friday's rounds were complete.

A figure stepped in front of me, jarring my vision. Jacob had a ladder hooked on his shoulder, and hands curled over a leg. He chewed a sprig of grass. "What are you looking at?"

"Nothing." I glanced toward the glass room. But Mrs. Burton had left, and Mr. Friday was closing the interior door.

"You're lazing," Jacob said.

"I'm not."

He jerked forward, the ladder swaying, then reached to tuck a strand of loose hair behind my ear.

"You scratched me."

"I didn't." The ladder wobbled as he took a step away. His face was a perfect orb of red. "Sorry."

"It's all right." I took the empty slop bucket in both hands and walked beside him. "What's the ladder for?"

"Need to repaint some corners of the sitting room I missed. Sorry again."

"Go off with you, then."

"Ayuh." He strode ahead, turning on his heel near the back door. "I was wrong. You're prettier than Mary Dawson."

I laughed. A great loud laugh.

He clenched his jaw and made to enter the house. The ladder caught on the frame and he tugged it through. "Shouldn't be like that, Lucy Blunt."

No, I shouldn't have laughed. He was just a boy, but he didn't need the reminder.

Cook chewed her pencil down to the nub while crafting menus. I carried each up to Mrs. Burton for approval, following her from room to room in the afternoon to read off the delicacies and treats—candied walnuts, eel in jelly, roasted lamb with tarragon butter, cold pheasant breast, garlic Brussel sprouts, meringue of lemon, pear tarts.

She waved a hand and turned her attention to straightening the trim on the davenports, then fluffed and rearranged the pillows at the corners. "Aurora doesn't like pears. Have Cook make it with plums."

"Plums it is." I followed her as she charted her course from the sofas to the game table, the game table to the piano. "Thursday's breakfast will be octopus in strawberry jam."

She rested her palm on the instrument's seat, then shifted it back an inch. "Apricot would go better. Though I defer to Cook's tastes."

"As you should."

She moved to the windows, smoothing the curtains and bending to the floor to drape the fabric just so.

"Centipedes drizzled with chocolate." I bent a knee to the piano seat and plonked a middle C. "Baby frogs. Baked."

"Ask her to add extra salt to keep them tender." She leaned a hip to the deep window frame and spread her hands across the lip of it. Her eyebrow lifted as she looked in my direction. "Baby frogs indeed."

"Does Aurora dislike those too?"

"How is the room?"

"Improved. Though Mr. Burton glares too much from his portrait above the fire."

"Does it show a dimple in his left cheek?"

I dropped my knee from the piano seat and turned to the painting. "I see a very small indent there."

"Then he's smiling." She pushed away from the frame, untying the apron from around her waist, twisting it round and round as she ambled close to me. I remained still, facing the painting, pressing my back against her when she stepped close. "Centipedes, hmm? Would you use a spoon or fork?"

"You're losing your touch at whist," I murmured. "I think I won two out of three sets last night." My attention was split between her fingers slipping into mine and keeping an eye toward the hall.

"I like when you win. You're generous with your earnings."

My skin flushed, as if her hands traveled me, and I thought I might faint from the pleasure. "Should I come tonight?"

"Every night."

Of course, this was impossible.

She heard Rebecca before I did. "There you are."

Rebecca wore a white cap and apron over an old frock of graying cotton. Her arms were full of crumpled muslin that trailed the floor. "Yes, here I am." She bit down on her lips and forced a smile.

"You look like Cinderella." I laughed.

"You look like a washer-up." Her eyes cut as deep as the comment. "Another menu?" She sauntered over and shoved the muslin at me, tugging the paper at the same time. "I'll look at this. You finish the nursery."

The nursery. For Aurora's boys, should they come. Aurora's last letter said her husband, Otto, wished to take them sailing instead. Jacob had hauled down two twin bedframes and unrolled two mattresses to air them out. The door, midway between Mr. Burton's room and Eugenie's, was never opened. She often paused in front of it, long enough to touch the wood panes before continuing. I thought of the family tree embroidered by her hand, each name remembered in silk: *Catherine, Josiah, Theodore, Aurora.*

None had thrived, she said. Her heart could take no more.

I forced myself up the stairs to the children's room, shifting a rocking horse from one corner to another. The saddle leather creaked, unused but in need of oil. The horsehair mane could use a comb to dislodge the dust and regain its sheen.

My hand hovered above the changing table, watching my gray shadow snake and slip along the painted surface. Mrs. Burton would have had a midwife, I thought, to soothe the passage of her children to this world. I had dropped my baby like an animal in a barn, my hands pierced with wood splinters from my grip on a post, my lip split and pulsing in my fight to keep silent, the straw slopped with afterbirth and the stench of the cows in the stalls across.

It was midspring, the mud turned putrid from the rains. All the coin Albert's wife dropped on the porch had been given to a Mrs. Framingham who promised she'd helped many other unfortunates. But she lied. There would be no good family for Ned in the future. The woman gave me a knife to cut the cord and a blanket to smother Ned. "There's no soft place for that one or you now," she said. "You can move on with no one the wiser."

But where was there to go?

I did not put the blanket to his nose and mouth. He was a miracle, with his blue-black eyes so like Albert's, frowning and reaching, tiny lingering touches. I wiped his black hair—so thick already, like my mother's—and pulled in breath after breath of his sour sweetness. "You will be called Edwin Roderick," I whispered. "After your grandfathers. You will be my Ned."

But he grew fretful, and no amount of coaxing would make him take milk. Not mine, not the cows' whose teats I twisted and squeezed for a few drops that I smeared inside his lips. His chest shrunk and stomach bloated, and I walked the length of the barn for three days to settle his colic.

On the third night, his face slackened, softening into a sweet composure. He stilled, then was silent, and then dead.

I was half mad; I muffled my screams in my palms and the fabric of my skirt. My skin burned where I scraped my nails, a useless effort to let out the bitterness that slid under my skin.

It was Albert's door I took him to. The rain roiled in the street and drummed in the gutters. But Ned was warm; I'd wrapped my cloak around him and held him tight to my chest.

Albert opened the door when I knocked, his skin graying as he recognized me. He sidled to the small porch, clicking the door shut. "What are you doing here?" His shirt and vest were unbuttoned; his fingers shook as he struggled to redress.

"Don't you want to see him?"

"Go away."

"Albert. Albert." My voice was a mewl. Not mine. Something else. "He looks like you. You should see him."

I pushed the cloak away from Ned's face, turned him to the lighted sconce.

Albert flinched. His jaw slackened. "What have you done?"

"He wouldn't eat. I tried—"

He flipped the cloth back to its place. "Bury the thing and be done."

"It's too dark. He'll be frightened. Hold him, Albert, hold him and—"

He grabbed my arm, yanking me down the steps and pulling me across the road. He glanced back at the house, at the windows alit and the immovable silhouette of his wife. He shoved me in front of him, grasping and grappling until we were past the neat houses and tree-lined streets, past the boarding houses and canals that snaked around mills, and tumbled down a slope to the Merrimack River. The water rumbled and roared, and Albert had to press his mouth close for me to hear him over its tumult.

"Give him here."

"What are you doing?"

"You poor girl. My poor sweet girl." His cheek pressed against mine, our skin slick with rain. "Give me the child."

I fell back, digging my heels in the ground, only to have it give way. "You'll throw him in the river."

"Dig a hole if you want him buried, then."

"No. No." With my free hand, I gripped the long grasses that clung near the water, only to find them pulled in clumps, sod and dripping roots, nothing to gain hold of. Albert kneeled over me, staring with his blue-black eyes. My head snapped at the slap of his hand.

He pushed me to the ground and twisted my fingers until my grip was no longer on the babe. With a sharp tug, he wrenched the boy from me, leaving my cloak and blanket to fall nearby.

"Give him back."

Albert held him in the crook of his arm, gentle as if the boy still drew breath, and pressed his lips to our son's forehead.

Then he pitched Ned into the river.

"I'm sorry." He wiped the back of his hand across his brow to push away the wet curls, took one last look at the water, then stepped over me and into the dark of the woods.

The nursery door clicked. Mrs. Burton stood at the entrance.

I squeezed my eyes shut to block the images, then roughed the heel of my hand at the tears I did not know had fallen. "Another quilt on each." I sniffed and grabbed a corner of the mattress to drag it onto the bedframe.

"Lucy."

"And bed warmers. This room doesn't seem to warm up."

"Lucy." She lifted her chin and swallowed. "What was the babe's name?"

"Ned." I let out a breath. "His name was Ned. He did not thrive."

She splayed her palm across her chest, over her heart. "It's hollow, isn't it? Here? I can never warm it all."

"I've nothing to complain about. You have four times the cold."

"One grief is not greater than another, Lucy. It is just grief." She lowered her hand to her waist. "You're a widow too young."

I startled, shifting up so my thighs bumped a headboard. "A widow?" I glanced up at the drapery, the striped damask in lime and fuchsia that held us in. A widow. She thought me a widow.

Such an easy lie. Conjure a husband and give him a death. No stain on her image of me and a bit of sympathy to bind us close. It pricked me then: what she thought of me mattered. "I feel a thousand years old."

We stood in silence, one on either side of the room, each alone with the mementos and marks of our pasts.

Chapter Sixteen

My life is measured in hours and minutes, breaths and regrets.

It seems only a flick of time, as if I'd just turned my head away from Cook, my attention caught on some immaterial object—a yellow leaf floating in a blue sky, a water stain browning a wall and awaiting Jacob's repair, the whoop of John Friday as he worked the horses. I could glance back, I think, and there would be Eugenie, reworking an embroidery pattern. Looking up, eyebrow raised, as I entered the morning room to change the ash bin or the flowers. "Good morning, Lucy," she would say, and return to her sewing.

I could count on my fingers the times we'd spent together or even passing each other in the hall. I even envied Mr. Burton his rare dinners with her, as silent and stilted as they seemed.

Then there were our nights, when she'd leave a slip of paper in the dust bin I carried, or folded in the linens brought down to wash. How I hungered for those nights. I wanted the taste of her kisses, the brush of her hand on my cheek, the soft words against my neck, the whispers as I read her correspondence aloud, and the titters at the cheap (but thrilling) romances she loved to hear. I tasted desire: round and spicy, pepper hot. I tasted life: sharp and rough and hungry.

If I glance the other way, there's no more kitchen and the sky is not blue and Eugenie does not hide a smile as I slip by and brush my hand to hers. But perhaps those were all lies anyway, lies I've told to keep myself sane. What does it matter, the story I tell? The words cannot undo what's been done nor give life back to all those who've lost it.

Words can be twisted any which way. Move a sentence here, change a name there, shift a day or desire. Put words in one mouth or take some from another.

She stands accused of murder.

She stole a horse to flee her crimes.

She screamed and screamed at the men who caught her. A harridan drenched in blood.

She stole a bracelet of gold and emeralds from the wrist of a gasping woman. A thief.

She crushed another's head and left the girl to freeze in the snow. Heartless.

She could account for none of it.

She could account for all of it.

She blamed the living.

She blamed the dead.

Unfortunately, the dead could not take the stand.

And the defense was too drunk to take advantage if they had.

Time slips. I never saw a reason to mark the cell wall: one way leads back to the horrible morning, the other runs in stitches to the gallows. Just a month ago, I stood in court. Or was it two? A young woman clutching a wood rail smoothed by the hands and sweat of those who gripped it before. My skirts didn't quite hide the chains that bound my ankles or when my knees knocked and trembled, setting the manacles to clank and thump.

Heavy breath rolled from the balcony, foul with tobacco and spittle. The wood groaned from the weight of the crowd. They'd come to witness the judgment. The magistrate realigned his black cap and stared all around with his pale eyes before smoothing the paper under the heel of his hand.

"Lucy Blunt." His voice was reedy and thin. The paper crackled and hissed as he pushed it across his bench. "You have been found guilty of the murders of Eugenie Charlotte Burton and Rebecca Louise White."

No gasps. No women fainting and men charging forward as they did so often in the penny papers. Silence instead, shaped like an egg.

"But it was not me . . ." My voice failed me, and the judge took up his words.

"You are condemned by this court to hang by the neck until dead. May God have mercy upon thy soul."

"It was not me . . ."

A single *thomp* of the gavel. An inward rush of air. Then the room a maze of sudden shouts and a crush of bodies jostling and shoving me from the box. I turned back to the balcony, my eyes scanning the swaying crowd. The woman I searched for was easy to spot, her red hair so shocking against the grays and tweeds of the audience and the white of her ermine stole. Once our eyes met, she kept hers steady upon me.

"Aurora—" I felt my throat swell with the fist of an impending sob. "Mrs. Kepple—"

But she could not stop this.

I was forced from the room and into the prison coach.

How black was the interior, the only illumination coming from a thin slatted opening near the roof. The light slipped and changed as the vehicle rocked and clattered on pavement and stone, my only window to what was left of the normal world—the bright-gold cupola of the courthouse narrowing to a blinding dot, the white-trimmed windows of brick buildings reflecting a wilted sky, the roil of dust at each corner the coach stopped, the smear of trees as we picked up speed.

My ankles stung, a crawling burn, where the cuffs bit the skin. I was near doubled over from the weight of the handcuffs and the chain that looped from my wrists to a metal ring on the coach's floor.

The air was dank with the ghosts of those who had been passengers before me. I had seen such coaches pass when I was younger. My father made sure of our bearing witness. He brought us to the edge of Tryon Brown's property, early, before we strode to the school and he took up his chalk and board. He tipped his hat to others who'd come to the fence to stare.

"There go the damned." His grip was so tight on my shoulder I lost feeling along my arm.

Mother held John against her breast, patting and cooing, her head turned away from the black hulking carriage, her gaze instead on the leafless trees. "There'll be buds soon. Look, John. Look, Lucy. Look up."

My stomach knotted against the reek and gloom of the carriage and revolted, searing my throat with bile.

With a jolt, the coach stopped. We were deep inside the high granite of prison walls, the coach growing chill in the shadows like a tomb.

A guard in rumpled blue and a crushed kepi unlatched the door and released the chain from its mooring. He looked up at me and twisted the chains in his tobacco-stained hands. "Should have hung you already."

A woman of no more than five foot and two stepped forward. Her dark hair was oiled to her skull and held in a tight roll at the base of her neck. Her brows were heavy and her chin cut sharp. She wore a woolen dress of indiscriminate color that I would come to know as matron gray. The wide leather belt was stiff and new, and four large keys hung from the leather.

"Let her down," she said.

The guard grabbed my elbow and pulled. My foot caught in the chain and my knee slammed to the compacted earth. I twisted to relieve his grip, and found myself released and dumped to the ground, blinking into the white sky.

I tensed and rolled from the hand held out. But it was the woman who kneeled beside me and pulled me to my feet. She stared at me, her gray-blue eyes unwavering. "If I dismiss the guard, will you walk willingly to your cell?"

My head was heavy and I left it to drop.

She must have taken it as a nod, for she dismissed the man and turned to the metal door. "Come."

The building was misshapen crumbling stone. The corridor was narrow, nine cell doors each side and nine above. The whole of it smelled of old shit and standing water. The first cell was shoved full of broken ladders and piles of tin lamps, the others—all full to the brim with trash and junk. The iron-barred door of the third cell was open. Waiting for me. The women's wing with a cell for precisely one.

She pointed at a cot with sagging cotton straps. "Sit."

Once I did, she cupped her hands, one resting in the other, and picked at her thumbnail. "I am your matron. If you are fair with me, I will be fair with you. Is that clear?"

I ran my tongue round my lips. "Yes."

She unhooked her key ring and bent to release me from the chains. She did not let the irons clatter to the floor, but set them down and examined the cuts and red bruises on my skin. "I do not believe in hanging." She scooped the irons and draped them over one arm. She stepped out to the hall and swung the door shut, turning the key in a well-oiled lock. "We will not lose hope."

Matron has brought lip ointment. She rests the tin in her lap and spreads it on her palm to warm it. Now she dabs a finger to it, leaning close enough I can see her thumbnail bit to the quick, red and raw. She is fraying, my matron. I see the sag around her eyes and the sallow haunting her cheeks. I see it in the extra holes pierced in her key belt and the new turns of fabric at her waist. She has grown thin as a broom. I think she wishes she'd never applied for the job.

There's peppermint in the ointment. It burns and freezes as she presses it to my lower lip. I grab for her hand but she's too quick. She's lifted it away. Sits back and fiddles with the tin, rolling it between her palms. It is black, with gold letters, and looks a cut above what she can spend.

She worries her lip, peering at me from under her lashes before shifting her gaze back to the ointment. Her narrow shoulders lift, just as they have in the past, though the confidence has grown faint. "Mrs. Kepple has written the governor directly. We could hear any time."

Matron holds much faith in Mrs. Kepple's sway over the governor. I hold much more faith in her husband's wallet.

My heart thuds. "Will you be there? When I—"

Matron presses a hand to her stomach, her fingers curling the clasp of her belt. "We will not lose hope."

"Do you still believe that?"

"I must." She raises an eyebrow, then leans in again. This time she runs the balm all along my lip. Allows me to dip my finger to it, to smooth the splits and scabs. "Better?"

She escorts me to the laundry, as she always does, but her shoulders tilt forward and she turns away once I've crossed through and Gert has signed the paper to mark my transfer. Matron slows at the outer door and turns back. Her brows are locked in a deep frown. She watches a bluebottle fly that's thumping the window glass. Then her gaze grazes her feet before landing on the grates along the windows.

"You must choose your last meal."

She shakes her head, quick and sharp, and strides again down the hall.

In between the squeezing of water from sheets and shirts, I think about food. If I'm to choose the best meal, the last meal, I want to make certain it's right. Cook said that flavors are particular and discerning in their friendships. Too much cinnamon can ruin a pork rub, and too little salt a chocolate cake. Beef tongue and a salad of pickled beets are quite a good mix, but pair the beetroot with capon and you've an ungodly disaster.

Arrowroot pudding.

Marmalade on crumbly biscuits.

Mint jelly.

Poached eggs.

Fresh milk.

Cook's Indian pudding.

I've added others I've never tasted. Pineapple. Mango.

Will solace be found in a familiar taste last taken, or a new taste as the last to try?

"Now, that's a question." Gert listens to my list, pulling a strand of her frazzled hair until it stretches taut, then releasing and stretching it again.

"I think a good haddock and a warm ale." She slaps her lap. "And snap peas. I've got a flush of them in the yard now." With a grunt, she lifts a mound of wet clothes to the sorting table.

I watch Gert work. Her hands are a permanent red from the lye and all the scrubbing. They're good hands. Strong and sure. I am confident she could get herself out of a muddle with one swing of her fist. She says she's only done so once, and that it was to her Archie coming home with the perfume of another on his clothes.

"That raised my Irish." She chucks her head and gives a *tsk* of her tongue. "I think an orange. What about an orange?"

Oranges were Eugenie's favorite. One night, not long before Aurora came to visit, she stole from the bedroom to the conservatory and returned with the single fruit yielded from the young tree. She dropped the peels in the ewer water and spread the segments on a plate.

She pressed a slice to my lips. "Next year the tree will be bounteous."

I bit down. But the fruit gave no juice, and the pulp was mealy and difficult to swallow. I poured water into a glass, watched a curled peel float on the surface. "What if I'm not here next year?"

Eugenie touched my cheek. "Then you will miss the fruit." She lifted her glass, which did not hold water, but a small draught of laudanum.

"Why do you drink that?"

She frowned at me, then swallowed the liquid. "It's hard for me to sleep."

"That will do you for two nights and the day in between."

"Don't talk to me like that."

I twisted from the bed and stood, shrugging out of her grasp. "I'm helping Cook in the morning anyway. We're putting up jams."

I push the trolley mounded high with shirts and trousers toward the tubs and set a brick at the wheel before grabbing an armload and slipping it to the water. Across from me, the mute Margaret drags the thick paddle round the tub edges. She doesn't talk to me; she has never once broken the rules. Her lips are puckered tight from too many years of scum-topped wash water and a large dollop of self-righteousness. She'll be first in line for tickets and no doubt shove her way to a seat at the foot of the gallows.

"What's your favorite food, Margaret?"

Her eyes bug and blink.

"I think you like stew. A good stew with mutton and new potatoes and onions and extra carrots."

A *blurp* of noise bubbles across her lips.

"Maybe a little sage and extra salt." I dump another load of clothes to the batch. "Hemlock tastes a lot like carrots. You wouldn't know that, though. But I do."

Her paddle clonks against the tin. She hisses.

"Well," I say, "maybe next time you'll follow that with words."

It's not just hemlock I'm familiar with. I have been schooled in the uses of arsenic (tasteless), strychnine (acidic). Bitter nightshade. Larkspur. Monkshood. Bleeding heart. Rhubarb. Thorn apple. Elderberry root and jack-in-the-pulpit.

The garden at the Burtons' was wild with death.

So said the prosecution.

So many choices, Miss Blunt. Which did you make?

John Dreye was called from Boston. He was a doctor of medicine well employed by the police. His opinion mattered. "Not a plant, at all. A more simply acquired poison, indeed," he stated. "Arsenic. A frightening lot of it."

"Of course there's arsenic." Cook shifted in the witness chair, and I knew her hip pained her much. She crossed her arms to her lap and shook her head. "You can't run a household without arsenic."

Arsenic in the larder for the mice. Arsenic in the conservatory for the bugs. Arsenic in the barn for the rats. Arsenic in the face cream for a velvet complexion.

The counsel pulled at the sleeves of his coat, then curled his knuckles to the table. "You do take inventory?"

"I do."

"As every competent housekeeper should. We took inventory too. It didn't match yours."

"That's not possible. It isn't possible." She squinted, then caught my eye where I stood in the dock. "I will not condemn her."

Chapter Seventeen

"I have a plan."

I startled awake, shifting to sit up but found my arms pinned under the sheet. Eugenie's face was inches from mine; her upper lip bore a sheen of sweat. I could not tell if it was from the warmth of my room or a midnight dose of laudanum. She had told me sleep was difficult for her, that night without day sometimes baffled her. She often paced the halls for hours, the creaks of the stairs and errant floorboards testament to her restlessness.

The June moonlight was murky, Eugenie's features indistinct. I ran my tongue over my lips and cleared my throat. "You'll cost me my job."

She shook her head and pressed her cheek to mine. The sheet tightened as she lowered her body on me, and her elbow jabbed my upper arm and pinched the skin.

"Let me up." I turned my head and gave her a peck on the jaw as she released me. I shimmied up to sit, rolling the pillow behind my back.

Outside, the katydid's song had grown faint. A tomcat yowled. It wouldn't do for her to be here. The house would soon stir, and how would I explain its mistress sitting on the edge of my bed? I cut a glance to the door to assure it was closed.

"You shouldn't be here. It's too—" My whisper hoarse with sleep.

Eugenie frowned and worried the fabric of her robe. "I can be anywhere I want."

"Not here." I leaned to the bed table and lit a candle. The light burred against the silver reflector and fell to dust at the corners. "Not here."

"Come, then." With a quick grasp, she pulled me from the bed to the door. My feet tangled, caught in the tail of the sheet. I snatched it from my ankles, irritated enough to sling it against the wall.

I took up the candle, following her as she crept the hall and stairs, slowing as she listened around corners and nodded to continue. My heart thudded as loud as the grandfather clock, and her self-satisfied smile did not ease it in the least.

She stopped in front of the conservatory, gripping both knobs before opening the glass doors wide and stepping inside. Her nightdress floated and settled in the gray light. "Close the doors."

The roses in the conservatory were heavy of bloom and steeped in the scents of musk and clove and lemon. Here there were no delicate tea roses, nothing pink-tipped and shy, nothing shrinking in violet. No dazzle of alabaster or splash of pale yellow to climb the posts and cover the glass. The sweet alyssums and gardenias of May had lost their luster to the roses of summer. Ruby now. Garnet. Crimson. Deep wine. Petals of velvet meant to handle and stroke. Perfumed air meant to encase like a cape.

Eugenie's thumb brushed a rose striped in plum and cranberry. She was careful of the stems, her touch hovering and choosing where to land.

I set the candle on a small wrought-iron table and dropped to a chair. My shoulders and feet ached with weariness—for hadn't we spent the last weeks preparing for the vaunted Aurora, and hadn't Cook commanded everything be washed and dusted to perfection? I rubbed my eyes. The air was viscous and the smell cloyed. "You can't come to my room like that."

Her hand stayed, then settled against her thigh. She picked at her thumb and frowned. "I'm sorry."

"We have to be careful."

Her expression brightened. "But we don't."

"We do." I sighed.

"I told you, I have a plan." She crossed toward me. I took her outstretched hand to guide her to a facing seat. She leaned forward, elbows on the table, not letting go my hand. She tightened her grip, pulling our hands to her chest. Her heart thumped sharp against her sternum, and her breath drew in as she settled my palm to her skin.

"You will be my companion," she said.

"Your—"

"No more Rebecca. Just you. Just you."

"What will we do with her?"

"She will wed." A slow smile grew as Eugenie said this. "You'll take her place. It's so simple, isn't it?"

I felt a twinge but could not discern the cause. I would share her morning table, keep her company through the hours of the day, leave the pots and pans for someone else to wash. Own more than one dress. Have rooms of my own. And I would have Eugenie.

"I'm desperate for you," she murmured.

"Do you have a suitor for her?"

"The choosing here is . . . well, sparse. I've written Aurora. She knows everyone from Concord to Portsmouth. Though I can't say I'll envy the man."

"We'll be free," I said.

She cupped my cheek and gave me the lightest of kisses. "We will be free."

That night, she sealed her intent with a tin of candied violets slipped under my pillow. When I opened the box, though, it contained two orange blossoms and a bracelet of emerald and gold.

I clutched the slither of band, then let it slide like liquid to hang and sway in the candle flame. My promise of freedom.

I couldn't say where it is now; it was stripped from my wrist when I was caught, and there's many a hand my jewel-stitched skirt passed through on its way into evidence. It is considered "officially missing." I am considered officially a lying thief. Among other things, of course.

They're taking Laura Reed away. She's parceled in muslin and leather belts, wrapped tight like an evening's fish. Two teeth bashed in and a gingham cloth tied to spread her jaw so she can't clamp down. I recognize the cloth; it's her favorite and I washed it just last week. Now it will end in the rag bin at the Asylum for the Insane.

She kicks a foot free from her captors, catching the stout one under his chin. He grabs at her ankle, squeezing tight until her moans serrate and cut the air to bits.

"Leave her be."

No one listens to me. Matron's tending to her, whispering to her as they move down the short hall—*DearLauraPoorLaura*—and the cloth she's pressed to the poor woman's mouth swells with blood. Matron drops it and pulls out her own white starched handkerchief.

They could have warned me. Matron should have given word as she walked me back from the laundry. *Laura's going to the asylum. It's very pleasant. She'll be looked after. You knew the day would come.* But she didn't. She went about serving our noonday meals and said nothing but her normal "Eat up."

"You can't take her." I grab the bars. "She's the only one left with me."

Doctor Prescott arrives with wire glasses atilt, fine pale hair mussed and flattened, threading his arm through his jacket. "You're early."

The entourage slows for him. Laura twists her head and stares at me. Her scalp is a maze of new scabs and old scars and seethes with the stench of pus and rotten flesh. She garbles some words and lets out a screech that fizzes bright with blood.

Doctor Prescott holds a wad of gauze to her nose and mouth. Ether. "You'll be a good girl now, won't you?"

Her eyes glaze over like frosted glass. I kneel and press my cheek to the iron, work my shoulder and arm out to reach her. But the tips of my fingers catch nothing as Matron takes up her singsong *OhLauraPoorLauraThereThereLaura* until they've locked themselves out and me in.

I roll back on my haunches, pushing at my eye sockets, and try to ratchet a breath.

What will happen to Laura now? All she did was steal a horse.

I stumble to my mattress, landing hard on my hip. I scream. I scream because Laura isn't here to do it. I'd grown used to her shrieks, used to her silences.

The main door hinges scrape and bristle. Matron has returned. She presses her hand to the wall to steady herself, takes wobbled steps to the middle of the floor. She's left her handkerchief and now she stares down at the sodden mess of it. The stone around it is stained dark. She yanks it up, twisting and pushing it against her stomach, and her face contorts in a grimace.

"You've killed her," I say. "As if you'd done it with your bare hands."

"Be quiet."

"You're as horrible as me."

She is trembling. Coiled. Then she spits and I'm too slow to avoid it. It rolls down my chin.

"That's honest, at least."

Her eyes are flat as she glares. Her mouth twists taut. Then she grabs the solid outer door of my cell with both hands.

"Please don't do that." My voice is thin and pleading. "Don't leave me here."

The air shards and shivers as she slams the iron shut.

I scramble up, smacking the door with the palms of my hand. I smack until I can't.

Mr. LeRocque sits on his stool, one hand curled over his knee, the other holding a proper porcelain plate with a slice of pie. The plate is thin, painted round with pea shoots and blossoms. The crust is dotted with butter and sugar.

"Rhubarb," he says, then raises his finger. His eyebrow lifts in a curve, and he does not let go my gaze as he sets the pie to the floor, nor as he reaches in his coat pocket to conjure a silver fork. He holds it aloft, so the tines and handle glimmer with a coat of oil light. With a clearing of his throat, he sets the fork on the plate and gestures for me to eat.

"I don't want it."

"My wife would be pleased if you did."

"They took Laura Reed."

"I heard."

"How did you . . ." But I must have dozed. Matron must have come and gone and left me now with LeRocque.

He's taken up the pie. The plate rests precariously on his knee. He presses the fork into the fruit and crust, folding a heap into his mouth. He hums as he chews and then swallows the lump. He blinks as he watches me with those infernally odd eyes, neither gray nor green nor brown and yet all of the colors at once.

He's changed his hair, let it grow so it curls at the collar. His mutton chops, wilder, threaded with gray, do not conceal the beginnings of a well-fed jowl. In a few years' time, his stomach will get the best of him and he'll eschew his plaid vests for the slim of solid black. He'll have a lover: a girl too young, but happy for the flat he loans her for the length of his interest. His wife will continue to bake cakes and trifles, and she'll still send a slice out the door with him, hoping he's found another issue of the day to exploit rather than a willing girl with no issues save her naivety and wiles. I should warn him now the girl will leave, and then his wife.

My portents will be waved away as another tale. I call it an educated guess.

Anyway, he's told me nothing about his absence, so I think I'll let the warning pass.

"She'll be better looked after," he says. The fork scrapes the plate as he takes up another bite. "The doctors are well versed in the mind's confounding and will be well involved in helping her improve her state."

"And what happens when she's improved?"

He gives a half shrug. Chews again and keeps blinking at me. "I cannot say."

But I could. She would be prodded and poked and her future measured by the tips of a caliper. The medicine men will map the peaks and troughs of her skull and pronounce her a good girl or bad.

She is a creature much determined by her combative and excitable nature. Come, look right here—the zygomatic arch is quite pronounced. And back here the protuberance is exceptional.

I turn to the wall and lean my forehead against it. "Go away."

She carries all the low traits associated with both. And I would add—

I squeeze my temples with forefinger and thumb. "Is there an Enoch Finch associated with this asylum?"

The fork clinks. The stool leg catches a crack and screeches. There's a rustle of cloth and the squeak of leather. "I believe he's on staff."

"Then God help Laura."

Enoch Finch came to the Burtons' as a guest of Mrs. Aurora Kepple. An odd couple they made, if one could call them that. She in her frippery and he in muted black. He was a little man, with the cockerel walk of someone who resented those with longer limbs and an easier stride. He strutted with his narrow chest thrust out against the day. His face seemed pinched and parched, shifting from one close-lipped smile to another. He often murmured, causing Mr. Burton and even Eugenie to lean in a bit closer and ask for a repeat of whatever was on his overstuffed mind.

"The mind," he said, with a jerking flip of his hand, "is an array of complications and ill-fitting pieces. And they don't always contribute to a whole."

He muttered something else then, as he sucked on his pipe and puffed out a cloud of smoke. It had taken him no time at all to ensconce himself in the Burtons' sitting room, legs straight before him and head resting against the divan. His lids were half closed against the late-morning sun.

Aurora Kepple rested her elbow on the piano, tilting her chin toward him. She wore the tightest bodice and widest hoop skirt I had ever seen—a gaudy nonsense of pink and lime-green flowers that flounced and swung like a bell. Her hair, a light auburn, was just beginning its fade to gray. "Mr. Finch believes us all preordained to chaos or order."

"Indeed." Another puff of tobacco. He ran his fingertip on the top of his glass, then held it out to me. I poured him another lemonade.

Mr. Burton lingered near the windows, arms crossed. He gave a flick of his fingers for me to pass him by, and turned his gaze to the fruit trees below.

"Mrs. Burton?" I rounded the piano toward her.

Eugenie was perched at the end of a settee. She looked at me. "I've left my glass—"

"It's right here." Rebecca slid forward on her chair. "I saw you left it—she's always leaving things round—"

"But you're here to pick them up." Mrs. Kepple gave Rebecca a hint of a smile. "She's an ever helpful girl, Mr. Finch."

Rebecca's skin stippled red. The glass she held wavered in her grasp. She set it down with a sharp clink. Then she lifted a second one and held it to me. "I would like some."

I poured the last drops to her glass.

"It's hot," Mr. Finch said. His eyes followed a smoke ring as it floated to the ceiling. "Is it always so hot?"

"It's June," Mr. Burton said.

"Yes. Yes, it is. Country and all that . . ."

I moved to return to the kitchen.

Mrs. Kepple clapped her hands. "Girl. Bring up sherry and four glasses."

"It's but eleven," Mr. Burton said.

"Which is an excellent time."

"Sister—"

"Brother—"

"Her name is Lucy." Eugenie's shoulders were tight.

Mrs. Kepple frowned. "Who?"

"Her name is Lucy. Not 'girl.'"

"I didn't mean—" She flicked a look at me and then at Eugenie. Her expression fell. "Gene . . ."

"I told you," Rebecca murmured.

"What does that mean?" Eugenie's voice was sharp.

"Nothing," Rebecca said, dipping her chin. "I didn't mean anything."

Mr. Finch twisted in his seat. "You see?" he said. "Chaos. Mmph."

Matron knocks on the iron door but doesn't wait for an answer. Just pulls the door wide and stands like a supplicant in front of the bars. "Forgive me."

"Go away."

She sinks down, palms in her lap. Her hair is haloed from the thin oil lamp in the sconce behind her. I cannot see her face, only her contours. "She did not survive the journey."

I stumble back. "How? It's no more than—"

"She swallowed glass. That's . . . There won't be an inquiry." Matron drops her head to her hands. I hear her gasps of breath.

I will not give her comfort. "We're all mad."

Chapter Eighteen

"James Clough was hanged in front of fifty spectators who cheered and foamed at the mouth with vengeance. Tell me the Christian mercy in that."

Aurora's voice floated through the open windows of the kitchen. I looked up from the tins and plates half scrubbed before me, glancing out to the back garden. I saw only the lazy swing of her buttoned boot and the flap of her skirt against her ankle. She had abandoned the stays and skirts as the temperature continued its upward rise during the week; now she wore only simple cottons that were not far in feature from the calico Cook had sewn for me.

The air hummed with cicadas. A dragonfly with indigo wings and a body shimmering like green glass hovered and landed on the window frame. It stretched and contracted its wings before settling into a corner of shadow.

Mr. Burton came into view in vest and rolled sleeves. He inspected the leaves and branches of an orchard cherry and glanced at her over his shoulder. "Was he guilty?"

"The point, Brother, is this: Was the punishment just?" She leaned forward, picked a leaf off the toe of her boot, then leaned back, out the edge of my window's frame.

"You think hanging not a deterrent?" There, beyond my view, the rasp of Mr. Finch's tongue.

"I think," Aurora said, "it is a crime as brutal as the first. I think it cheapens us."

"Indeed, indeed . . ."

Mr. Burton wiped his palms on his pant legs and strode the grass to take a seat next to Aurora, his long legs crossed and foot swaying in time with hers. "So, you fought to save that Blaisdell woman who has confessed, freely confessed, to murder. She killed with malice, Aurora."

"We ourselves would have killed with malice in the hanging of Letitia."

Mr. Finch's pipe smoke twisted and snaked in the air, slowing and stilling before dissipating. "It is brutal, Mrs. Kepple, these ropes and gallows, but what about the crime that spurs the judgment . . ." Here another voice mumbled something and spit out another round of smoke. ". . . separated from the wheat, and those not deterred more ably watched and a tight rein taken to constrain the sinner inherent."

"Your pronouncement," Aurora said, "leaves no room for human correction."

"I would be much interested in studying Mr. Clough's head. There would, I believe, be very little surprise to it." Finch jerked into view, his pipe caught between his teeth. He stretched his arms, then swung them across his chest before tramping out toward the orchard.

"You can't tell me Otto approves of your friendship with this man," Mr. Burton said. "He's an insufferable egotistic—"

"Otto's not the one who needs to approve of him. I wish to bring him into the cause. And Gene—"

Cook clattered a pan in the water, sending a dollop to soak my apron and dress.

"What was that for?"

"Little pitchers get their ears boxed."

I stepped away from the pans and snatched a towel from the table rack to dab my apron and dress. "Now look."

"If it was black, there'd be naught to see."

Cook disapproved of my new dress, though she said nothing to Mr. Beede as he handed her the bolt of cloth and gave a nod that it was indeed a calico and indeed more lilac than blue. I couldn't keep my hands to myself, but pinched and brushed the flowered pattern. Cook's tuts were admirable, to say the least. After we'd cut and measured and pinned and hemmed, the tuts turned to mutters and shakes of the head.

She trundled back to her mixing bowl, dumping handfuls of dark raisins into the batter. "You give yourself airs in that."

"I don't."

"I've seen you. Pride—"

"It's a dress, Cook. I didn't ask for it, and I didn't choose the fabric. And you of anyone should be pleased with the economy of it. Mrs. Burton didn't need it, Rebecca didn't want it, so here it is." I flapped my hands against my skirt and turned back to the sink.

"That's airs."

"Oh, for God's—"

"Lucy." Cook slammed the whisk on the wood, spraying batter across the table.

"Say two psalms tonight. For my salvation."

Mr. Burton and Mr. Finch were at the far end of the orchard. Aurora's seat was empty. The dragonfly lifted from the casing and slipped away in the haze of yellow light.

I probably did have airs. I had not owned a dress of such fine smooth cotton since my mother passed and left me to Father's meager care. I liked how the folds of it swirled when I turned. How my hands slid along the fabric and how the turns in the bodice showed off my waist.

I did not look like a vagabond or a maid. Just a woman, almost pretty, in a dress of lilac flowers.

"Oh good," Rebecca said when passing me on the stairs. "That will save sending it to the rag man."

But I saw the envy.

It wasn't the piano that caught my attention later, though it was the first time it had been played in many months. It was the voice that accompanied it.

I was meant to be filling the lamps; instead, I paused at the doorway and listened to Aurora sing a tune I had never heard before. Something in French, with trills and long, winding turns of notes. Her head was tipped back, eyes closed and a glaze of pleasure on her face. Her fingers faltered on the keys, and she stopped and started a phrase. But it mattered little when the tune was again alive and her voice caught and held before dropping to a whisper.

"Not as good as Jenny Lind, cat, but damn near close enough. I should have stuck with the stage." She reached down to pat Mr. Quimby, who flopped on his back and purred. She straightened and closed the lid, then drummed her fingers as she looked about the room.

"I'm told you play a decent hand of whist." She cocked her head and turned to me, speaking before I could step out of her view. "Come in and close the door."

I pressed the doors shut and set my oil can on the floor near the cabinet.

"So you are Lucy Blunt."

"Yes."

"I'm not fond of the country," she said. "Pastoral as it all seems. There's always a stench." She stood and spread her arms, palms up. "But here I am. And there you are, Miss Blunt." She knocked her knuckle on the piano lid and moved toward me. "Most girls like you want only silver."

"Ma'am?"

"You've charmed Gene into foolishness and wild fancies."

"I don't know what—"

"Don't insult me." Aurora dipped her chin and stared with hard eyes. "Do you think you're the first?" Her lips curled into a smile. "Of course you do."

I dug my nails into my skirts, then flattened my hands to my thighs.

"Right now, you're the wonder of her day. It's getting tiring to read about it. Letters from her, missives from Rebecca . . ." She trailed a hand along the back of the settee as she moved closer. "Eugenie has a proclivity for this sort of thing. Something to pass the time. Her world is quite small. You're just *un caprice*. I think you're a clever enough girl to understand that."

I clenched my jaw. "Eugenie and I . . ." My words withered as she stared. "She's asked me to be her companion."

"I am aware."

"I'm not a caprice."

"Hm. Mary Dawson said just the same."

My stomach gave a twist. "Mary . . ."

"This scheme you two have . . . Rebecca has no money and fewer charms. Even I can't help with that. I'm afraid Eugenie is stuck with her. And as dull as he is, my brother cares deeply for his wife. I'm afraid she is stuck with him too. You, of course, can leave at any point in time."

"I'm not leaving."

"That will be your heartbreak."

"Of that you will be wrong." I grabbed the oil can and snapped the door wide, nearly careening into Eugenie and Rebecca. Mr. Quimby escaped like a shot, his bell jangling as he weaved past all the legs and jumped the stairs.

Eugenie gasped and stepped back, one hand outstretched, the tips of her fingers finding my arm. She frowned, then dropped her hand to her skirts and smoothed them. "You frightened me."

I pressed my lips tight and stepped to the side. I could not look at her, nor at Rebecca. Was I just a curio to be eventually packed on a shelf in the attic?

Aurora leaned a shoulder to the doorframe. "Come keep me company, Gene. I can only entertain myself for so long." She laced her arm through Eugenie's. Her gaze traveled to me, but she said not a word.

Rebecca lingered. "Bring us some cakes, Lucy. When you've finished your other chore, of course." She gestured to the oil can and then flicked her fingers on her skirt as if the sight of the can had dirtied her hands.

Here it was: the gnawing ache of doubt. It grabbed at my gut and wouldn't let go. It clung to me, teeth deep and razored. Mary Dawson. Who before her? And who after me?

My nails bit into my palms as I stomped out of the house later, ignoring Cook, waving her away and saying that it was Monday anyway, my afternoon off. I tore down the hill, away from the house. The path was stone hard, dried and baked and wavering with heat. Not even the canopy of red maple and silver-barked birch could abate the crush of it. I fumbled with the buttons at my neck until two had come loose. I shoved my bonnet back so it dangled against my back.

I scrambled off the road to catch my breath and wipe the oil of tears away and found myself at a stream of jumbled gold and silt, its bank littered white with the last blooms of the wild plum trees. Iris and Queen Anne's lace ribboned the water's edge. A bevy of stone shingled out over a precipice of hollowed earth, and water bubbled and coiled round exposed roots.

I glanced back toward the road. This turn of the stream was concealed from view, hidden behind buckthorn and sheep laurel, and in winter would remain nearly so. And I couldn't help but think: Mary Dawson died in a spot much the same.

There was a rustle and snap of branches from across the stream. "Ah. Ah hah." Enoch Finch twisted to unhook the edge of his coat from the clutches of bush. He flicked his fingers over the hem and tidied his collar. "Are you lost?"

"Lost?"

He stretched his mouth into a wide smile. "I am perfectly lost myself. I was on my way to find the tobacconist. And my wandering mind . . . mmph."

I pointed behind me. "The road is right here. You just follow it down."

"Indeed." He poked a boot in the water, then took a step and waded across the shallows. "Come. We will walk together."

"You see, even here one can rely on the tobacconist." Mr. Finch sat on the bench outside the shop, then stood again with a gesture for me to take a seat. "My apology."

I sat and fanned myself with my bonnet while he packed the bowl of his pipe. Across the street, a mule dozed in his traces, one ear flicking away a clutch of black flies.

"We will, of course, not hear the last of this." He struck a match on his shoe.

"This what?"

"You there. Me here. Without a chaperone. I suggest we not mention it." His cheeks billowed and sunk as he worked to light the pipe. He turned and peered at me. "But I think your character tends to secretiveness, which sets me at ease."

"You are an odd man."

"I am a perceptive man. But underestimated."

"What is it you do?"

He puckered his lips and then settled back. "I am an intellectualist. I've written a book or two."

"What are they?"

He shrugged. "Well, rather pamphlets, but so . . . *The Laws of Hereditary Descent* was a recent. *The Symbolical Head* was a favorite. My mapping of phrenological organs is making a name for itself. For me." He twisted and leaned back to peer at me. "You would be quite the study."

"Would I?"

"Indeed. Quite." With a clamp of the pipe between his teeth, he stood. "I am giving a demonstration in phrenology tonight. I will ask for you especially."

"As a guest?"

"As my subject, Miss Blunt." He knocked the pipe against his shoe, dumping the ashes and remaining tobacco to the ground. "Come, show me your fine town." He hooked out an elbow for me, and when I took it he clamped my arm tight to his ribs.

It was uncomfortably hot and his hold clammy; I was glad as we neared the shade of trees near the church and moved to take rest under the bowers.

Mr. Finch tensed and tipped to his toes, his attention off somewhere in the graveyard. He pointed, then waved. "Ah. Miss White!" He pointed and waved again before dragging me past the low fence rails and among the flat headstones. "Miss White!"

Rebecca stood by a grave still raw with earth and a simple wood post. Mary Dawson's last bed, awaiting its granite stone. She stepped back, gave a quick shake of her head, and dropped a small wrapped parcel into her reticule. I feared she might snap the drawstring as she pulled the cord tight. But she composed herself and settled a smile on her face. "What an odd pair you make."

"What an odd place to find you."

"Ah. Miss White." Finch gave a tight bow. "I was just discussing our need for a chaperone. And here you are."

"Why *are* you here?" I asked, for Rebecca was not of the habit of leaving the house and grounds.

She blinked at me. "Giving regards to poor Mary. Isn't that why one goes to a cemetery?"

"Indeed it is, Miss White. Mmph."

I was glad to leave the evening washing that night. Not one pot escaped a return to the scrub and rinse. Cook was in a churlish mood. She had made a fine meal of asparagus soup, duck confit, quail eggs in aspic, and raisin cake with brown-sugar glaze, and not one word of regard came down from above. Just a request for me.

All the lights were lit in the piano room, softening the walls to warm butter. Jacob stood near the door like a tin soldier, but he gave a lift of his eyebrow and a quick roll of his eyes as I entered. A round table had been moved to the center of the room, its top covered in a length of white tulle. Placed on top was a plaster cast of a man's head. Upon its surface appeared to be diagrams writ in black lettering. Mr. Finch stood holding a large pair of calipers to the back of the sculpture's head. Mr. Beede hovered near Mr. Burton's shoulder, a bottle of wine cocked over his glass. Aurora's arm draped along the back of a settee, her fingers playing with the fringe of Eugenie's shawl.

I waited a moment at the door, watching Mr. Finch twirl the caliper and point at various bits of diagram. Watching Aurora fiddle and smooth that shawl. Watching Rebecca as she watched the two women whisper and titter and laugh.

Eugenie nodded at Mr. Beede when he proffered wine. She leaned then to Aurora to ask, "What is he doing now?"

"He's got the calipers above the left eyebrow." I crossed to Mr. Finch and peered at the plaster bust. "I can't read this. What does it say, Mr. Finch?"

"Ah. She is here. We have our study." He settled his measurement tool on the table and gave a light clap. "A chair. Let us get this girl a chair."

Eugenie straightened and moved to the edge of the seat. "What now?"

"Enoch is measuring your maid," Aurora said. "What secrets will you find, Enoch?"

Mr. Beede set a bentwood chair next to the bust.

"No secrets." Mr. Finch gestured for me to sit. He cleared his throat and planted his fist on a hip. "Physiology. The brain. Character and morality."

Mr. Burton glowered and slunk down in his seat.

"Why is Lucy here?" Eugenie asked.

"Why not?" Aurora took a sip of her wine.

"Get to the parlor trick, Mr. Finch. Without the lecture." The room went quiet and all eyes turned to Mr. Burton.

"That came out wrong," he said. "I apologize."

"This is a science, sir." Enoch's cheeks reddened. He gave a *tsk* and grabbed the calipers, touching the cold tips to the exact spot above my brow, just as he'd done to the bust. Section by section I was measured. Section by section the measurements were scribbled to a notebook. Section by section Mr. Beede poured the wine and Jacob shuffled from foot to foot and Mr. Burton dozed. Aurora hummed and finally wandered to the window.

Rebecca stared at me. "Can you tell us her secrets, Mr. Finch?"

Eugenie grew anxious, biting her lip, rocking forward and pushing back against the cushions. Then she laughed, though it came out rough and dry.

"It seems we've all forgotten I can't see."

Rebecca stood up. "Of course not. There's just nothing very interesting to explain. Yet."

"It's not your place to determine that."

"Mr. Finch has the caliper tips stuck underneath my right earlobe." I glared at Rebecca. "They are quite cold."

"Mm."

"Mr. Finch, can you explain exactly what you're doing?" I grabbed at the calipers. "Out loud."

Mr. Finch cleared his throat again. "You are confirming my measurements."

"Mrs. Burton?" I held out my hand. "I'm two steps away. Come see the parlor trick."

How deep was her frown as she touched the caliper, exploring the metal, following its curves to the tips.

"Moving slightly up from the crest of the ear," Finch said, "we approach the ridge that determines combativeness. Can you feel that, Mrs. Burton? It is not large. But neither is it average. Not ungovernable but tinged, unfortunately, with fire. You would be well advised to watch the girl's temper. Shall we move further round the skull? Come, come." He lifted the caliper and pressed his index finger to the spot above my ear. "You should each have a touch."

For the court records, I present my findings of the accused from the original diagnoses made in June '54 and the recent appointment of Dec '54.

She is a creature much determined by her combative and excitable nature. The zygomatic arch is quite pronounced. The protuberance at No. 6-7 is overlarge, and in both sittings, I was troubled by the measurements and took them twice to confirm. Together we have evidence of unqualified bitterness, hatefulness, and when roused, a desperate wrath.

I suppose, the next week, I should have thought twice before punching Enoch Finch.

But I didn't.

For the record, Mr. Finch, you caught me unawares. You're lucky I didn't pick up a slop bucket and sling that at you.

I do apologize (for the record—not that it will do me any good) for taking my roused wrath out on you. You slobbered on my breasts and bruised my waist, but those were only the final straws to your trying personality.

"Tell me about Mary."

Eugenie bolted in her bed, but I would not let go her shoulder. "What are you doing in here?"

I pressed my cheek against hers, my lips hard against her ear. "Did you tell her she would be your companion too?"

Her mouth was slack, and she breathed in quick rations of air.

"Did you love her?"

"Let me go."

"Do you love me?" I clamped my fingers to her jaw and turned her head to face mine. "Tell me. Tell me the truth."

Eugenie did not answer in words but in quick bites and caresses that marked my skin. I pushed my mouth into her shoulder to stifle a cry and left before she could conjure a lie.

Chapter Nineteen

Truth is a rather pliable object, isn't it? Something molded and recreated and told as an entertaining story.

Evidence. Me. Sitting here now, Mr. LeRocque.

I was observed pushing Rebecca down the stairs. That is true if you're the girl looking up from the bottom step. That is not true if your view is from the landing above.

And it is true I had quite the inventory of jewels in my valise. And men's clothing. It is not true that I stole them.

And I did punch Mr. Finch that summer. That was, alas, also true.

Mr. Finch says I have committed calumny. That he instigated nothing at all, and certainly not the last bit behind the barn that caused his ensuing black eye. Not accosting me on the steep back stairs as I brought down the plates. Not with a hand over my mouth and the muffled rumble of Cook's snores filtering from her bedroom to mine. Not at Wheeler's Inn where he took longer, and was crueler, and gave me a coin to spend any way I wanted during the remaining threads of my afternoon off.

But *that* morning, he followed me to the barn as I lugged the slop buckets to the pigs. He hummed and kept stride, thumbs hooked in his vest pockets and eyes squinting at the light.

"You're a fine, strong girl, Miss Blunt. I can see it in your forearms."

We passed the side of the barn, the shadows nipped with the last of the night, and then came to the hog pens. The brutes pushed against each other, solid bodies of brown vying for the first bucket of the day. Steam curled from their nostrils as they snorted and bunched close to the fence. I set down the buckets, reached in, and tugged a few ears. "You're a hungry sty of pork today."

I stepped down and lifted a bucket. Mr. Finch stood a few paces back from the animals, his hands still clamped to his vest pockets. He peered at me with eyes both dispassionate and wanting at the same time. I'd seen the look before. Albert's version of it melted me. Mr. Finch's made me laugh.

I slung the bucket's contents over the rail, then switched to another and moved down the pen.

"Why are you laughing, Miss Blunt?"

I couldn't say out loud that he looked like a woodpecker in heat. I couldn't say that he frightened me. I just shrugged, tipped the last of the buckets, and then gathered them up by the handles.

He sauntered toward me. As I slipped past, he reached for me. The buckets clattered to the ground. His thumb pressed deep in my elbow as he twisted me to face him and pulled me tight. To breath rank of coffee and his ever-present pipe. To his thin chest and extruding rib cage. To his thighs and hardness. "You shouldn't laugh."

I kept laughing. For wasn't it ridiculous? I laughed and his thumb dug deeper, and then he let go just to grab the scruff of my neck. Like a dog. He shook me once and twisted up the neck of my dress. Marched us past the hogs to the back of the barn where the night still lingered.

The boards were flaked and in want of a coat of paint. He pushed my face to the wood and held it there. It didn't take long. A few grunts on his part, a spittle of paint chips on mine.

"Put your skirt down." He buttoned up his trousers.

I touched the back of my hand to the stinging skin on my cheek, then curled my fingers to a fist.

He stared at my fist, one brow lifting. "That would be unadvisable." He tilted his head. "Wouldn't it? Yes, yes, I think it would . . ."

He glanced then at the field beyond us, and the trees that circled the pasture. "Sheep. There's so damn many sheep here. It's—"

That's when I punched him.

He staggered, more from surprise than the strike of the blow. He covered his eye, stumbling back in a flail of feet and elbows, landing with an *umph* on the ground. "What the hell was that for?"

"You're a pathetic man."

His mouth flopped open and closed shut. He cupped his eye and rolled to his back. His ribs expanded and flattened and his chest rumbled in a chortle of amusement. "You shouldn't have done that. Shouldn't have done that at all."

Rebecca stopped me as I returned that afternoon. Her arms were full of cut flowers from the garden. "What happened to your cheek?"

"I tripped."

Her eyes narrowed, her gaze slipped past to the edge of the orchard and then cut back to me. "You must be more careful."

Eugenie stopped me that day, stilling the water can I had lifted to a rose so dark it was nearly indigo. Her touch was so soft on my arm, I thought I would break in two. "You've been avoiding me. Are you well?"

I crushed my lips to keep from speaking. For what would that possibly gain? Her disapproval at best and her disgust at worst. Either way, I could lose this position and the one I craved.

"You have guests."

She crossed her arms at the waist. Her dress was cotton, frilled round the collars and cuffs with yellow daisies, the fabric patterned in a snarl of vines.

"Where did you get the dress?"

"It's one of Aurora's. Do you like it?"

"No."

"You're out of sorts."

"I have work to do."

I caught sight of Rebecca turning from the stairs, her hand still on the curved banister as she peered in the dim hall. She approached us and stood in a square of light.

"There you are."

Eugenie gave a sharp smile. "Here I am."

"I thought Mr. Friday took care of this hothouse."

"He's taken Mr. Finch to town," I said. "He wishes to tour the mill."

"How attentive you are of Mr. Finch." She slipped her arm through Eugenie's. "Come along. Aurora wants you to accompany her while she sings."

Eugenie hesitated. When she turned to me, her expression was troubled.

I've been summoned to the warden's house. There is a visitor, though Matron was not told the name, only to bring me post haste. It is early; the ground still shimmers a bluish hue. The only others astir are the guards tending to the boilers in the kitchens and laundry.

The warden's dwelling sits in the center of the prison, a red-brick house with black-paint window frames and a tidy garden along the walkway to the door.

I wonder about a man who would bring his wife and daughters to live in such a domicile. No matter the window, the view is as grim as the last.

Matron holds my elbow instead of tugging at the short chain between my handcuffs. She glances at me, then away, then back again. "Stop."

She pushes her fingers through my hair, tugging at the tangles until my head jerks and scalp stings from all the pulling. Her hands slow and smooth, draping a tress over my shoulder, curling it round her finger before letting go. Then she nods and takes up my elbow, and our feet crunch over the gravel-and-rock path to the warden's door.

Whoever it is has been granted entry before visiting hours.

Matron grips my elbow. "Perhaps it's Mrs. Kepple with news . . ." But she can't say more; saying it means there's hope someone believed me when I told the truth.

I slowed before the morning room door as I passed and stared at the tableau round the breakfast table. Aurora held her teacup halfway to her lips. Mr. Finch bit into a strip of bacon, his jaw shifting side to side as he chewed. His left eye was a swell of purple and red.

"She threw herself at me. Dropped the buckets, spun right around, clawed my collar. Like a harridan. Mmph."

"I warned you," Aurora said.

"There was no reason for her to give me such a blow. I might lose my vision."

"You won't lose your vision, don't be daft." (Saith Aurora.) "But you can't say Rebecca and I didn't warn you about that girl. I hope Eugenie listens now."

"She's a horrid little creature." A cup returned with a click to the table, and Finch's voice cut sharp edged and smug. "I should have minded my own findings."

I followed Mr. Beede, my satchel in hand. It held only the dress and coat I came in, my comb, and the paper folded with Ned's hair. I concealed Eugenie's gifts in the hem of my lilac dress. Ribbons and lace. A bracelet of emeralds. A pair of garnet earrings.

A mural ran the length of the wall behind Mr. Burton's desk: a fuddled landscape of wilting trees and splotches of brown that denoted horses or four-legged boys. The houses tumbled along a blue lick of water. The buildings in the corner looked to be the mill and the sawyer's, though the sawyer must not have paid the artist, for his building was half out of the frame.

The other walls were black, the flatness interrupted only by paintings as somber in color as the rest of the room. A table ran through the middle, and on it lay a map of a sinuous river. The curling corners were held in place by a cast-iron model of a train car, a paperweight of amber glass, two leather-bound books, and a vase filled with a drooping daisy and yellowed water.

Rebecca perched at the far end, her embroidery round held in her hands. She did not look up when I entered. Just a long sigh and a needle poked to the fabric.

Mr. Burton sat behind his desk, elbows planted atop a twisted stack of bound papers. "What have you to say?"

"Does it matter?"

"You have injured a guest of my house."

"He injured me."

Mr. Beede set a hand on my shoulder, but I twisted away.

"Whatever the circumstance," Mr. Burton said, "we do not tolerate violence in this house."

"He deserved that black eye," I said. "It wasn't the first time—"

"You seemed content with him when I ran into you in town." Rebecca peered at me, then out the window. "Fawning around beyond your place. Goodness knows the rumors, Cousin. If you hear any, you—"

"I didn't ask his attention then. I certainly haven't asked it after."

"No? Not the attention you really want, is it, Lucy?"

"Why do you do this?"

"I don't know what you're talking about. She needs to be dismissed."

"You pathetic—"

Mr. Burton flattened his hands to his desk and stood. "Enough."

"I'll speak my mind as I wish. Mr. Finch is a baboon. Which is all very fine to all of you, as long as it's me he accosted. What if it had been your wife?"

Mr. Burton's mouth curled. "My wife would not be in such a position to begin with."

"No. God forbid she's allowed to walk two steps on her own."

"I will not have you—"

I stepped back. "I'll be on my way. I'd just like to say my goodbye to Cook."

Mr. Burton gestured to Beede and then turned his back to me.

"Here are your wages." Mr. Beede handed me an envelope. "Cook will have a basket for you in the kitchen."

Mr. Burton strode to the door and grabbed the knob. The corners of his mouth pulled down and set in a deep frown. He glared at me, then looked above to the horrible fronded trees of the mural. I crimped the envelope in my fist.

"I would like to see Mrs. Burton."

Rebecca glanced up from the embroidery loop she worked, then returned to sliding the needle and pulling the thread taut. "She has a headache." With a flick of her wrist she hooked the thread. "Close the door as you go, Mr. Beede."

"Oh, Lucy." Cook fingered the edge of the psalm book in her pocket, then rested her hands on my arms. She had left a pheasant half plucked on the counter. The floor was littered with feathers striated in yellows and whites and browns. I whisked them into a pile to be sifted into boxes for later use, the soft hackle set aside for pillows and fishing lures, the long tail plumes to be added to a vase in the hall. I kept my eyes on the patterns of the plumes, not the throb of the split skin on my knuckles. I kept my attention on the sorting rather than the stir of acid in my stomach.

"You'll find another girl, Cook."

She wiped her eyes with the back of her hand, then turned to the pheasant and plucked the final quills from its skin. "I've made a good basket for you. There's two slices of raisin cake, and I've slipped in a bottle of cider. Victuals enough to tide you for a few days."

"You didn't need to."

"And there's a note to give my sister in Keene. Mrs. Cyrus Elfton. There's just her now, her husband fell to the cholera a few summers back. She could sorely use help."

"Is she like you?"

"Fiercer."

"Then it's I who will need the help." I grabbed her then, arms wrapped round before she could grumble away.

"That'll do." She bent her head, and her lips moved with silent words. Then she gave a sigh and turned back to the pheasant. "Be off, then."

I picked up the basket and shifted the shoulder strap of my satchel. I slowed at the door. "Cook? What's your name? I've never asked your real name."

Cook wiped her hands with her apron. "Connors. Emma Connors. But I wouldn't know it to answer to."

"God keep you, Emma Connors."

The warden's wife meets us at the door. She is a small woman, smaller than Matron, and her blond hair is graying. She worries the brooch at her throat as she leads us through the dark-walled hall. The parlor is washed with gray light that has reflected from the stone wall of the building opposite. The oil lamps placed round the low-slung room, the bright-red rag rugs, the gaudy pillows, and random cut-glass ornaments attest to a feminine hand but a losing battle.

There are two figures at the window, one large with feet planted wide. The warden, brash with confidence. Then the other turns toward us. My skin chills and then flushes with prickling heat. I press my hand to my mouth, pulling in gasps of air, the iron chain swinging and the shackle hitting my jaw.

"Ah. Miss Blunt."

Enoch Finch. With the same rasp of a voice and cocky thrust of chest.

"Sit." He gestures to a tufted velveteen chair. "Make her sit."

Matron grips my elbow and I topple into the seat. She steps behind, and her hand rests on the seat back.

The warden looks at me. His eyes give away nothing. They never do. They are hard as glass. It's not surprising given his position. He nods at Finch. "I'll be in my office."

Finch leans against the deep window frame and takes his time packing and lighting his pipe. He puffs and blinks, his head tilted one way and then the other. "Are you well?"

My lips are numb, cold, though the room is heated from the stove in the corner. "What do you want?"

"Still so bellicose." He kicks out a shiny shoe and steps toward me. He leans down, resting a hand to his knee, biting the pipe in his teeth. His eyes dart back and forth as he peers at me. "Your time slips like sand. Mmph."

Then with a twist of his trunk, he settles into the sofa. He sets the pipe on a plate of rose glass, the tobacco glinting orange and sifting to ash as it lands.

"We wonder why we were called here," Matron says.

"Do they give you a precise time to hang? Or is it a range of hours, say, sometime between lunch and evensong?"

"Ten fifteen a.m." I can't stop the needles prickling under my skin.

"Ten fifteen a.m." He leans back and snakes his arm across the top of the sofa, his finger tapping the curved wood of the frame. "Or not."

His eyebrow lifts. "Mrs. Kepple is a worthy ally to you. She has gained a hearing on the floor of the statehouse."

I sit forward with a gasp.

"I have been asked to report on your character. As an authority on psychological conditions, of course the request came to me. Aurora will plead for your life. I will confirm if it's worth it."

My clench is so tight on the arm rests, my fingers have numbed.

"There is hope," Matron murmurs.

"The warden isn't keen on you women. His last report was the third time he's complained that you don't earn your keep. At least the men have a hand in the sale of cabinets. And shoes." He shifted. "The asylum is on offer. If I deem you fit. You see, Miss Blunt, I hold your life in my hands."

My stomach heaves and I swallow back bile. "No." I lunge from the chair.

He winces, shrinking into the seat. "You are not helping yourself."

"I could press this chain against your neck and be happy for the crack. But you are not worth the effort."

"Guard!" he calls. His voice is tremulous and thin. "Guard!"

"Why, Lucy?" Matron's got her arms wrapped tight around her waist. There are others out as we make our way back across the yard. Men in a wobbly line of black stripes and manacles. On their way to nail soles or turn a lathe as they did the morning before and will do the mornings after.

"I'd rather hang."

Chapter Twenty

I am certain Keene has much of interest, vital things that set it apart from Goffstown or Peterboro or Harrowboro. I wasn't of much mind to care. When I arrived, I was still full of spleen at my unfair (though not unforeseen) circumstances. The stage from Harrowboro to the township had been a jarring six hours on heavily potted roads. The sun baked the exterior of the coach and steamed the interior. On our approach to the town, the road paralleled the new train, which billowed smoke of oily coal dust that crusted my clothes and teeth.

Mrs. Cyrus Elfton's house was a simple saltbox of weathered white paint and a door that hung just off square. It was easy to find—Cook wrote on the outside of her original letter to take a turn right from the stage stop, turn again past the First Church bell tower, and there behind the blueberry bushes at X-marks-the-spot would she be. And so she was.

"I have no money for you."

"I ask for none."

Mrs. Elfton, grim and hard edged, stared up from the note I brought from Cook. "She says you were grievous treated."

"Did she?"

"Aye." She flicked the paper near her wind-burnt nose and cheeks as if it would bring both a waft of cool air and some solution for the wayward girl on her steps.

I lowered my chin and shrugged. Perhaps Cook didn't exactly say *grievous treated*. It was a small postscript embellishment I made at the stopover in Jaffrey. And though I had confidence in the forgery of the letters themselves, I felt a twinge of unease in the phrasing.

The woman glanced again at the paper, then her eyes caught the basket. "Is there raisin cake?"

"And cider."

"Ach. There's nothing to match my sister's raisin cake." She pointed to a square table away under a sugar maple. "We'll sit."

Mrs. Elfton ate the cake and drank the cider, then ambled over to the blueberries. She picked a handful and brought them back to the table. Her hands were twisted from hard use and age. But I saw Cook in her gestures and swallowed back a rush of grief that it wasn't the woman herself.

The light was fading. I rubbed my eyes and blinked, as if that were all it would take to clear this away. As if with a shake of my head I would be returned to the kitchen table to take up the mending as Cook murmured bible stories. Manna in the desert. Lot's wife and the pillar of salt. The raising of Lazarus. All while her voice matched the rhythm of our needles and Jacob's cloth as he shined the silverware. Jacob's lips mirroring hers, and when he remembered a fragment of a story, his voice weaving into hers.

If I had been more pliant, not let my temper go, not lashed out at Mr. Finch, I would still be there and not in Keene staring at Cook's sister and her pale eyes.

But there was nothing to return to. Rebecca would have told the sad story to Eugenie and poisoned any thoughts she had of me with lies. All in the name of protecting her, and all, I am certain, with her hand slipped gently in Eugenie's, and basking yet again in her attention.

My chin trembled. I dropped my head and pressed my palms to my mouth. But I could not hold back the sobs that pummeled my ribs.

Mrs. Elfton remained quiet, observing me as she ate a solitary blueberry, then another, until there were none left.

I gulped in a breath and wiped my eyes with the back of my arm.

"Are you finished?"

"I'm finished."

"Is she well, then? My sister."

"Yes. I think so."

"Still the psalms at night?"

"At least one."

"Good." She folded the rest of the raisin cake in its cloth and placed it back in the basket with the empty cider bottle. "We'll tend the goats now."

I don't know what Mrs. Elfton—Marietta—really thought of me. She allowed me to stay, and I helped her deliver goat cheese and milk and soap to households. She rose earlier even than Cook, with a quick whistle to awaken me and a *chookchook* to the mule. We loaded the jugs and bottles on the short cart and walked each side of the mule without passing much of any word during the deliveries.

She never gave a name for the mule, so I called him Fred, and he wasn't averse to me scratching his long, tufted ears as we plodded along.

His one good eye, a deep, soft brown, was level with mine on our local travels, and his look was often baleful, as if this lot in life both disappointed and annoyed him. I thought of the peddler's mule and his fine ears pricked forward to the possibility of each new adventure.

The long whistle of the railroad perked Fred up. He pranced and shifted in the traces, his tail high angled and flicking. We watched the plume of smoke as the Cheshire Railroad approached the Ashuelot River and clattered over the stone-arch bridge, wheels squealing and sparking and slowing their revolutions as the train pulled to the depot. We sold blueberries and gooseberries and red currants in small paper cones to the few passengers coming from Concord and points east. A few alighted, but most remained in the single car squeezed between the engine and the beds of timber and cotton and brass and wool. Mrs. Elfton walked the windows with a cone lifted and a singsong "Sweet berries from Keene."

"She'd sell more with a smile," I told Fred. But she was as tightfisted with her smiles as she was with her words.

Fred dozed in the swelter of sun and ignored me.

Dear Cook,

I am well here in Keene, and your sister has been kind to me. I hear from your letter to her that you have hired another girl. I hope she is serving the house well. I thought of you today—I made Marietta a pudding that turned out more clots than cream and I thought—Cook would know how to fix this. Unfortunately, I did not, and we settled instead for chokeberry jam.

I have learned much about the business of goats. They are stubborn creatures, and I've found myself face first in the ground when I wasn't careful. You can't bribe them as you can a horse. They've got their own mind, and the best to do is sit and nod and pretend to listen to their litany of inconveniences. One is named Medusa, and I am careful to keep my distance from her.

Please let Jacob, Mr. Beede, and Friday know that I ask after them and hope they are well.

And if you can, would you be so kind as to give Mrs. Burton a greeting from me?

Yours Sincerely,

Lucy B.—

At night we kept the windows flung wide, awaiting any purchase of breeze. It was too hot to do much but sprawl across the bedsheet in the room I now occupied, my thin shift stuck to my chest with sweat. Sleep evaded me. I stared yet again at a meandering crack in the ceiling plaster that journeyed from the doorframe to the window jamb on the wall opposite. The plaster had crumbled, exposing narrow strips of lath and horsehair. It was a high moon, bright enough to add to my restlessness. I bunched my pillow over my head and twisted toward the wall.

Marietta's voice drifted up from the yard. I turned my head to the window. The moon was directly overhead, casting its pallor on the bell tower of the church. Late. Too late for callers.

Her voice drew me to the window. I peered down to the yard and spied her walking the rows of red currants. She bent to pick weeds from around the bases, tossing them to the path and walking on. There was no one beside her, though she lifted her head and nodded and curled her fingers as if her hand held another's. She spoke then, though too softly to hear the meaning.

She turned to the next row, reaching to cradle a branch of the fruit in her palm. Then her hand dropped and the currant bunch swung and settled. She closed her eyes, dropping her head back and pressing her palms together. Her smile seemed too private for my witness. I stepped into the dark and made my way back to the bed.

Mrs. Elfton spoke to the dead. It was not the only conversation I overheard. On Tuesdays she shared the ledger books with her late husband, and on Fridays she walked the graveyard across the road and touched her hands to the weathered stones.

"Do they speak back?" I asked once as we sat under a tree in respite from the heat and watched Fred chew the shards of grass against a stone fence.

"Only if I listen."

"Mr. Elfton?"

"He's never been able to give up the books. Well, can't say as I'm any good with numbers without him."

Mr. Finch would have a grand time with her.

> *My dear Lucy,*
> *How kind of you to correspond with Cook. She gives her*
> *regards as requested. Mrs. Burton, however, asks that you*

not write to this address again. She states it is distressing
to all involved.
   To your best health—
   R. White

I crumpled the paper, shoved it in my pocket, and pushed a goat away with my hip. Then I turned back to it, staring into its strange, elongated pupils before giving its shoulder a sharp shove.

"I hate you."

It shook its head, ears flapping, mouthful of half-sodden hay splattering my skirt. I grabbed its horns and shoved it back until its rump hit the back rails of the pen, then gave another push before grabbing up my skirts and scrambling over the rails.

I didn't have a destination; I knew little of Keene but the route we took to peddle the berries and milk. I ran, my back to the barn and the cottage and the church spires and bell towers, the sawmills and machine shops and brickyards. I felt the sting of branches and cockleburs on my palms as I slapped them away, darting farther into the forest, away and away from Mrs. Elfton and her mumblings to a husband dead of cholera and rotted to nothing but soil and loam.

The light splintered between the trees into gold and oranges. My lungs pulled in shallow breaths, and the air burned as it entered. There was a rustle of leaves from the maple branches above, then a flash of blue and white as a kingfisher darted in front of me, its call rattling the air before it dove and disappeared. I skidded to a stop. A burble and rush of river lay just beyond me. My chest heaved and I stumbled to the river's edge.

Here, upstream of the textile mill's dam, falling leaves stained the water a deep mahogany. The river slipped like oil over boulders and slowed and stilled in lazy eddies alit with black water striders and iridescent damselflies. Too wide and too deep to cross.

I wasn't the only one there.

Below the water's skin, opaque and then cobwebbed with filtered light, Mary Dawson stared.

"Oh God." I kicked until the silt lifted and swirled and buried her to the riverbed.

I was certain she had flung herself in the ice of that stream. Had gripped the rocks to hold herself there until the rime coated and silenced her lips. She threw away her life. Mrs. Burton's fading fancy.

Was it grief or guilt that kept Eugenie in the carriage while Mary lay in repose? Perhaps, in one of her intemperate moments, she'd locked the girl out of the house, as she had Rebecca. Or was it Rebecca who turned the key?

I would never know, for there was no chance to ask. Any query I sent would be intercepted by Rebecca. No answer, if possibly returned, could I fully believe.

My feet and arms were heavy as I returned through the woods. I perused the matter, turning from the absolute conviction that Eugenie truly loved me, to the desolate acceptance that Aurora had been right. The closer I came to the cottage and the sour stink of goats and curdled milk, the more futile my future became. My meager savings were nearly depleted, and to sell the earrings or bracelet would call attention, and most likely send me to jail as a thief.

I wandered out of the woods to the tumbling racket of the town. I stopped at a corner, aware of eyes catching mine and then quickly averting. I glanced in the window of the tobacconist. My hair was unkempt, loose from the bonnet that hung down my back. My dress was covered in burrs and twigs, stained and crinkled at the hem. As if it were I, and not Mary, who'd inhabited the waters and arose.

I lifted my chin and gave myself a nod. I was not her. I would never be her.

I was wrong, of course.

George Farley (so named in gold letters on his door) was grandly tall, and when he leaned upon the travel office counter, the wood grunted. I stood in the midst of maps pinned to walls and rolled in cubbyholes, of train schedules that displayed departures and arrivals from Boston to South Carolina and the far reaches of Missouri.

My finger traversed the Cheshire Railroad line, whose map was pressed between glass and the counter. The line continued west from Keene to Bellows Falls, Vermont. There it joined the Central Vermont line, and from there one could travel most directions.

I grabbed the counter edge to steady myself and took in the wall maps: all the roads and bridges, the confluence of the Mississippi and Missouri rivers, the inked-in mountains, the great empty desert, a tiny dot signifying San Francisco. So many possibilities, I felt lightheaded.

Albert said the same once, in a room we'd rented for an afternoon. He was on his side, chin cupped in his hand, stroking my waist with his finger. "The world has so many possibilities. Why, it's all just a ship away."

I brushed my palm across his chest, curled the dark hairs and nipped kisses. "Where would you go?"

"Timbuktu," he said.

I pressed my nose to his skin and sniggered. "Timbuktu."

"Or Edo Bay."

"Japan?"

"I could meet the emperor."

"Would you take me?"

"Mmm." He rolled to his back and stuck his hand under his head. I smoothed his mustache as he stared at the ceiling, eyebrows pulled tight in thought. "I couldn't take the children. You, however, would be a grand companion."

He didn't mean it. It was another of his flights of fancy. Even then, he kept a close eye on his pocket watch, lifting it from the bed stand to check and recheck the time.

With a scratch of his beard, he said, "You're my girl."

"Yes. Here or Timbuktu. Or the Andes, if that suits."

"Right." He gave a soft smack to my rump and sat up.

We dressed, backs to each other, and left ten minutes apart.

"How much to San Francisco?"

The travel agent raised and lowered his eyebrow as he looked at me. He cleared his throat. "I can get you to St. Joseph by train, then you'll need to find a wagon going and—"

"Get me to St. Joseph, then. That's in Missouri?" I rummaged in my waist purse and slid the last of my coins across the counter. "Would you barter for the rest of the fare? I've some old jewelry."

"Better if you had some old companion with you."

"I can take care of myself."

He reached for his fare book, opening it to a half-filled page. "What's the name?"

"Tessa Marks."

I turned and pushed through the door before I could change my mind. So simple. A ticket and another new life.

Mrs. Elfton had company.

A red brougham sat on the dirt street. A pair of mismatched horses, one dapple gray and the other a freckled white, lingered in their traces. I slowed as I came to it, my heart punching my chest. I clenched and twisted my skirts as I rounded it, following the voices to Marietta's yard. I stopped at the hedge of blueberries. Dappled light fell through the wide-armed sugar maple, and it caught the movement of a jade-green silk fan: the flutter up, the quick flick down, the twist and click as it closed. Then its owner leaned forward, her free hand gripping the table. My heart tumbled in my chest, and I misstepped as I neared. Eugenie. With Mr. Burton sitting across, his dark-gray suit vest sifted with a fine layer of dust. And there, by the porch, Mr. Friday just stepping down and carrying a large pitcher of iced tea, followed by Marietta, who carried a plate of biscuits and the chokeberry jam we'd put up the previous week.

"Mrs. Burton?" The word raced from my mouth.

Eugenie turned her head with a slight cock, and her mouth quivered and drew into an uncertain smile. "Lucy."

Her cheeks stretched along the bone, for she had lost weight and her skin was so pale I could see the pulse of blood along her throat. Her dark hair had come loose from her bonnet, and her yellow calico dress was dulled with dust.

I darted my eyes across the yard and peered into the shadowed porch. "Is Rebecca . . ."

Eugenie pressed her glove to the corner of her eye and then let out a breath with a short laugh. "She's at the house. Sorting out the new maid."

Mr. Friday set down the pitcher and clasped his hands behind him. He had not removed his coat; when he flicked at a mosquito, I saw a ring of sweat under his arms.

Mr. Burton pressed his lips together and gazed at me. "My wife says I was wrong. About you." He swallowed. "Mr. Finch . . . He and Aurora are no longer at the house."

"I don't understand why you're here."

Eugenie spread her palms. "We've come to take you home."

Mr. Friday's gaze caught mine. As he regarded me, his expression grew dour and then seemed to coil to a sort of pity. Perhaps it was his only way to warn me; he was never one for words, after all.

My words caught in my throat, a riotous mix that would come out a meaningless keen were I to let them go. "But you fired me."

"You did nothing wrong, Lucy." Her voice grew tremulous. "Please. For me."

Chapter Twenty-One

So, I was collected.

In bright moods I think: she loved me.

In my darker moods I think: I was collected like an object for her shelf.

We lodged in town that night. Mr. Burton made the arrangements, and we sat in a lobby of ferns and horsehair seats while the room was procured. Mr. Friday passed bags and a trunk to the desk clerk.

"Is it a nice hotel?" Eugenie whispered, wiping her gloved hands along her skirt, the fan at her wrist bumping and twisting with the motion.

"Very nice."

"Good." She nodded, her mouth curling down before settling into a thin line. "Are we ready, husband? I think I'll have Lucy take me in to my room."

That evening, a summer thunderstorm made good on its threat. The tassels on the heavy curtains in the Burtons' room swayed and bumped against the wall with each successive clap. The room—with its excess of tables and silk chairs and a wide swatch of fabric that hung over the bed—held in the heat and static air.

Mr. Burton had excused himself to the men's parlor two floors below, no doubt puffing cigars with other mill men and rolling dice for penny antes. Or not. He could indeed come up any moment, and only the turn of the key would sound the alarm. We lay on the bed, listening to the rolls of thunder and the plonks of rain against the half-open windows. I kept one ear toward the knob, and with each creak in the hall felt my blood pulse quick and hard.

"God is very grumbly tonight," Eugenie said.

"You don't believe in God."

"Thor, then. Zeus on Olympus. Nattering about his indigestion." She bit her lip, a smile caught between. "Six more seconds," she whispered.

Our fingers weaved together when the thunder shook the glass precisely six seconds, or nine, or twelve—for she was right every time—and we rolled toward each other and laughed and kissed and tangled the thin blanket around our knees.

"How do you do it?"

"It's a matter of listening." She nuzzled my nose and I breathed in the sweet of brandy, of lemon cream, of our joint bodies.

I ran my thumb down the soft curve of her arm. "I love you."

We both stilled. Eugenie rose to her elbow, caressing my chin. Then her lips touched and rested on mine. "Tomorrow I will buy you a beautiful dress."

"Will you?"

"There is a dressmaker in this town, isn't there?"

"More than one."

"And I will take you home to your very own room. Right next to mine."

"The nursery is right next to yours."

"It's yours now. You can decorate it any way you want."

She reached to touch my cheek, a quick caress, then ran her hand down my arm and circled her thumb on my wrist. "I'll give you anything."

A fractured slice of lightning and loud clap sent us under the covers. The glass beads on the lampshades clinked and chimed.

I pulled the cover from my head and sat against the headboard, pulling my knees to my chest. Leaden clouds pushed and darkened the window glass. "Rebecca—"

"Rebecca doesn't matter."

"But she does."

Eugenie crawled up, stretching her legs before her and clasping her hands to her lap. Her expression was veiled. "I don't care."

The cloudbank thinned and swirled, revealing and then obscuring streams of moonlight.

"You came for me."

"I did."

"And Rebecca? How were you able to leave without her?"

She shrugged. "I made sure she overslept."

I shivered. "Not sorting out the new maid, then."

"Are you cold?" she asked.

"No."

"I am. Can you find my shawl?"

"In that heap? Give me an hour." But I found it quickly, glad to leave that conversation behind. Had she given Rebecca a dose of laudanum, or a sleeping draught of morphine, or belladonna from the yard? Did I really want to know?

I turned to the task of brushing and hanging her clothing in the hotel wardrobe. I lit the lamp, tidying and listening as she described the fulsome horror of the long trip and the roar of the railroad as they entered the town.

"It's a beast. Like the Minotaur let loose from his cave."

A necklace dropped from her jewelry case, causing its locket to flip open.

Two miniatures, precisely painted. Eugenie still plumped with youth and covered in her wedding silks. Mr. Burton with hair still fully black, curling around the ears, his collar high and brushing his jaw. They looked hopeful, as if in time they might come to grow fond of the other. As if it all were not merely an arrangement of money and a shift of responsibility from Gene's father to her husband. Just an artist's trick, those gazes. Or at least that's what I made myself believe.

"It's time to dress you for dinner. And I still need to find my room."

I had seen the necklace before; she wore it often, stroking the gold casing as she sat listening to me read. I closed it with a snap and pushed it and a sliver of unease under her pins and bracelets. Then I placed the box on the dressing table.

"Hold still unless you want this pin stuck in your neck." Gert fusses over a piece of collar lace. She's adamant I be dressed right for God and has fitted me in a dress of serge, midnight blue with white posies. She's smuggled in the pins one by one and stitched the pattern pieces to the underside of her petticoats to evade the inspections. Here a quick measurement, there a hasty turn of the hem. All the elements now assembled and draped and fitted.

It seems a shame to waste it on me.

She circles. "Step up on the bench."

The boiler knocks and hisses steam. "Think the warden will replace that one too?"

"When the Irish learn to wash their mouths out." She shakes her head and bends to the skirt hem. "I don't want you tripping."

Almira and Margaret stand over their vat, two witches with a brew of lye and tepid water and thin, tattered sheets.

"What are you looking at?" I ask.

Almira shakes her head, a frizz of gray and black wobbling on her scalp. "Can I have that dress when you're done with it? My girl could use it."

Margaret keeps her head down. "That's a horrible thing to joke about."

With a twist of her paddle, Almira lifts a bundle of sheets and slaps it back with a spray of water. "I don't really want it. You'll piss and shit and ruin it anyway."

I stumble from the bench, Gert's shoulder grabbed tight in my fist. I lurch over, breath burning my chest, mouth wide gasping for air. Gert settles me to the floor, grousing about the pins and smoothing out the skirts.

"You've got no heart, Almira."

But she's right. I'll shit and piss and my tongue will swell and go black. If I'm lucky, the rope will be the precise right length and I won't notice anything but the drop of the floor. The doctor's weighed me; the cut of the rope's in the hangman's hands now.

Gert grabs me by the chin with a shake. "You listen to me. You're going to put your shoulders back and give us a goodbye and you'll be quick to the Promised Land, leaving all the rest of us envious you got there first. And not a stain will mark this dress. Now, take a good deep breath and let me get back to the hemming."

"She's not headed for the Promised Land."

Gert pushes to her feet, her face red as she turns on Almira. "I'll have you switched to the latrines quick as I can snap my fingers."

The seamstress at Mrs. Dempsey's Millinery bore the patience of someone who'd been handed triple the fee. She held up ready-made dresses for Eugenie's exploration: how smooth the fabric, how fine the stitches, what material the buttons, which tone exactly did Mrs. Dempsey mean by green, does it suit her companion's complexion?

Eugenie's cheeks maintained a high flush, and she often laughed and reached to make certain I was consistently near.

She settled finally on a teal dress of silk and cotton, patterned with peacock feathers and a modest scoop collar. It fit nearly as if made for me, and Mrs. Dempsey said the alterations would be complete by noon.

I should have demurred then. Urged Eugenie toward one of the simpler dresses in plainer fabrics.

Vanity, Lucy.

A drop of ice water hits my cheek. I flail my hands and struggle upright, blinking against the dark.

"Who's there?"

I can hear it: the shift of a body, the intake of breath.

I can smell it. A boggy rot.

I can taste it. Silt and iron.

"Mary?"

It's cold here.

Her voice is like crystallized breath.

Do you want to know what she did to me?

"Who?"

But you already know, don't you?

The chaplain is insistent I speak with God. Since I have refused the good man's pleas too many times to count, he has given me full run of the prison chapel. I catch him staring at my leg irons.

"Here you may talk to God, Lucy Blunt. He is listening."

I sit in the plain room, white boards, long worn pews, a visitor's gallery boarded over, the hymnals locked in a cabinet near the chaplain's dais. The tall windows allow light through the rusting iron lattices, and it patterns the walls and floor like a limitless game of hopscotch.

Mr. Smith has unlocked the cabinet and removed a hymnal. He holds it in his palm, weighing the value of sharing it with me. His hand trembles and he grips the spine tight before turning to meet me in the second pew.

"He will listen," he says. But he stares at the cover of the hymnal instead of me, and I know it's because he doubts.

I do not take the book. He leans forward and sets it near my side. His lips form into an indifferent smile. He taps the cover, then takes his leave of me.

Now I sit in an empty pew in an empty church. The pew seat is scratched and scarred; fingernails have dug through the oil-dark surface, littering it with yellow-white hieroglyphs. Jan 1813 Carlyle Martin; Goffstown; Jesus C; Nov; Mirabel—names and dates and smatters of pictographs crisscross and tangle from one arm to the other. I walk each aisle, my fingertips tracing the ridges and furrows of lives spent kneeling and praying and whittling.

It is the first I have been in this place; it taxes the chaplain to provide two sets of sermons, and the few women here don't warrant the effort.

I return to my seat. I shove the hymnal off the pew, and it lands with a satisfying thwack. Beyond the clang of the irons, it's the only sound in the room. I click my tongue and turn my head from left to right, listening for echoes that chirrup and bleat and break to pieces in the air.

Cook would smack the back of my head if she were here. Faith simmered under her skin. She told me once that God resided between our thoughts and spoke in the quiet spaces. "You don't leave enough room, Lucy."

But Cook is not here. Though I would like to know if, at her passing, all her prayers and pieties bring her face-to-face with him for at least a quick chat and holy embrace.

Behind the dais hangs a large embroidered cross. It is as plain as the room, and the gold has browned at the edges.

"You took my child," I say.

The room is still. Only the sound from outside the windows of the workers replacing the cabinet-room boilers, a whoop of the foreman and the pound of hammer to metal.

"You took everything."

He's not listening. Mary—at the other end of the pew. Her form shifts and varies, her face concealed behind a graying veil. Her back curves as she cuts her name into the wood.

I close my eyes and press the heels of my fists to my lids. When I look again, the seat is empty.

But there is her name, etched and ribboned into the dark wood. *Mary Dawson.*

Eugenie's arm pressed to mine during the trip back to Harrowboro. Mr. Burton departed at the mill, ensuring he would be home for dinner. Mr. Friday took the narrow lane to the house. I rolled down the window to take in fresh air. The trees curved above, limbs weaved and creating a path that limned to shadows with the onset of dusk.

The horses quickened their pace as they recognized home. Mr. Friday's churrings could be heard through the glass, and his hands worked the reins to keep the animals at pace.

Then the carriage shot out of the woods and into the clearing, washing the interior with the last rays of the day.

Eugenie pressed my fingers, then released them, shifting in her seat until there was space between us. "She will be waiting."

The horses slowed, swaying the carriage forward and then settling back. I looked through the glass at Rebecca framed by the columns, her hands held across her waist, hair twisted into tight loops, her smile set in a brittle curve. She stepped to the door.

"Lucy. You're back." Her words came clipped through that careful, wary smile.

"You were told. I assume."

"I was not." She lifted and dropped a shoulder. "Well. We do need you. The new maid is worthless."

Her welcome—both polite and spiked with displeasure—was what I expected.

Eugenie untied her bonnet and handed it to me. We descended to the gravel drive. I shook out the wrinkles in my skirt. The teal fabric gleamed. Eugenie slipped her hand to my elbow and leaned past me. "Lucy's bags go with mine, Mr. Friday."

I saw it then—the flash of surprise in Rebecca's eyes.

"And Rebecca. Will you ask Cook for two trays? Just something light."

"I've eaten," Rebecca said.

"I'm glad."

Rebecca fought to keep the smile on her face, clenching her teeth. "Two trays, then." She turned, her shoulders pinched tight, the bell of her skirt swinging as she strode to the steps. Her foot faltered on the first stair. She glanced over her shoulder, her gaze fixed to the ground. "Is she your new companion?"

"Rebecca . . ."

Her flinch was palpable. "Then she can tell Cook about the trays."

Chapter Twenty-Two

I was begrudged nothing upon my return, or at least nothing that involved my physical well-being. If I wanted damask curtains and velvet coverlets, Eugenie placed the order for two of each, in blue or teal, amber or ochre. If I merely mentioned a yen for rose water, or a flush of white calla lilies to brighten a corner, or sugared peaches, by the next day they were procured and presented with a child's glee.

"Is it not all you wanted?" Eugenie clasped her hands to her chest, then spread her arms and reached for me, waiting with an expectant smile for her kiss of thanks.

I was given my own bed. My own desk. Fine thin paper. A crystal ink bottle. A shelf of the latest romances. Feather bolsters. A tortoiseshell comb-and-mirror set. A chemise in the smoothest cotton. Hairpins tipped with pearls.

Like a well-kept whore.

It is a hard word, I do grant, but appropriate nonetheless. And yes, it dogged the edge of my conscience, though I was able to ignore it most hours of most days.

I had all I desired in the palm of my hand. What did it matter that the door between us locked from her side and not mine? That some nights she invited her husband to cards and an evening's reading and my patience grew taut enough to snap? Those nights I closed my windows and pressed my hands to my ears. I paced the corners of my room, slowing at the keyhole to watch the flits of shadows and light from the other side, but not stopping, never stopping my pace until the bruise of morning light. Then the clock on the wall above my desk chimed, and the sonorous clock in the hall answered. Six o'clock. A brush of my skirt, a pat of my cheeks, a trip down the stairs for the morning trays, for the new maid's sly glance, for Cook's silent disapproval.

"I see you less now than before. I hate it."

Eugenie rubbed her nose with the back of her index finger and sighed. She leaned her elbow on the armchair, resting her chin in her palm, fingers curled in, and looked in my direction. "It's too early in the morning. Don't you think—"

"I don't care about the time."

"Such ill humor."

I picked a curl of paint from the sill. Flattened it. Picked again. I cut a glance to the open door and the dark hall beyond. With a shove away from the window I crossed the floor, making wide berth as she grasped for my wrist. I peered into the hall and turned my gaze to a scuff of sound beyond the stairs. Delphine, I assumed, for there was another scrape, chair legs against the floor and a rectangle of light washing from the open doors of the piano room. "She's always skulking. And not very kind to the furniture." I glanced back to Eugenie. "Why did Mr. Beede choose her?"

"Miss?"

I swung my head round. Delphine stood in the hallway, twisting a feather duster. Her mass of black curls haloed her head and looked seconds from bursting into a chaotic tangle. Her eyes slanted up, as did her dark eyebrows, and with a sharp chin, gave her an obdurate expression.

"Yes, Delphine?"

"Oui?"

My fingers pressed into the doorframe and then I tapped them against the wood. "I didn't call for you."

"I know." She turned back to the room, giving a quick swipe to a hall table. Her lips curled with the threat of a smirk. "I don't answer to you anyway."

I shook my head, at a loss. My grasp lingered on the knob after I shut the door.

"Are you afraid of our little French-Canadian?" Eugenie asked.

"I think I am."

"Josiah's hired a group of them for the mill. He expects to save money."

"The Irish are cheaper."

"But they're so few and far between here."

A breeze lifted the summer curtains. Eugenie sat in the light. "Come, read to me from your romance. Our nun is quite on the verge of losing her habit."

My shoulders dropped and I rested my forehead against the wood. "Will I eat in my room or with you tonight?"

"I'm dining with Josiah. You could eat with Cook. Or Rebecca, if you like."

"Why would I do that?" I gritted my teeth and turned the knob. "Can you embroider instead? I'm tired of that story."

"Lucy." Her skirts rustled as she walked to me, circled her arm around my waist. Capturing me. Her head on my shoulder, her breath a muddle of bitter coffee and ginger preserves. "You know you have my heart."

"Do I?" I grabbed her elbows and pushed myself from her. "You're right," I said. "I am ill-tempered. And afraid of the new maid."

She gave a quavering smile, then nodded and smoothed her hands over her vest, settling them on her hips. "You are forgiven. Will you come up and read, after all?"

"I don't think so. It really is a tiring story. I think I'll take a walk."

"Of course." She dipped her head and moved to the hall, fingers trailing the lip of the wainscoting. Mr. Quimby sauntered down the stairs, his bell tinkling and his stomach rubbing the risers. I had given him too many treats in an effort to win his affection. He flattened his ears when he kenned my presence and only perked them upon greeting Eugenie.

"There you are, my little love," she said. "There you are." She stopped to synchronize her watch with the grandfather clock. Directly across was a stilted image of Eugenie in a dark blue bonnet. Paint on wood. Her left ear was a good half inch lower than the right. The painter should have given up on detailing—indeed should have forsaken painting altogether and gone into an honest trade.

"Let's go to town tomorrow," I said.

"Is that what you wish?"

"You can treat me to lunch."

"I'll tell Mr. Burton we'll join him on the morning ride."

"Thank you."

But her attention was drawn away. "Delphine?"

And there the girl was, pressed in the inset to Mr. Burton's study. "Ma'am?"

"Perhaps you, like the cat, should wear a bell." Her lips curved in a smile. "It will warn Lucy you're lurking about."

I changed my mind and did not take a walk. The day had grown too dreary. It was the end of September, and the flat gray skies spared no warmth. Instead, I meandered the hall to the piano room and dropped onto a settee. I lifted my arm to my forehead and stretched out. The windows were latched shut, the air stale. The room was too yellow. Like dried mustard. I reached behind to the table, my fingers finding a porcelain figurine of a cat. A coating of dust dulled the surface. I wondered what Delphine had been so industriously doing in there.

A thought slid by. I pondered looking for Eugenie's laudanum and passing the time as she did when she thought I wasn't paying attention.

"What a life of leisure you've made yourself." Rebecca rounded the settee and hovered over me. She gave a quick signal for me to move my feet, then settled, her skirts crowding against mine. "I don't know how you've made the time. I never seemed to have it. There was so much to attend to." She frowned. "Hm."

"She doesn't need caretaking."

"Oh, but she does."

"What do you want?"

She shrugged, then shimmied further into the seat, crossing her hands on her lap. "I'm just sharing the free time. I'm at a loss myself as to what to do. Now that time is all I have."

"Do you have any friends, Rebecca?"

"I wonder the same about you. I wonder a lot about you. I've never quite grasped your story. It disquiets me."

"My father is a tutor; my mother and brother are dead. Our means were modest and I was required to work. There is no story but that."

"Are you estranged? From your father?"

I moved to rise, but my skirts caught under hers. I tugged them clear. "There is no story but what I told."

She sighed and her curls swayed as she shook her head. "I think there is more." Her smile lifted the corners of her mouth. "It's terrible to lose everything you love. Isn't it?"

I am to have my picture taken. A daguerreotype for posterity. A sketch of it for the broadsheets. I can see the peddler's eyes now, as he hands round this latest sordid tale. *I knew this girl,* he'd say. *Look how far the road can run.*

Matron's brought my dress full finished from Gert. She's done my hair in neat braids and a smattering of white wildflowers to match the pattern of the dress.

I asked that the portrait be taken under the box elder by the laundry, but Matron worries we won't be able to hide the manacles I'll have to wear on my wrists. I think she's more concerned that they will take attention away from the seashell brooch she has loaned me. It is thin as paper, opaque and pearled.

"It belonged to my mother," she said, though I don't quite fathom the need to tell me so. Still, it sits well on the ribbon of crossed lace, and when I touch it, it holds the warmth.

I sit in the ladderback chair Matron's brought to my cell. She circles around me, straightening my skirt here, shifting a flower bud there, with little hums and *mmm*s.

"Am I pretty?" I ask.

She stops in front of me, her hands clasped and nods. "Would you like to see?"

"Do you find me pretty?"

Her lips clamp tight, then soften. "Would that make you happy if I did?"

"It wouldn't make me any way. It was just a question to pass the time. Although with what's left I should be more particular." I swallowed. "Yes, it matters."

"Well." It is not an answer. "Just let me . . ." She pinches my cheeks to pink them, then lifts a mirror from a weave basket. It is a plain wood, the handle smooth from use. Not ivory and silver filigree like Eugenie's or the tortoiseshell set she surprised me with on my birthday. I take it from Matron with both hands, palms slick with sweat. My thumb leaves a sticky print mark on the glass as I turn it toward me.

"Oh."

This is not me. I am not pretty. This is a stranger who frowns when I do, and cants her head to see tight braids, a nose sat just off center, cheekbones sharp enough to push against the skin, sunken sockets. The stranger stretches her lips into a simulacrum of a smile.

"This is not me."

I fling the mirror to the ground, tumbling the chair as I rise, and crush the heel of my shoe into the looking glass. It cracks and splinters into shards. But I cannot escape the burn of the stranger's gaze and the dark charred edges already run to ash.

Matron uses the side of her boot to shift the glass bits to the corner.

"Leave me a piece."

Her mouth pinches, and she twists her boot against the last bits of glass, setting her basket atop the chips and flakes of silver. "That was my mother's too."

I would like to answer, but I think it might be harsh, and Matron is patient enough with me. There's a turn of the lock on the door. Matron glances at it, then picks up the chair. "Sit."

A guard swings the door wide. He gives a nod to Matron, his eyes lingering on her before dropping to me and giving a chortle.

"You make Matron blush," I say to him.

He smiles, lifting an eyebrow. His eyes are laughing warm. "It wouldn't be the first—"

But the photographer trots his way in, forcing the guard to suck in his belly to make space at the door.

"I'm Jonas Bowdin, and we've got about seventeen minutes of good light." His hair is greased tight to his scalp, and his beard runs a circle round his jaw, neat trimmed. He combs it with his thumb, then sets his hands on his hips, flipping his jacket tails up and down as he peers at me and then at the high window. His shoulders are narrow, his waist wide with the buttons on his vest straining. One has popped loose and threatens to slip the brown thread. He twists his neck as if to stretch out a crick, and then he pulls a measuring tape from his jacket pocket, unfurling it and handing me the end. I've not seen eyes so pale.

"Hold this to your nose."

He takes a step backward, then another, then walks his index finger a few inches more on the cloth rule.

"Stand, please. Don't move the tape." He stares up at the window, quick blinks with long lashes. Then he steps around Matron and maneuvers the chair four inches to the left. "You can sit again."

I hold the tape to my nose, tethered to his hand holding the other end, and sink to the seat.

He plucks the tape from me and rolls it back in a neat circle before pocketing it.

LeRocque has slipped in and stands shoulder to shoulder with Matron. She patently ignores him, even though he's lifted his bowler to her. "You're looking fine, Lucy."

"Don't lie."

Jonas Bowdin raises an eyebrow and stares at LeRocque. Then another man lugs in a wooden box and an assortment of cases slung every which way on his shoulders. His pocked cheeks blow out like balloons, and he stares everywhere but at me, his cheeks deflating and skin sheening with sweat.

"We'll set up here," Bowdin says. He takes the box and waits for the younger man to organize the cases and set up a tripod and stand. He squeezes his fists tight, then scrubs his palms on his trousers and his hands shake as he returns to his task.

"What's your name?"

He jerks back when I speak.

"Tom. Tom Nash."

"Well, Tom Nash. Have you never seen a murderess before?"

"No."

"LeRocque will hound you for an interview. What will you title it, Mr. LeRocque? 'My Encounter with a Woman of Evil and All Her Temptations'? Yes. I like that."

"Who are you talk—"

"Sixteen minutes, let's move along." Bowdin unlatches a small box, sliding out a black plate and placing it into the side of the camera.

"How does it work, Mr. Bowdin?"

"Bromine, mercury, and mystery." He opens the camera front, releasing the bellows and cupping the black-capped lens.

"I've never had my image taken."

"Once I pull off the cap, you'll stay very still." He shakes out a black cloth, draping it over the camera, then flapping it over his head. He sticks his hand out and reaches for the lens cap.

"Wait." Matron pushes away from the wall and straightens the collar. "Don't fuss."

"Yes," she says in a low breath. "I think you are. Pretty."

I grab her arms and shove her away. "Take the picture." White petals fall from my hair, and I can't stop the shake of my head, my teeth clenched hard enough I think they might crack.

"Breathe, Lucy." LeRocque mimics a great inhalation, his chest expanding and deflating.

"Eyes forward," Bowdin says. "One large breath. Hold it. Ready?"

"I'm ready."

He removes the cap, holding it out to his side. The lens is a cold round eye of ground glass, reflecting my image back as if in a warped mirror.

I will never know if he made me pretty or left me plain. Never know if it will be a stranger or myself fixed forever in quicksilver to a copper plate.

I keep my breath. Hold still. Play my part. No doubt LeRocque will sell the image to the highest bidder. *Lucy Blunt. Murderess.*

Chapter Twenty-Three

"Delphine has quite the propensity for cards." Rebecca dabbed a narrow paintbrush tipped in yellow to the vase set on the table. She glanced at me, then returned to her task. "But not so much for her chores. I'm sure you've discussed it with her."

My mouth filled with bitterness, as if I'd taken a swallow of vinegar. I closed the book on my lap, marking my page with my thumb, though it didn't matter. I'd not read a word. Even now, as I passed wearisome time in the sitting room with Rebecca, Delphine was ensconced in a chair in Eugenie's room, dealing a few quick hands. "Isn't that for Mr. Beede to sort out? Or Cook?"

She shrugged and gave a little *tsk*. "If you wish some authority, then no."

My lids fluttered. I could not look at her directly, just watched the bristles separate and unite as she swirled the colors across the stoneware. "If Mrs. Burton wishes to—"

"Be careful what Mrs. Burton wishes." She lifted an eyebrow and then held out the brush. "What do you think?"

I stood, dropping the book to the divan. "Another vase with posies."

Rebecca scowled and tipped the vase to the light. "But I've added dahlias."

"Hands out of the boysenberries." Cook gave me a swat, though not hard enough to dislodge the fruit from my fingers.

I held it out. "Just the one?"

The windows beaded with steam. Jars floated and clicked in great pots of boiling water. There was sugar at hand, and wax at the ready for the canning. She eyed me, then pointed at the bowls of berries on the table. "There's not enough here as it is. You'll be glad for it in November."

I dropped it back in the bowl with a sting of regret.

"If you'd get out of your finery and put on an apron, we'd make quick work of it."

"It's not finery. And I'm happy to help. Mrs. Burton has decided Delphine makes a better partner for whist."

Cook snorted and tossed me an apron and a masher. We took to the chore without conversation, and I was content for the scrape of the mashers against the bowls and the hiss of water on the iron stove.

The door to the garden was open, allowing in the cooling air. A maple leaf in burnished copper slid across the slate floor, its motion stopped as the stem caught on a cabinet leg.

I'd brought one to Eugenie early that morning, placing it in her open palms. She sat forward in bed, head bowed over the leaf to breathe in its smell. Her thumbs skimmed the curled brown edges, then tracked the stalk and splay of brittle veins. Then she grazed it over her lips.

"Have they all turned?"

"It's just beginning."

Her mouth softened and her eyes flicked. "This I remember best. So much color. The hills draped in fire." She closed the leaf in her palms. "I remember."

My thoughts returned to the kitchen, and I wondered if I should bring her the leaf of copper. Or perhaps a walk with the leaves crunching underfoot and snapping in the air. I glanced out the garden door. "It feels like frost."

Cook shifted the bowl and set to work on another. "Mr. Friday will harvest the pigs soon." She pressed her lips and made a small sound in her throat. "The Almanack says a mild October, but when has a sane man ever gone by its divinations? It's felt in the bones, isn't it? And I feel winter early."

I jumped at the screech of the cat and a heavy crash on the floor above. Cook and I stared at each other, mashers frozen in our hands. There was a clatter of feet down the stairs. Delphine pushed through the door, hand to her chest and breath ragged.

"The mistress . . ."

I dropped the masher to the bowl. "What happened?"

Delphine pulled in a breath and shook her head, pointing behind her to the stairs and landing.

I grabbed my skirts and pushed her aside, following the sounds of commotion to the second-floor landing.

Eugenie lay on her side. Jacob kneeled over her half-prone form, dabbing a cloth that came back red. He turned his rag and folded it in fourths. "I think her nose is broken."

The blood flowed freely from her nose and beaded in a wide cut on her forehead. Rebecca put her arms under Eugenie's shoulders and strained to get her upright. She moved her knees at an angle and took the weight of Eugenie's body. "There, there, it's all right."

My heart hammered in my chest. I touched the back of my hand to her cheek and throat.

"This is your fault," Rebecca said through thinned lips. "Your fault."

"I wasn't here."

"You should have been."

"I'm not her jailer."

"We need more rags," Jacob said.

"Gene."

She moaned.

"Go get gauze and a bowl of water, Jacob." Rebecca wrapped an arm around Eugenie's waist, her nails digging and pulling at the fabric. "Where were you, Lucy? It's your job, you stupid girl."

I caught a glimpse of movement under the hall cabinet. Mr. Quimby crept low, then dug his claws into the carpet and burst from underneath, careening to Eugenie's open door.

"Where's his bell?" I asked.

Eugenie jerked away from Rebecca, her hands flailing the air, then stopping her fall forward as she wrestled to all fours. She tried to speak but instead coughed and sputtered blood that had run from her nose. "Delphine?"

"It's Lucy." I smoothed her hair. "You've had a fall."

"Lucy."

"Don't talk." My fingers stopped on her cheek, thumb touching the tacky blood at the edge of her lip. I settled behind her and tipped her chin to slow the bleeding.

There was a grumble from the stairs. Cook took the banister with one hand and held the medicine bag with the other. Delphine and Jacob followed two paces behind. "What's the fuss and muss up here?" She blew out a breath as she took in the three of us. "Looks like you fell on your head, Mrs. Burton." She waved a hand. "Lord, you're all useless. Jacob, Lucy, take her by the arms and get her to bed."

Cook daubed the last of a poultice on Eugenie's nose and wiped her hands on her apron. "You might have a crook to your nose when all is said and done, Mrs. Burton, but I think it will be serviceable for breathing."

Eugenie pulled in a cracked breath. She patted the pillow next to her. "Where's Mr. Quimby?"

"You tripped over him." Rebecca sat at the foot of the bed. "He lost his bell."

"Did I hurt him?"

"I've warned you about that cat."

I gave Rebecca a sharp glance, then tapped Eugenie's hand. "He's hiding. I'll look for him when you're resting."

Cook lifted her psalm book and leaned the pages to the window for light. "I think a small reading . . ."

I glanced at the bedside table and the drawer half ajar. The laudanum bottle was tilted against it, the cork resting on the table by the oil lamp.

I bit the inside of my cheek to quell the wave of anger. If she hadn't been under its influence, she would have heard the cat, bell or not. I set the bottle upright, corked it, and slid it into my skirt pocket.

Rebecca saw the bottle, too, and her eyes caught mine with a hard glance. "I told you."

Delphine wasted no time in spreading the word, catching Mr. Burton the minute he set his hat on the rack, jabbering at him half in French while shushing me to be quiet. She relayed a story so exaggerated one would have thought Cook had to sew Eugenie's head back on and whittle her new legs.

"It's not at all like that, Mr. Burton."

He stared down at me. "She is your sole responsibility."

"Come up, Cousin." Rebecca leaned over the railing. "She's been calling for you."

Mr. Burton pushed past me and climbed the stairs.

Delphine let out a low whistle.

"Be quiet." I stepped forward and shook her shoulder. "Just be quiet."

My grip tensed like a claw and she winced. Her face wavered in front of me, her lower jaw pushed out, pugnacious. "Let go of my arm."

"You were upstairs with her." I knew I would leave bruises. I wanted to let go. Delphine was annoying, but she did not deserve this seething wrath that coated the edge of my vision and kept my hand clamped tight.

"Let her go." Rebecca's voice was flat and low pitched. She stood beside me, her hands resting on her skirts.

We locked eyes. My grip loosened and Delphine jerked herself back, rubbing her shoulder.

"There." Rebecca's shoulders dropped an inch. "We'll keep this between us."

"But she—"

"It wasn't your place to tell him, Delphine. That was Lucy's place. And Lucy's apology."

"What am I apologizing for?"

"She could have broken her neck."

"But she didn't."

Rebecca's gaze had not left mine. "Your temper will be your undoing, Lucy."

Mr. Burton glowered down at me as I remained seated on a horsehair divan. He did not say a word.

I raked my nails on the brocade and stared at the tips of my boots. "She tripped over the cat. It could have happened to any of us."

"She could have broken her neck."

"I've already heard that scenario."

"Your only responsibility, Miss Blunt, is the well-being of my wife."

"What will you have me do? Kill the cat? Lock her in her room? She's not a child."

"The cat will be taken care of."

A shiver traveled my spine. "It's not Mr. Quimby's fault."

"He's a hazard. Jacob—"

I stood and crossed to the door. "Jacob will do nothing to the cat. I forbid it."

"Who are you that you can answer to me like that?"

My temples throbbed. I had gone too far.

"I want Rebecca to see to Eugenie."

"She does not want Rebecca. I am her companion now."

He took a step back, then crossed his arms and rolled his shoulders. His skin reddened. The light from the sconce traced shadows under his cheeks and along the deep lines round his mouth. "She is fond of you."

A quaver of heat pressed from my chest. I forced myself to take a breath. "Yes."

"And you?"

"I am fond of my employer too."

With a slow nod, he dropped into his desk chair. He laid his hands on the scatter of papers and I noticed how elegant they were, so at odds with the angles and rust that made the rest of him.

"I need to minister to your wife. She'll require quiet the next few days and nights. You can trust me to provide that succor, Mr. Burton."

"'There is a curious animal, a native of South America, which is called the preaching monkey.'" I pulled a chair close to the bed, flopped back, and stretched my legs and bare feet to the coverlet. "'It has a dark, thick beard, three inches long, hanging down from the chin. This gives it the mock air of a Capuchin friar.'"

"It reminds me more of Mr. Finch."

I curled the newspaper. "He is clean shaven."

"Is he?"

With a shake of the paper I continued. "'In their evening meetings they assemble in vast multitudes. At these times the leader mounts the highest tree and the rest take their places below. Having by a sign commanded silence—'"

"Have you found him?" Her voice was rough and nasal. Though it had been five days, the swelling was still apparent and the bruising purple. The cut at the edge of her hairline would scar.

"He's hiding. Cats are good at it." I did not tell her I feared him dead: I had seen Delphine toss him to the edge of the woods late at night, and my morning calls brought nothing.

She pressed the heels of her hands to the ridge above her eyes. Then she twisted and reached to the drawer at her table, riffling through the handkerchiefs. "Where is it?"

I folded the paper, pushed it against the cushion, and dropped my feet to the floor. "You don't need that."

She turned her head to me, then reinvigorated her search, yanking the drawer to the floor, then grappling across the sheets and quilt to find purchase at the other table.

"Gene."

Her search grew frantic, her fingers shaking as she combed them over the tabletop, dislodging and nearly knocking over a table lamp. She clutched the correspondence I'd brought up, crumpling the envelopes and dropping them in a heap.

"Gene—" When I grasped for her she swung out an arm, knocking me back with a sharp strike to the cheek.

Her lips were so taut they'd turned white. She kneeled on the mattress, fists clenched to her chest. "It was your fault."

"How was it my fault?"

"You didn't tell me . . . I didn't know where you were. All I heard was the creak of that damn rocking horse you insist on keeping."

"You imagined it. You were dreaming. I was downstairs with Cook."

Her skin grew pallid and sweat clung to her forehead. "He's dead. I know he's dead. It's your fault."

I pressed my palms to my temple to soothe the pounding. Everyone blamed me for something I was not even present for. And then to have Eugenie turn on me was too much. She should have been paying attention. "No. It's your fault. You tripped over the cat. How much laudanum did you have?"

"I didn't—"

"God, don't lie about that." I picked up the letters and slapped them on her writing desk.

"I was ill. And calling for you. Why didn't you hear me?"

I smacked my hand on the table. "Because you didn't call. And you weren't ill. No wonder they rarely let you out of this house." With a gasp, I covered my mouth. "I didn't mean that."

She was still as a statue, and her expression hardened to marble.

"Gene—"

"Get out."

"I didn't mean it." My pulse thumped in my throat. "Please."

She seized the base of the oil lamp and slung it. I ducked, avoiding the worst. The brass base slammed into the wall and fell to the floor. I sprinted over to turn it upright before the oil could seep out. The globe spun and slowed on the carpet.

She breathed in and out through her mouth. "Why are you still here?"

A bird has settled on the window and tips her head to watch me. A crow. She likes to sun herself against the glass. Sometimes she carries moss or twigs, other times a strand of meat. If I stay still, she trusts enough to doze. Once she came in the rain, and thick drops flashed from her wings and her claws tapped the window thrice before she took off again.

Today she paces the ledge. Back and forth. Her head dips and elongates. Her beak stutters open and snaps shut. Back and forth on a ledge so narrow her blue-sheened wing presses the glass.

The shift of my foot on the cell floor startles her. She opens her wide wings and rushes away.

I waited at a turn in the path Delphine took to her boarding house. The trees' shadows were sharp as spears and the dead leaves hissed in the wind. She was bent to the chill, wrapping her wool shawl around her shoulders, her woven reticule tucked tight under her arms.

I stepped in front of her, pushing a hand to her chest until she was backed to a maple's trunk.

Her eyes were wide and blinked rapidly. Her mouth formed an O but had no words behind it.

"You will find that cat, or I'll make sure you're shipped back where you came from."

She struggled and pushed at my arms. I pressed harder against her chest.

"Do you hear me?"

"You're pathetic." Her lips twisted into an ugly shape. "Do you know what we call women like you? *Chienne*."

I took a step back. *Whore. Bitch.*

"The cat is dead." She rolled a shoulder and straightened her shawl. "Let me by. Or do you want me to tell your mistress you tried to seduce me in the woods?"

Chapter Twenty-Four

Eugenie refused my entreaties and apologies. I made them through the keyhole between her room and mine, then grew tired of her silence on the other side. I finally left my bedroom and made my way down the stairs, each step away from her joined with a growing resentment of her pride. I had done nothing wrong. I did not deserve the ill treatment.

Rebecca caught me at the turn to the kitchen. "Where are you going?"

"To find the cat."

I stopped in the kitchen, my gloves crushed between my fists. Delphine was at the sink, her arms up to her elbows in dishwater. She held a sopped rag, and it wagged from her fingers as she mopped her brow with the back of her forearm.

Cook sat at the table, a bundle of mending on her lap. Her boot heels hooked over the spindle of an empty chair she'd pulled to face her.

"What's Mr. Quimby's favorite food?"

"Rabbit," Cook said. "Liver. Hearts, especially."

I shoved on a glove. "Cooked or raw?"

"I've some salted."

"Delphine's coming with me."

We strode across to the barn. Delphine glared over her shoulder and held her bag of salted offal straight out from her side. Her other hand grappled and clawed at her shawl. She didn't have gloves and I didn't care.

"If I were a cat, and thrown out of my warm lodging, a barn would be my first choice to survive the night." The space echoed. The horses and brougham were absent. The air was gray with dust from the hay and icy on my lips. I peeked over the first stall at the banked straw, unhitched the latch, and toed the bedding aside. "Mr. Quimby. We've got your favorite food."

The straw yielded nothing. I hesitated before setting out a bit of meat, for any creature could steal it and most would find it a great delicacy. Delphine stood next to me, shifting the straw with her foot. I saw it then, woven in her hair. Pink ribbon. Grosgrain. From the third roll in the sewing chest.

"What's this?"

Delphine flinched when I hooked my finger near the knot of ribbon tying her mess of hair from her face. "It's a ribbon."

"I see that."

"Do you want to talk about the ribbon or find the stupid cat?"

I handed the pouch to Delphine and pointed to the loft ladder. "Go up there and see."

I opened and then clamped the lid back to a grain bin and turned to find Jacob standing with a hoe slung over his shoulder. He made a quick gesture to the field. "He only comes to the missus. You're just wasting breath out here."

"She thinks he's hiding in the house."

"He's got a taste of the wild life." He squinted to the door I'd left hanging wide. "Now he doesn't have a bell."

Delphine started back down the ladder. Jacob swung the hoe from his shoulder and set it against a stall wall, then loped over. "Watch yourself on the way down."

"We'll try the woods."

Matron has brought another chair to my cell so we both avoid the floor. I've been watching the water seep and puddle in the corner under the window. Flecks of rust from the bars float on the surface, and when I blow on the water, the ripples send them swirling like minuscule ships. Two have landed on the damp shore, and I like to think the others will find a destination.

Now we sit together and she watches me lift my spoon from the tin bowl. I press the oats to the roof of my mouth and swallow. "I like the raisins."

"I thought you would."

Her hands play her skirts, folding and creasing and twisting and smoothing. She slows them when she catches me following their patterns. Sets them, first left, then right, on her thighs. She coerces a smile, though I can see it takes effort for her to retain.

I like her eyes. I like the way she lifts her eyebrow when she wants to say something and decides against it and how the bones of her wrists round. She works very hard at sternness, but I see the sag of her shoulders when she knows she's failed. I notice her footfall outside my cell late at night and that she stops for a moment and mumbles *God rest you* before turning away.

"Do you say it to the other women?"

She looks at me with surprise. "Do I say what?"

"Do you say good night to them?"

She shifts her hips and points at my meal. "You should finish before it goes cold."

I lay the bowl in between my legs. "It was cold when you brought it. But the raisins were nice. Almost as good as the peach cobbler LeRocque—"

"You shouldn't talk of him."

"I'm aware you aren't keen on the man." I stick the spoon to my tongue and lick the hollow clean. "I think you're jealous of my time with him."

Her cheeks flame and her smile tenses and drops.

"Or his time with me? Is that more accurate? Do you have a yen for Mr. LeRocque? I'm afraid he'll never leave his wife. And he's leaving soon for the West, he's leaving right after . . . Well, maybe a day after." I set the spoon in my bowl and the bowl to the ground, then stand and move to the puddle. I lean down and set a large curled strip of rust and white paint to spin. "He says the inns are bursting, the taverns are empty of beer, and there's a line to the warden's for the lottery to see me hang. Is that true?" The little boat twists and sinks. "I can hear them build the gallows. They start so early with the hammering. Are they building viewing stands, or will they just pull the pews from the church for the day?" I know they stop when Matron and I cross the yard to the laundry. Their eyes burn into my skin as we pass. The yard smells of sweet green wood.

I lurch forward as if punched in the gut.

Matron comes to me. Her arms are strong around my waist, her hips and legs are tight to the back of mine. She rests her cheek on my shoulder blade. Her grasp is firm, but the trace of her thumb along my waist is soft.

"Your Mr. LeRocque makes up half of his stories and steals the other half." We are upright, but still she holds me. Her breath heats my neck. "The men are replacing the boilers in the shoe shop and the rotten roof above the kitchens." Her keys and the prong of her belt buckle jab my hip. "There is no lottery. And there is still possibility."

It didn't take long to find Mr. Quimby. His carcass lay in a shallow divot in the orchard, his entrails blackened. His orange coat was an easy target for a fox or a bobcat. Jacob removed his collar and rolled him to a tarp with the blunt end of a rake. We folded the canvas and tied the ends with twine.

Delphine stood a length away and rolled her eyes. "You should leave it for the animals. He's nothing but food now."

"The missus will want to bury him, I think." Jacob sniffed and glanced up at the sky.

I looked at Delphine and that stupid ribbon. "She'll also want to know who threw him out the door."

"No." Delphine shook her head and stepped back, her foot and ankle wobbling on the exposed root of a cherry tree. "I'll lose everything."

"You should have thought of that before."

"My brother—"

"Mr. Burton won't want him at the mill. Not after this. He might be kind enough to buy you a ticket back to . . . Where are you from?"

Jacob tugged at my elbow. "You leave her now."

I ignored him.

Delphine trembled. She held a hand to her mouth and her gaze swam from me to Jacob. "She told me to do it."

"Rebecca—"

She gave a sharp nod.

"You don't answer to her."

"What would you have me do?" Her hand dropped to her throat. "Michel and I have nothing. Please. There's no food. There's no family. Please."

"She's got nothing. Let her be." Jacob lifted the tarp by the twined ends. "We need to bury the cat before dark." He trudged past us.

Delphine caught my coat in her grip. Her stare was flint, all pretense of impending tears evaporated. "You can lose things just as easily as me. Positions. People. So, if you say anything, I'll tell about you. Will you tell?"

"No. I suppose I won't."

"Then I will keep your secret too."

Mr. Quimby was buried behind the barn, with a fine view of the fields and a wide swath of forest.

Eugenie had allowed me to guide her to the small grave, but she let go my arm and stood alone, her jaw muscles shifting and tensing as Cook read from Psalm 103.

The Lord is merciful and gracious . . .

The daylight had lost its luster, the tips of the hills of maple and beech tamped to a dull gray. Jacob shifted his hip, his arm resting on the shovel. He glanced to Delphine and patted her arm once. Rebecca stood on the other side of Eugenie, one hand tapping the back of the other, lips pursed to contain her smug look. I crushed a handful of soil until it was a dense ball, then pressed my thumb against it to crumble it to the earth. It smelled of dead leaves and rot.

For he knoweth our frame; he remembereth that we are dust . . .

I lay in my bed that night as awake as if it were morn. My position in the household felt tenuous. Nothing to grasp on to. I heard my father's drink-tinged voice, the words knife-edge sharp. *You're nothing.* I heard Delphine's threat and the echo of Aurora's warning.

The lock tumbled in the door. I sat up, swinging my legs over the edge of my bed. My toes curled in surprise at the cold floor. The stove, with its dwindling embers, left no warmth and a dim glow.

"Will you undress me?" she asked.

"Of course."

She padded toward me, feet bare, and I took her hands and held them until she stepped between my legs.

"I'm so sorry." I leaned to her, my forehead pressed to her stomach. Then I ratcheted in a breath and unhooked the buttons from the plaid bodice. Her warm tears fell to my knuckles. I continued, removing the bodice and skirt and draping them on the chairback, untying the cage hoop and watching it coil to the floor. I rolled the corset and left it on the desk. "Forgive me." I unpinned her hair, combing my fingers through long strands that straightened and curled against my skin.

She stood in her chemise and drawers, her arms clasped around her middle. "Will you hold me?"

"Hold me."

Matron's arms slip under mine, crossing and pressing, her palms cupping my breasts.

"I don't know what's real," I say.

She tightens her grasp.

"You are, though? Aren't you?" I turn in her embrace. "You are."

Her lashes lower and flick open. Her eyes shadow and cloud but she does not look away.

"I'm afraid."

She lifts her hand, hesitates, then touches the edge of my mouth with her thumb, traces it like a whisper. "I am here."

We returned to our habits, though the air snapped with unease. I smoothed the letters Eugenie had crumpled and discarded those nights past, laying them in a neat pile on her writing desk. She twisted the ink pen and played with the wire in her writing template, half listening with her head resting in a palm. Her demeanor was prickly.

I sat next to her in a ladderback chair, my posture straight and wary, and how I wished for the comfort of the armchair. "Mrs. A. Martin asks again if you will attend the dinner and fund-raiser for the county poorhouse."

"No." She waved her hand. "Answer as you will and get a draft from Mr. Beede of an appropriate amount."

"Do you ever go to these?"

She frowned and motioned for the next letter.

I sighed, arched my back to relieve a crick, and glanced at the return address. Aurora, whose handwriting was as familiar to me now as my own. I slit the seal with the letter opener and unfolded the missive. Certainly, it held another boast of a soiree well held or a speech to an academy of overeducated women or a rousing put-down by one of her husband's acquaintances or the latest height in inches of each of the boys. "It's from Aurora."

I took in a breath and then clamped my mouth shut as the words sliced my vision.

> *Dear Josiah—*
> *Your Lucy Blunt is not who she says she is—*

"Oh." I pressed my hands over the letter and stared at Eugenie.

She raised an eyebrow.

"Her handwriting is atrocious." I cleared my throat. "Let's see . . . Oh, look, Theo's a third of an inch taller. And Portsmouth was a grand season this summer, though the mosquitos were close to unbearable. Celia Wainwright (you don't know her, she's younger than us by too many years to count, but you might remember Clarissa) is betrothed to . . ." My heart drummed in my ears. I stared at my hand, at the hangnail on my index finger and my nails that needed a trim, and made up stories of Aurora's adventures in Portsmouth and then Dover in August. Could she hear the waver of my breath? The stutter between my assembled fictions?

"'Write back! Write back, my dearest. Your loving Aurora.'"

I folded the pages. "Well then."

"She had a busy summer."

"Yes."

I stood, the letter clamped tight. "I think I would like a coffee. Would you like one?"

She cocked her head. "Are you all right?"

"Just tired." I pecked the top of her head. "And wanting a coffee. I'll bring you one. And a sweet."

I crossed the yard and took the path to the woods, to the turn by the brook, and picked my way through bramble and vines. I sank to the piled leaves by the water's edge and unfolded the pages of the letter.

> *Dear Josiah—*
> *Your Lucy Blunt is not who she says she is—*
> *I have been much concerned, as you know, for the girl wields inordinate influence on Eugenie and I am afraid she is bent on a game Eugenie cannot win.*
> *It was Rebecca who first cautioned me, and to her I will be always grateful. She has been keeping me informed of the situation and has been kind enough to procure from your man the original letters of reference that came with the girl.*
> *Neither family knows of a Lucy Blunt. This alone should be enough to send her away—but I fear there is something darker, for both turned out a maid for theft of jewelry, and in one case the wife's wall safe was plundered.*

They describe the girl as middling tall with dark hair and eyes, with education beyond her position and a sharp temper. The Damons gave the police the name Martha Adams. The Temples stated her name as Alice Pratt.

Lucy Blunt is recorded as having died in Goffstown in 1834—at the age of 3.

I crushed the pages and bent over, hitting my forehead with my fist. "No. No." I crawled to the brook and flattened the papers on a stone. "No." I tore each into shreds and bits, scattering them to the channels of water, waiting until all had slipped under the surface or frayed against stone and branch.

Chapter Twenty-Five

Names are curious inventions. They can stand for nothing and every-thing, be dropped and forgotten or fought for to the death. I put them on like cloaks and discarded them when they started to wear thin and let in the cold.

In Henniker, as Martha Adams, I did steal a pair of pearl drop earrings, two gold bracelets, and a silver-and-onyx ring from Mrs. Rachel Damon. The objects were not declared missing until weeks had passed, for they were fripperies collecting dust and only noted during the housekeeper's annual inventory of an overstuffed household.

The takings were not for me. My father had found me. Stepped in front of me as I made my way along the river on my afternoon off. He was gaunt, his beard a forest of gray, his suit coat much repaired at the cuffs and collar.

"I've been looking for you."

"You mistake me for someone else." I turned on my heel to leave, to be anywhere but with him.

"Daughter." He rested his hand on my forearm. I turned my head from the stench of him—the mildew sweet of his clothes, the heavy round of his breath, the sweat of his poverty. "Will you not look kindly on me?"

My limbs shook. "I have nothing for you."

"You look like your mother." His fingers gripped and held me. "Anything you can give me."

"I have nothing."

He smiled then, and I was jolted by memories, the way the skin wrinkled around his eyes, and the warm comfort of his arm curled upon my shoulder. *There's my little girl.*

I swayed against him, allowed the kiss to the top of my head, just as before when Mother still lived.

His breath was warm on my scalp. "Does your employer know about the babe? Such a tragic end."

I grew chilled, fixed to the spot. How could he know? Only Albert knew the truth. Only Albert. He must have tracked down Albert in his search for me and any penny he could grapple from my fist.

"Just a little coin to tide me?"

In Concord, as Alice Pratt, I tended to the Temples' pimply teenage daughters. Delia and Nancy simpered and pouted and spent most of their time in front of mirrors. Their mother wasn't much better and left me—Alice—to fetch both necklaces and allowance money for the days she and the girls paraded the town. Concord was low on nightlife, but the days were filled with the intrigue of bored wives and political husbands.

Father found me again in the Temples' parlor. He pulled at his beard and drank a small tipple of sherry while nodding to his long-faced host. When I made to leave with a tray of empty glasses, he cut in front and stopped my way. "I will always find you. When I need you."

Mrs. Temple was lax about closing her safe. The door was ajar and the painting of lilies and flax tilted and bulged from the wall. I had an apron with a large pocket.

Father got the necklace and I used the money to gain another life. Lucy Blunt's, to be precise. A name carved on a gravestone half buried in snow.

I am not a thief, though I have stolen.

I am not murderer, though I have killed.

Rebecca turned in surprise from the small secretary in her attic rooms. I had never had opportunity to call on her there. The room was plain: pot stove, chaise longue in faded blue, a single lamp on the secretary, a single chair. The low ceiling made me want to hunch over and cover my head against a bump. Through a narrow door I spied a bed with a neat coverlet, a cherry dresser, and a standing mirror tarnished black at the corners. The room smelled of rose water and naphthalene, though I doubted a moth could breach the windows, shut tight as they were.

She did not move from her desk nor did she say a word in greeting. Her hands clamped round the desk's edge. Yellow-red knuckles. She touched the scar at the edge of her lip with her tongue. The desk itself was bare of all but an ink bottle, pen, and sheet of paper half blackened with words.

Her eyes darted from me to the hall, and I turned to see what caught her attention. Nothing was there, save the upturned frame of a child's bed that had been removed from the nursery and replaced with the full sleigh bed I called my own.

"What do you know?" I asked.

Her pale eyebrows lifted slightly. She relaxed against the desk and stared. "Oh, quite enough, Lucy Blunt."

Which meant she knew next to nothing.

I stepped toward her, examining the wallpaper (parallel lines of roses on damask), straightening a still life of vase and dying flowers, then reached past her to pick up the letter.

> *Dearest Aurora,*
> *I am afraid she means Eugenie great harm. Just yesterday,*
> *I came across her tipping an extra dose of laudanum in*
> *the coffee and then rummaging through drawers looking*
> *for—oh! I don't know what, I'm not of that criminal*
> *persuasion to hazard a guess.*

Josiah does not listen to me, though I have been clear there is much amiss. Although, I think he remains home more often these evenings because he is beginning to doubt the girl's intentions. Have you—

I folded the letter and laid it back on the desk. "Did you take the bell off the cat?"

She blanched. "Why would I do that?"

It took one more step to press my cheek against hers. She leaned away but did not secede her position. "Because you seethe with jealousy."

"I protect her."

"You love her." I pushed my nose against the cartilage of her ear. "And she doesn't love you."

She wrenched away, slapping me hard enough that I stumbled back. I grabbed her wrist as she lifted her hand again, forcing it to her side.

"What lies did you tell Aurora?"

"What lies have you told us? What do you want?" Her lip quivered and she dropped to the chaise longue. "What do you want from us?"

"All of this."

"It's not yours to have."

"I already have it, Rebecca." I slid the folded letter toward me, moved to the stove, and opened the grate with the tongs. The embers sputtered and lit white gold as the fire consumed the paper.

Aurora's coming. Matron says she will be here. "She'll be by in the morning." That's what Matron says. "She's bringing news of the petition."

I can't sleep. I stand at the door and wait as the moon crosses the wall in an arc.

After I'm dead, they're tearing down this building. I'm the last of its inhabitants. Sometimes I can hear the murmurs of its past guests. We've all complained about the damp. The warden plans to replace it with a brand-new cellblock of red brick and black iron and a stove at each end for warmth.

Matron says . . .

Matron says . . .

I put the flat of my hands between the cell bars and against the rough iron door that keeps me locked tight for the night. But she'll be by to open it soon and Aurora will be here, and I think Mr. LeRocque is bringing me a lemon curd tart and telling me which papers will carry the news of my hanging. He says that's important, not just for his own pocket, but for the public to know a woman's been hung. He promises to write me in the right way and that's why he comes every day, though sometimes not. Sometimes he looks askance and doesn't believe that I'm innocent of at least some of the charges.

I am afraid for my life.

When did you write that, Gene?

I am afraid for my life.

In those stilted block letters you labored over for hours. No one believed me when I said it was about Rebecca.

I don't like this time. Cook called it Devil's Purgatory. She rose early as she did to get round it. She said a brisk start to the day takes care of the Devil's play.

Lucy . . .

No. Stare at the door. Matron's coming soon.

A touch of ice on my shoulder. I twist away. There they are, lined like dolls on the floor, legs splayed, bare feet, blackened soles. Mary's lace is half receded and her empty eye gapes at the floor. Eugenie—

I screw my eyes shut but it doesn't matter. How she stares. Her hands cross at her chest. Her hands stained black and flecked with dried blood and vomit.

"Look what you've done, Lucy." Rebecca peers at me, then coos down at the baby coddled in her arms, lifting his hand to kiss each tiny blue finger. "Look what you've done."

God, how my body remembered the thrum of the millworks. I rolled my shoulders forward and hurried past. I had begged off the afternoon reading with Eugenie, saying Cook was in need of vanilla and lard for the night's dessert. Jacob was not free to go. Yes, I would bring a present back.

I was under no delusion regarding my status at the house, no matter how I might have frightened Rebecca. The opportunity would not come again to waylay any letter Aurora might send her brother, and there would be even less opportunity to defend myself against the charges.

There was no choice but to flee, though the thought wearied me. I stopped in an alley and allowed myself tears before gathering my wits.

I made my way to the chemist's. The travel office sat at the rear of the shop. I took a seat in a cane chair and waited for the proprietor, Mr. Elijah Watts, to complete his arrangements with a man who wanted a round-trip stage and train junket to Durham. The traveler tucked his tickets into his jacket pocket and tipped his hat to me before exiting.

I knew I was far short of the monies required to traverse the counties and territories between Harrowboro, New Hampshire, and St. Joseph, Missouri. I had regained my deposit from the depot in Keene. Well, Mr. Friday did. Still, it would do until I could sell or trade the bracelet.

Mr. Watts gave a gesture for me, then spread his hands across the counter and waited for me to speak. His lunch of gherkins and a wedge of farm cheese sat on a table just beyond a thin set of curtains. He gave it a yearning look, then returned his eyes to me.

"I would like you to map for me the quickest route to St. Joseph. And the cheapest."

"There's nothing cheap about that sort of journey."

"See what you can do."

His fingers smoothed the crinkled corner of a blotter, and his eyes traveled my dress. My finery, Cook had said. Finery enough he would not pick the cheapest route.

He cleared his throat and opened two thick books of timetables, licking his fingers to turn pages and pointing and tapping in approval of this departure or that. "It's late in the season. You'll be stuck in Missouri for the winter. If you're thinking of crossing the plains west."

I glared at him. "Just St. Joseph."

Winter. My heart thumped hard and slow. The prospect of a winter with little sustenance and a gambling chance of employment subdued me.

"I assume there's lodging houses."

"Plenty."

"Then I'll need a list of the affordable ones."

He peered at the shelves on the side wall and pulled out another booklet, this with a sketch of a prairie schooner and a pair of oxen embossed on the soft cover.

While he perused the lodgings, I glanced back to the chemist's and the door to the street. The wind gusted, and the leaves lifted and circled before careening away.

"Will you be traveling with someone?"

"Hm?" I turned to him. "A single reservation. I'm meeting my uncle and aunt."

We came to an agreement and I left a deposit with a promise to return by midweek with the remainder of the fare.

"One other question. How frequent is the stage to Boston?"

Another walk to the warden's. Matron's got her head lowered. She pulls my elbow and then the chain at my waist.

"What's wrong with you?"

Her breath notches as she pulls it in. She shakes her head and knocks on the door. A pebble's gotten in her shoe; she twists her ankle to the side and keeps the weight on her left leg.

A young girl opens the door. She's lean and angular like a colt. The warden's daughter. "You're her."

Her mother comes forward, hands worrying the pin at her throat. "Come in."

The daughter follows behind us, and when I look back she's bug-eyed and no doubt formulating what she'll tell her friends at school.

Matron has tamed her expression to a blank mask and only lifts her mouth in a smile when the mother comments on the day.

"I'll be outside." Matron moves aside for the daughter to close the door.

The room is not changed from the last, though the space seems brighter without the presence of Mr. Finch. Or perhaps it's the reflection of Aurora's cream linen dress bordered with ribbons of velvet gold. She moves toward me, the light from behind casting her face in shadows.

"You look as I expected." She swerves to the sofa. "Sit."

"I'd like to stand."

"Suit yourself." She sits and rests her arm along the cushions. "There's tea on the tray if you wish it."

"Will I hang?"

"I forget you are so plainspoken. Not if I can help it. Though the odds—"

"I won't go with Mr. Finch."

"You won't have much say in that." She presses her hands to her knees and rises, moving to the window. "Tomorrow I speak before the assembly to plead for your clemency. They gave mercy to Letitia Blaisdell when I fought for it three years back. Even though she confessed." She lifts the teapot, then sets it back in place. "I will be frank with you, Lucy. Your petition has gone nowhere, as I thought it might. You don't show remorse. Not even a little. But there are men in that room who abhor capital punishment, and it is to them I will aim my speech."

"And then?"

"Mr. Finch will give his report on your state of mind."

"And then?"

"They will vote on commutation or execution. If it's the latter, the only hope is the governor."

"And if it's the former?"

"You'll be ordered to the asylum." She turns again to the tea, pouring herself a cup and adding two spoons of sugar. "You have tested my principles."

The steam snakes around her chin and along the ridge of her cheek. She blows over the cup and ventures a small sip. "I believe the death penalty degrades all of us. I believe it does no good in deterring crime or forcing penance. It is as brutal as the crimes that precede it. So I will speak for you."

Another sip.

"But the lives you have wrecked, Lucy . . . In my heart I wish that you hang."

Chapter Twenty-Six

"It's a good tract of land. Spruce and hardwoods." Mr. Burton pierced the lamb chop on Eugenie's plate and sliced the meat into cubes. "More northern than I wish, near Bethlehem, but it's to be had for a song."

Rebecca sat across the dinner table from me, with the Burtons flanking the ends. A silver candelabrum graced the middle of the table, the flames reflecting the tonic in Mr. Burton's hair and the oils in the three of ours. We sat quite close, for the table leaf had not been added. Mr. Burton's elbow jostled my own as he sliced the meat and then bent to the task of quartering her potatoes.

I slipped my hands to my lap and pulled in my arms, waiting until he had completed his quite unnecessary task.

Eugenie inclined her head and ran her fingers lightly over the rim. "I was capable of this myself, Josiah."

"But we'd all be finished and on our dessert by the time you'd done it."

"That's not true."

He speared a large bite of his own meat, his hand hovering above the plate. "And I like to spoil you." He bit and chewed, lifting his wine goblet to swallow down the last dregs. "I'll be leaving in the morning."

Rebecca jolted forward—not enough for Mr. Burton to notice, but I could see the coil in her, and the questioning way she peered at him. "So soon?"

"Mm. If we're to make the White Mountains before the weather."

"I see." She folded back in her seat and stabbed at her lima beans. "Well, we will certainly keep the house to order until your return."

Mr. Burton tapped the stem of his glass with his ring, staring at her until her lids fluttered and her skin flamed. I followed his gaze as he turned to Eugenie. "You are nearly healed."

She touched the bridge of her nose, then the edge of the cut on her forehead that was but a line now fading from red to pink. "Yes."

"How does it sound, my Gene? Being the wife of a timber magnate."

"Is the mill not enough?" She folded her napkin, pressing the corner to her lips before returning it to her lap. "Or do you grow bored with wool?"

"The mill needs a rail spur and we don't have it. Not yet. But if I provide the timber, they might be amenable to laying the iron. I'll be stopping in Concord."

The blood blanched under my skin, leaving me with a sudden chill. "To see Aurora?"

"Among others."

Rebecca's fork scraped her plate. "I'm sure she'll have much news for you, Cousin." She smirked at me. "And if you'd be so kind as to pass a letter to Aurora, I'd be in your debt."

"We'll have a guest on our return." Mr. Burton pushed his chair back and crossed his legs, draping his hands over his knees. He tipped his head toward Rebecca and then Eugenie. "Shall we tell her?"

"Not now, Josiah." She twisted her fork and set it on her plate.

"But it's fine news, isn't it?"

"Josiah—"

Rebecca glanced from one to the other. "What's the secret?"

"You, my dear, have had a proposal."

"I'm sorry?"

"You can thank Eugenie for the wherewithal to mend the fence, but it seems Mr. Finch is quite fond of you."

"Mr. Finch?" Rebecca pressed her hands to her cheeks. But they were not flamed with any pleasure. Her skin paled. She shook her head and then stared at Eugenie. "No."

My stomach dropped. Eugenie had mentioned none of this to me. And as much as I disliked Rebecca, I would never give her to Finch. "Gene?"

"It's something to consider, Rebecca. You should consider it." Eugenie picked up her fork and returned to her meal.

Mr. Burton lifted his eyebrows and gave a self-satisfied smile before turning toward Jacob. "More wine."

Jacob grabbed a decanter and tipped it. The wine spilled like liquid garnets into Mr. Burton's glass. He turned then to Rebecca, who covered her own small glass and shook her head. "I think these few sips have gone well enough to my head."

"Lucy?" Mr. Burton asked.

"Lucy's not fond of spirits," Eugenie said.

Rebecca rolled her napkin tight in her fist and stood. "If I may be excused." She didn't wait for an answer but jerked away from the table and lurched to the hall.

Mr. Burton watched after her, sipping his wine. "Hm."

I cleared my throat. "How long will you be gone?"

"I think a fortnight."

A fortnight. Both a gift and a sentence. My funds had purchased the stagecoach ticket but I had not the money for the train, nor to switch to a different route after a number of stops. I had a fortnight to trade the bracelet from Eugenie somewhere, to escape the past—and the police—sure to return with Mr. Burton and Mr. Finch.

"Will Mr. Friday remain here?" I asked. I could hear the sawdust in my voice. Friday would be silent were I to ask him to take me to Peterboro or Jaffrey. No one would have an idea where the jewelry came from there. I could pretend to be a widow and simper and flirt with the dealer of silver and gold.

"Friday will accompany me. And Beede, of course."

"Of course." My shoulders grew heavy.

"Jacob will be the man of the house. And you'll have the mule, should you need to hitch the cart for town."

"When do you leave?" I asked.

"First light." He lifted his glass. "I leave you to your house of women."

I do wonder if he had some premonition when he mounted his horse, his leather bag slung across his chest like a soldier going to war, fearing his household undone on his return. His horse, the darker gelding, was skittish, and Mr. Burton circled him round with a shush while Mr. Beede and Friday loaded foodstuffs and supplies to the wagon.

Across the narrow valley, the mist strung along the treetops and rose in funnels through the bare limbs. The air was harsh and sharp, the frost hardening the ground and spitting sparks from the gelding's shoe as he pawed the soil.

Jacob held the reins, and Mr. Burton patted the horse's neck with hands cloaked in leather gloves. But the horse's flank and shoulders already glistened with an anxious sweat.

"He doesn't want to leave." Mr. Burton threw a smile as we all stood on the steps. "Are we met, Mr. Beede?"

Mr. Beede waved from his seat next to Friday. "We are met." And the wagon rumbled on the drive.

Jacob let loose the reins. Mr. Burton whirled his mount and loped after the wagon. But then he slowed and trotted back, reining in before Eugenie. She shivered under her robes, for we had not dressed for the morn and stood knock-kneed in our nightdresses and wraps.

He pulled his beaver hat from his head. "Be well, wife." Then he settled the hat back and gave a squeeze to the horse, bounding across the yard to join the men.

Rebecca lifted and dropped her chin, then took the stairs, patting my arm as she passed. "Just us, then."

"Rebecca. I didn't know."

"Of course not."

"It's what we planned, Lucy."

"But, Finch? That horrible . . . Of all people, Gene."

"You can't deny they're well matched." She pressed her hands to the door of her bedroom and laughed. "And now we have a fortnight together."

"It's too late."

"I thought you'd be happy."

I pulled my robe tight and paced the windows, lifting up and discarding an amber paperweight, a wingless fly caught forever in resin. Her pen threatened to tip from her writing desk, and I picked it up and set it on its holder. A fortnight. I cataloged Mr. Burton's study, curious if he kept cash in a safe or a drawer I could pry with a hairpin. But when could I do that, with Rebecca always nearby and Delphine now staying the nights as the days grew too short and too dark to traverse the woods?

Another pace to another window. A view of the dead garden and the most delicate of plants covered in domes of glass. I flicked at a curtain. "We need to change these."

"Change what?"

"The curtains." I shook them and let them drop. "The curtains."

"Come. Stop being so fractious." Her voice dropped low. "We'll make our own little world right here, like we did in Keene. There's just us, now."

"There's not just us."

"Of course there is."

"No, there's not. There's Delphine. There's—never mind."

"Delphine? Your jealousy is quite misplaced."

"Where should I place it, then?"

"You're who matters. Why do you not believe it?"

"There's Mary Dawson."

Her face paled. "Poor Mary."

I clenched my fists. "Tell me about Mary."

"But there's nothing to tell." She slid along the wall and lowered herself to a chair. "Why are you like this? I thought you'd be—"

"I think Mary killed herself because of you."

She took in a harsh breath and clamped her mouth tight.

"Nothing to say?"

"I rarely spoke to her."

"Did she come to your bed too?"

I picked at this, though I'm not certain I would have found peace with any answer she gave. She was either cruel for using and spurning the girl or cold for thinking nothing of her when she died. Perhaps it wasn't peace I was after, but confirmation she felt as little for Mary as she would eventually for me, and thus my leave-taking could be done clean in anger, rather than muddled with regret.

"There is nothing to know." She spread her hands across the chair arms and sat back with a sigh. "She was a simple young woman who liked to please. Not as you're thinking."

"What should I be thinking?" My gaze ticked upon each painting in the room. I should have mapped the safe much before this point. Kept the knowledge tucked like a rabbit's foot in my pocket.

"She brought flowers and I don't know, a crème from town, or I don't really know. I don't remember." She gave a dismissive wave. "Rebecca no doubt noted every indiscretion. It doesn't matter, it—"

There was a quick rap at the door, then a jiggle of the handle. "Hallo? Mrs. Burton?"

I strode over, twisted the key and opened the door to a slit. "What?"

"Good morning to you too." Delphine held up a pail of kindling. "May I enter? Unless you wish to freeze."

I grabbed the handle. "I'll do it."

"You're leaving us? Is that true?"

"No."

"But I saw the stagecoach ticket. In your room."

The pail dropped from my grasp, clanging and spilling out strips of wood. "What were you doing—"

"Was I not supposed to—"

I slammed the door. My hand gripped the key tight enough the metal bit into my skin.

The room was silent. Eugenie remained in her seat; only the flush on her chest gave anything away.

I let go of the key, curling my hands into fists and rubbing them against my skirts. "Delphine doesn't know what she's . . ."

She shook her head in confusion. "I don't understand."

"I'm in trouble, Gene." My breath felt trapped and I forced the air through my teeth. "I need money. And I need to leave."

She loved me. I know she did.

"No."

Where is Matron? My hands are blue with cold. My fingers draw lines of ice on the wall, and my breath freezes into shards of glass.

"I won't listen to you." With a flick, I lift my soiled skirt over my head, crouching and retreating as far into the corner as I can. It's warmer here under the skirts, and dark. And if I wrinkle up the skirt hems, I can press them to my ears and keep Mary out.

There, there.

She tilts her head and she is whole, wide eyed, skin clear and plumped.

Don't hide. Her fingers gentle away my skirt. *There, there.*

She draws so close, her legs straddling my lap, knees pushed to hips, her dress thawing and dripping, soaking my skirts and the skin of my thighs. Her breath is like sleet.

You shiver. I shivered.

"She didn't love you."

I should have killed her. It was too late by the time you did. Too late.

Mary leans back on her haunches and studies me. The moonlight slides through her, splintering against the cell door.

So many lies.

My nails scrape the floor. I can't turn without her shifting in front of me.

She lets out a long keen and grabs the back of her head. Then she straightens and turns her palms in a plea.

She was kind to me. She was my friend.

It's not safe to walk in the woods, she said.

Let me walk you home, she said.

Mary blinks. Mary kisses my lips.

So many lies.

The day before my trial, the constable stood watch as the gravedigger dug into the soil. Shovelful by shovelful he dug, until the metal made dull contact with Mary Dawson's coffin. Her body was transferred to the cellar of the Justice of the Peace. I can imagine the stench.

The back of her skull was crushed. As if from a large stone and calculated anger. The bone fragmented and there was no chance she could rescue herself from the water.

"It was Rebecca," I whispered.

"Not guilty," my counsel noted, this time without the smell of spirits on his breath. "The force of the stream. The crush of the ice. A drop from our gravedigger's hands. Let us promptly reinter this poor drowned girl before her family finds the grave amiss. I think two charges of murder are enough anyway. Don't you, gentlemen?"

"I've got a surprise for you, so squeeze your eyes tight and stay sat."

Gert shuffles away, leaving me standing by the drying racks. The boiler bangs and wheezes, and I wonder when the warden will get around to replacing it. Low on the list, I think, as the laundry doesn't bring in money like the shoes and the cabinets. It's damp here and nothing fully dries. All the bedding and clothes go out with a tinge of mildew and return the same.

"Don't say your Gert hasn't done something for you."

"You've done more than enough."

"For your last shift here." She turns my hands, hers puckered and cold from the tubs still, and lowers a cloth bundle to my open palms.

I close my fingers around it, feel the slim stalks and trace the petals soft as silk and velvet. I lift the bouquet to my nose. Open my eyes to the spray of color. Wildflowers. Orange and purple and brightest red. Yellow pollen flaked across browns and spring blue.

We turn over two tubs, sit between the mounds of sodden clothes. Gert unknots another cloth and breaks a ginger cake in two, never minding the crumbs settling in her lap. Spicy and sweet and thick. Cook would approve of the addition of the apple.

"My boys always liked the apple in it."

The black hand on the clock ticks away a minute. The scrollwork is intricate, made for a place kinder than this. "Mrs. Kepple will be speaking before the legislature now."

"Will she be?" Gert chews, her jaw twisting around and her eyebrows drawn down. "She's a fearsome one. She'll set the tail between some legs, that'll be certain." With a click of her tongue, she shoves the last of the cake in her mouth and swallows it down. "One last thing." She half stands to peer across the racks, sits again when she's certain the other two women aren't paying us attention. She takes a small folded paper from the cloth that held the cake and sets it atop the flowers.

I unfold it.

Rough thick scrawl: *Youv bin a good help with the laundry. Don't forget Gert when she comes to knock at Peter's. And Remembr—God do not hold you to yer sins.*

The safe was not behind a painting, but rather cut into the closet wall directly behind Eugenie's dresses. We kneeled shoulder to shoulder, the skirts that I'd tugged from the hangers bunched and crumpled behind us, bills and silver coins stacked in front of us. I held up the lamp, turning again to the closet door to make certain it was shut.

"Does Mr. Burton hold any Boston notes?" I asked.

"I don't know."

My throat contracted in panic. All the notes from Eugenie's safe were worth little ten miles beyond Harrowboro, even less by Stockbridge, Mass., and nothing at all by Hartford.

"Bank of New York?" I grabbed at her.

She startled and pulled her arm away. "Don't do that. You know not to do that."

"I'm sorry."

"God." With a shake of her head she stood, stepping on the bills and scattering the coins. "Why did you tell me this? Why did you tell me any of this?"

I set the lamp to my side, gathering the money and the strands of pearls that now snaked and tangled. I laid a hand to her ankle to prevent her from kicking over the lamp. She wrangled her leg from my grasp, pressing her back to the inset drawers and biting her lip. "Will he find you? Your father?"

"I don't know." I pulled my handkerchief from my sleeve to mop my forehead and neck. "It's suffocating in here."

"Where will you go?"

"Boston, St. Joseph, somewhere in between or beyond. I have to go."

"When?"

"Two days. Three at the most. Rebecca sent a letter with Mr. Burton. To Aurora. Rebecca will do anything."

"I want you to stay."

"I can't, Gene."

"Anyone would understand. Josiah could—"

"All my father needs to say is I murdered my child."

"But you didn't. It's your word against his."

"And who would be believed?" I threaded my hands in my hair, dropped my elbows to my knees, and swallowed a sob. Then I gathered myself and counted out enough money for the train and a few days' reprieve. "I promise to repay you."

"No. Please." She slid to the floor, her hands roaming my back and tugging at my hair, pulling me by the waist until my back was against her chest. "You can't. I can't . . ."

"Gene—" I strained against her hold, stuffing bills and coins in my waist purse.

Her body shook, tears dropping from her cheeks to slip along the nape of my neck. I trembled when her teeth grazed my spine.

I turned around to face her. "Come with me."

Her eyes shifted back and forth. "How? You're—"

I leaned close, her mouth near to mine. "Come with me."

I pressed and coaxed, lowering us to the floor. My kiss was hard, the nip on her lip would bruise. "We could become anyone. We could see those monkeys we read about. In South America."

She pressed her hands to my cheeks and dragged them down to my chest. She had always been tireless in the moments she wanted my affection. Her fingers caressed me. Possessed me. She memorized me bit by bit, much like she explored the raised maps I made for her that late summer. Sometimes she'd frown, as if she expected a different turn in the map, a different curve on me. But her hands continued their journey. "Yes," she said. "Yes."

"Stop," I said, and grabbed her wrists to hold her away. "You would really leave?"

"For you."

This time, I possessed her.

Afterward, her fingers trailed my stomach, smoothing and petting my sensitive skin. The remaining coins dug into my back, and I eased onto my side. "Is this all your money?"

"There's a lockbox under Josiah's desk. But I don't have a key."

I scrambled up, straightening my nightdress.

"One bag. You can do that, can't you? We'll switch stage to rail . . . back again somewhere. We'll sell these pearls . . . I don't know . . ." My head pounded; I rubbed my forehead. "How could they not find us, Gene?"

"Cut my hair."

"What?"

"I'll wear trousers, Josiah's not much taller than I, and—"

My heart thudded. "Yes."

"Yes."

"Come." I took her hand and pulled her to her feet. "We'll pack your valise." I reached to the top shelf and swung the leather satchel to the floor. "Pick the underthings you want. And give me the jewelry. I can stitch it in our travel clothes tomorrow." My words tumbled, and I pulled her to me. "We'll plan to leave on Friday's stage to Boston, I think. Oh, Gene. You'll really leave?"

She put her finger to my lips and tensed. "Sh."

There it was: the smallest scuff of a foot against wood. A clink of glass.

Then silence. As if whoever was in the room knew they'd given themselves away.

Eugenie pressed her ear to the closet door. Her hand found my arm and she gripped into the soft of my wrist, letting go to stroke the tendons and down to my palm. "Delphine?"

My heart thumped hard enough I thought Eugenie would shush me again.

"It's . . . it's Rebecca." She tapped the door. "Are you both in there?"

"Rebecca?" Eugenie's voice was a brittle lilt. "What do you need?"

"It's snowing."

"Rebecca?"

There was no answer but the muffled thud of the outer door.

"Oh, Lucy. How much did she hear?"

"I'll pack the bags tonight. Leave your shears out and I'll cut your hair along the way. We'll change stages in Goffstown."

"And go where?"

"Somewhere without her."

The flakes were fine as dust, flitting and lifting and settling on our shoulders. Cook stood with her hands on her hips and eyes to the sky, her lashes and cap sparkled white.

"Would you look at that?" Jacob stuck out his tongue to catch the flakes.

Rebecca kept her gaze on the granite steps. She wrapped her scarf round her neck and tugged at the knot of her wool bonnet. "You've not dressed yet?"

The chill air seeped through the thin slippers I had tugged on and slipped under my nightdress and up my bare calves. "Come, Gene." I stole an arm around her waist and tugged enough for her to follow me down the steps to the drive and the sloping yard.

She turned her palms to the snow, grasping at the chips and flecks that shimmered silver on her teal shawl. "It's too early. It's barely November."

A wind whipped the fine snow, surrounding us in white. The black of the tree line disappeared; the house and the others blurred and came into focus in bits and pieces only to scatter again with another flurry.

I folded her arm under mine, pulling her close. "Have her play the piano after dinner. I'll gather what we need," I said, my voice low.

She nodded.

"Are you sure, Gene?"

But Jacob's whoops covered her words.

I couldn't stop the chatter of my teeth.

"It's too cold," Rebecca called. "You'll catch your death."

Chapter Twenty-Seven

Eugenie was wrong about Josiah's height. He was taller than she by at least a head. When I held up his jacket, I was dismayed at the breadth of the shoulders.

Yet, there were so many pockets to secrete the jewels and cash. Local notes, for quick use, folded in the cuffs. Boston notes tacked under the felt of the high collar. Coins to a leather purse I'd found on Mr. Burton's dresser were tucked into one breast pocket, and the spare watch with its fine filigreed plating rested in the other. The pearls snaked their way down the lining of the lapel.

I kicked my foot at the bottom of my skirt. It was heavy with the earrings and brooches I'd stitched into the fold of the hem. I wore the emerald-and-gold bracelet.

How Rebecca mauled the keys of the pianoforte. The horrid grate of it set my teeth to edge. I perched on my bed, scanning what remained to pack. The valise yawed open, awaiting the coat. I tucked the trousers and shoulder braces to the bottom, along with the shears. Underclothing. Hairbrush. Two pairs of wool stockings. Mr. Quimby's collar, most insisted upon. Camisoles, petticoats, a pair of stays, a wrap to later bind Eugenie's breasts. A white-and-blue striped shirt. Hard collar. A round of bread and square of cheese I'd slipped from the larder, along with a tin of tea I scooped from the container Cook had left open on the counter. My envelope with Ned's hair kissed and slipped into the inner pocket. The silk embroidered memento mori of Eugenie's children, a keepsake I was certain she would come to miss.

I bent the needle to the hem of the left sleeve, stitching away an ambergris cameo and a pair of cufflinks set with onyx and diamonds.

One jewel at a time to trade. One depot at a time to plan the next.

The pianoforte stopped. I raised my head, pricking my thumb. I sucked the drop of blood. Shook out the sting of it. Zebidah would be alarmed that my sewing had not improved in the arching years since my struggles with the samplers.

There. The bass notes of a quadrille, the beat slowing and stuttering and then proceeding with confidence. I tied off the last knot, bit the thread, shoved the needle into the wrist cushion and set it aside. I rolled the coat into the valise, then shut the clasp and slid it under my bed for the morning.

The room had grown cool; I opened the stove and stoked the fire, then did the same in Eugenie's room. The embers flared red and glowed through the glass window.

One last thing.

A letter to be written.

To Aurora.

From Eugenie.

I sat at her desk, sliding the writing tablet forward, then took a sheet of paper from the drawer and slipped it under the wires. My stomach grumbled; Cook had sent up only cold cuts, a thin pea soup, and molasses bread, with a message she was ailing and taking herself to bed early.

How often I had watched Eugenie at this desk: how she held her pen near to vertical, how her thumb and forefinger, stained with ink, traced the wire.

A pluck of a match, the hiss of the wick. I turned the burner on the oil lamp and replaced the chimney.

My Dearest Aurora, Josiah has shared your concerns re Lucy. The situation is to hand. We have forgiven her and wish you will not mention any of this to Josiah when he visits. Rebecca is an idle

I pulled the page and rocked the ink blotter over the words, then followed with a sprinkle of powder. To the other side then.

woman and prone to fits of fancy. Ignore whatever else she should choose to vex you with.
  Your Dearest Friend
  E.—

I would leave it at the coach stop for the Concord-bound mail. With luck, it would be delivered to Aurora by the evening. Just a note to gain me more time.

"Lucy? What are you doing in here?"

I startled, dropping the pen to the wires. Ink splashed from the nib. "I'm packing your letter case."

Eugenie leaned her shoulder against the wall. Her head tipped, and she ran her tongue along her lower lip. "All right."

My stomach lurched. "Laudanum or brandy?" But I knew which it would be.

"You would have had a sip, too, if you had to listen to that playing."

"Give it here."

"She says I've betrayed her. That it's unforgivable, what I've done." She listed back, planting her foot and holding her arm out to the side to restore herself before she tumbled over.

I launched from the chair and dug at her skirts, grabbing through the folds to find the pockets. I pulled the small laudanum bottle from the right pocket, not caring the seam ripped.

"You're not my keeper." Her words slurred flat.

"No, I'm not."

"Good." She walked to the bed, unsteady enough to reach for the bedpost. "Go away." She made a heaving sound and covered her mouth.

I sprung to the bed, grabbing the chamber pot from underneath and shoving it at her just in time for her to be sick.

She gulped in a breath, then spit the dregs of her vomit into the pot. I set it to the floor, then kicked it underneath the bedframe.

"Will you be sober enough to travel?" I lifted the water ewer from the dresser, glad it was full, and poured her a tall glass. "Drink this."

She took a small sip and grimaced.

"Drink it down. It'll help."

I waited for her to finish, then took the glass and set it on her bedside table.

"Turn around. I'll undress you." The buttons fought me as I undid them. Or was it the shake of my hands? "Where did you get the laudanum?"

A laugh rolled in her throat. "That particular bottle was in the clock case. You didn't think to look there, did you?"

I lifted her arms one at a time, tugging at the sleeves and pulling the top of the dress so it folded at her waist. My hands twisted the buttons of the skirt and wrangled it down to the floor. "Step out."

She pinched the side of her waist and fumbled with the buttons. When I moved to help, she slapped me away. She left the underskirts to fall atop the dress and sank to the bed.

"I need to loosen your stays."

"How are we getting to . . . the . . ."

"We walk."

"In the snow? My skirts—"

"You'll lift them and walk."

"In the snow."

"I have woolen stockings for you. You'll be perfectly warm."

She pulled the pins from her hair, and it fell in heavy waves every which way. She gathered and twisted it to a loose bun. "Do you know how I met Josiah?"

"No."

"I was in the servants' corridor at . . . someone's. And he found me. He said, 'I think you're quite turned around.' He found me." She sank to the bed. Her shoulders slumped and she rested her elbows on her thighs. "Oh, Lucy. You want too much."

"You're not going." My chest constricted against the sharp sting of those words. The room spun away. Settled again in place. I yanked the clothing from the floor, snapping them smooth and laying them along the hope chest at the foot of the bed.

"Don't be angry."

"I'm not angry. There isn't time to be angry." I smacked the pillows into shape.

"You're angry anyway."

She fell back, rubbing at her face as I lifted her feet to the mattress and unrolled her stockings.

"Scoot up. Take your nightdress."

She rolled it on and then caught my hand as I moved to straighten the neck of it. "Don't be angry."

My throat was tight, holding in the pleas I knew would be useless. I moved the ewer from the dresser and tipped it to the glass. "Finish the water tonight."

"Forgive me."

I kissed her forehead. "I never saw you dressed as a man, anyway. It was a ridiculous idea."

Then I waited. Rebecca had not settled to bed. I could hear her footsteps crossing the boards above in the ritual of getting ready to sleep. Clothes to the wardrobe, nightdress from a drawer. A washcloth to the face and underarms. Wood to the stove. The creak of the mattress. There.

Eugenie's breathing slowed and steadied. God knows what her slurried dreams would conjure. I stroked her hair, slowing to caress the small scar. "Goodbye."

I slipped off my boots and passed through her closet to the narrow servants' hall, treading close to the wall to avoid loose boards. There was no light; I traced the wall and curled my toes over the stair risers as I descended to the first floor.

I opened the door a crack. The lamps in the hall had been snuffed. The grandfather clock ticked. My chest clutched as I thought of the bottles and vials sitting below the pendulum's swing. I hesitated, wondering if I should bring some, a balm for my unease, then thrust off the thought, turning my attention instead to the door hard to the right.

A quick step from my hiding place, and in one movement I twisted the knob to Mr. Burton's office and sneaked inside.

The room was snow bright; none of the curtains had been drawn. I crept to his desk and lowered myself to my knees. Ledgers and loose papers circled the legs and sat in stacks around his chair. I slid a stack and peered into the space. Then I lay on my stomach and swung my arm until it connected with something hard and metal and heavy. I grappled to find the lock's strike plate, then wrapped my hand on a corner and turned the box so the lock faced me. With my free hand I pulled a long hairpin from the crown of my head and pushed the tip into the keyhole. I felt the shift of a tumbler, and the pin slid closer to its prize.

Another dull click. The pin snapped.

I pressed my hands to my chest to slow my heart. Then I rejoined the task with another pin.

But the other jammed in the tumblers, and there was no egress for another. There was nothing to do then but lug it upstairs and hope I had the strength to carry it until I found another way in.

I reversed my route, my steps burdened with the load, and once in my room lowered it to the floor, lighting a candle to keep sentry until morning. The brass fittings gleamed. Inside that box was freedom from my father, and enough money, at last, to stop running.

I collapsed back on my bed.

Soon.

I woke with a jolt, my slumber and a shifting image of Eugenie in black trousers and a topcoat fading with the pounding at the door.

"What is it?" My eyes were glued with sleep. I rubbed the crystals from my lids and stood. "Stop pounding." I lit the stub of candle, holding the pewter base as I unlocked the door.

Delphine stood in front of me, her hair half wild. "There's something wrong with Mrs. Burton." She twisted her fingers and gasped as if she could not get a full breath. "I came to light the fires."

"With Gene?" I stared at her.

"Rebecca said to wake you."

I turned to grab the door handle that adjoined our rooms. But the door held tight. Locked. My skin prickled and a heavy dread filled my chest. "No. It's all wrong." My foot caught the heavy hem of my skirt. "Where's Jacob?"

"At the barn."

"Go down and fetch Cook."

She took to the stairs, her boot heels echoing as she crossed the floor below.

Eugenie's door was open. I kept the candle in front of me, a feeble shield against the blackness that streamed around. I stepped into the room. Stopped. Set the candle on her desk. I grabbed the edge to stop another fall as my skirts, heavy with jewelry, caught under me.

The candle threw a half circle, catching the damasked wallpaper. My eyes slid along the walls and windows, to the warp of the trees and the yellowing sky.

The water glass lay on its side, just a breadth out of her reach. The empty ewer rested on her splayed bare arm. Her skin was a horrible gray. She lay on her stomach, the sheets coiled like ropes round her legs. The pillows were soaked a scarlet red. Her head lolled over the edge of the mattress, hair cascading and curling in a pool of bloody black vomit.

Rebecca stood on the other side of the bed. Her fingers played with the silk ribbons that braided the collar of her nightdress. She twisted them round her fingers and unfurled them. Her gaze flicked to Eugenie's body. "Oh," she said, and took in a shuddering breath. "Oh." Her fingers wound the ribbons again, rose pink and mint green.

"What have you done, Rebecca?"

"Now she's no one's." She stepped round the bed and moved to the door, gripping her hand to the frame.

I swallowed back bile. "What have you done?"

Her lips stretched into a grimace. "Monster." She took a step back, a quick glance to the balcony and when she looked to me, her mouth quivered open and closed and her nose bled down her chin. "You've murdered her." She grabbed the railing and raised her voice, like an actor pitching words to the very last stall. "Get the constable. Lucy's murdered her."

My vision blurred and spattered red. With a lunge, I grabbed at her throat, tightening my hold as I pushed her backward on the landing. My thumbs hooked into the soft space. Her arms flailed. She scratched my cheek and dug her nails into my gripped hands. Her skin blued and paled. I kept pushing forward, not letting go. Her hip caught the corner of a curio cabinet, weaving us to the banister and the stairs. Her foot slipped off the top step. I let go. I let her fall.

Her neck snapped somewhere along the way. I heard it. One snap. Like the pin in the lockbox.

She landed in a heap, her leg bent at an angle, her hand flopping to the wood.

Delphine cowered at the bottom, whimpering like a trapped rat.

"If you scream," I said, "I'll kill you too."

Arsenic has no smell.

No taste.

Like water.

A tick of a watch. Eugenie's, sitting on the dresser. It was out of rhythm. I picked it up, pulled the crown to silence it, then opened the glass case to stop the minute hand.

Jacob had gone for the constable. I promised Cook I would not run.

The windows stammered, the ice scratching. I lit the fire.

Eugenie did not mind when I situated her aright on the bed. I fluffed the pillows, wiped her mouth as best I could. Brushed her hair and picked through the tangles. My fingers left pink stains on her cheeks and chin. On the sheets and cases. I pulled the comforter around us, my arm circling her waist and my head resting on her chest. "There, there." The thin lilac light snaked and slipped across the bed's striped canopy. "There, there."

Chapter Twenty-Eight

Truth is a rather pliable object, isn't it? Something molded and recreated and told as an entertaining story.

I was observed pushing Rebecca down the stairs. That is true if you're the girl looking up from the bottom step. That is not true if your view is from the landing above.

I choked Rebecca. I don't think I'd have stopped. That is the truth. But she was responsible for her own fall.

As I am responsible for mine.

"Lucy Blunt, variously known as Martha Adams and Alice Pratt." The paper crackled and hissed as the justice pushed it across his high desk. "You have been found guilty of the murders of Eugenie Charlotte Burton and Rebecca Louise White."

No gasps. No women fainting and men charging forward as they did in the penny papers. Silence instead, shaped like an egg.

"But it was not me . . ." My voice failed me, and the justice took up his words.

"You will be taken hence to the state prison, and on Thursday the seventeenth day of May in the year of our Lord one thousand and eight hundred and fifty-five, within the walls of the prison yard will be hanged by the neck until dead. May God have mercy upon thy soul."

"It was not me . . ."

A single *thomp* of the gavel. An inward rush of air. Then the room a maze of sudden shouts and a crush of bodies jostling and shoving me from the box. I turned to the balcony, my eyes scanning the swaying crowd.

The woman I searched for was easy to spot, her red hair so shocking against the grays and tweeds of the audience and the white of her ermine stole. She remained sitting. Once our eyes met, she kept hers steady upon me.

"Aurora—Mrs. Kepple—" Next to her sat Mr. Burton, his face buried in his hands, his shoulders shaking with grief.

"I loved her," I said. "I loved her."

He could not hear me through the throng.

So little time. It is gossamer now, frayed at its ends. I sit on the chair and count the drips of water from the ledge to the corner. I have been given an orange.

Cook sits with me. "I think Psalm 51 tonight, Lucy."

"As you wish."

"It's a comfort to share this with you." She turns her head and peers at me. "A nod of the head to God is good for the soul."

"Will he nod back?"

She licks her pinky, pressing the tip to the corner of the book and shuffling the pages. Her lips purse and then pull into a smile. "Here we are."

Her voice weaves itself round me like a shawl, a shroud, a twist of air that thins to a single fading note, leaving me to the drips of water and my orange.

It is morning. Matron twists a sponge above the bucket she's brought. Warm water that steams with lavender.

"Lift your arms," she murmurs, and her breath is sweet against my skin as she drags the sponge across my shoulders and down my back.

Another dip and twist of the sponge. Long strokes along my thighs, behind my knees. Droplets cool and slide down my ankles.

"It will be warm today," I say.

"It will."

It is morning and Matron bathes me and plaits my hair. In the corner of the cell, the dress Gert made is laid across a chair.

Mrs. Kepple did not convince.

"You are not a poisoner, Miss Blunt." Mr. Finch stands two steps out of my reach, his hands slung behind his back. He spreads his elbows and settles them to his waist. "Impetuous and headstrong, yes, but not a poisoner." He turns a foot and brings the other to match it, two paces to the left and two to the right. "Mrs. Kepple tried. I tried. But not a single vote went our way. Ignorant minds, mmph." His step hitches and he comes to a halt. His eyebrows furrow and he sucks air between his teeth. "Or I am mistaken in my findings. But I think not."

"I hate you."

"I have something to show you. Would you like to see?"

"What could you—"

"This, Miss Blunt." With a flick of his wrist he flips open a small leather case and holds it in front of the bars. Red velvet lining, a curve of glass. Me.

White petals strewn across a dress and a brooch so fine it is near translucent.

"Me."

"Yes." With a bounce of his knees he snaps the case shut. "Not a poisoner at all."

I have been granted the sun. No cuffs or chains. Ten minutes. It is fair warm. I loosen the buttons at my collar and fold back the lace. The leaves on the elm are spring green and curled still. In a week, perhaps two, this bench will be full shaded. For now, I turn my face to the dappling and watch the light hop and shimmer above.

A shadow then.

"You're in my sun, Mr. LeRocque."

He's swinging his hat and knocking it to his hip. He's had a barber trim his mustache. There's a nick on his chin and a crust of styptic powder threatening to fall.

He rubs his boot against his calf and points to the space beside me, a questioning lift to his eyebrow.

"You've never not sat when you wanted to."

"That's true."

"What's the newest headline?"

He hangs his head, twirling his hat. "Justice."

"For whom?"

"I thought—"

I take his hand and look again at the new furled leaves. "You've been good to me."

"Are you ready?" It is Matron, and it is her hand I hold.

She wears a woolen dress of indiscriminate color. Her dark hair is oiled to her skull and held in a tight roll at the base of her neck. Her brows are too heavy and her chin cut sharp. Her gray-blue eyes do not waver.

"What is your name, Matron?"

"Coraline."

"It's a nice name." A breeze quivers the leaves. "I'm ready."

The watchman holds my elbow. He drags me across the packed earth yard. The chaplain trots behind me with his hails to God and contentions of forgiveness. My heart thumps so loud it echoes across the granite blocks.

The gallows stands rough-hewn and weeping sap. Twelve steps and I twist to get away.

"I can't breathe. I can't—"

I scan the yard for Matron. She'll be there. She promised. In the shadows, the constable and warden and two men from the jury and Gert. There's Gert. She's nodding her head at me.

There's a buzz of noise and heavy stamping from the men's prison. I stare up at the iron-barred windows and catch the flutters of hands waving as I pass.

Where's Matron?

I'm sick. All down the new dress, and the watchman shakes my arm hard.

"No. Oh, please, no." I catch my toe on the first step, and it's the hangman in his black hood who lifts me from under the arm and drags me the rest of the way. It's so hot.

There's the noose. There's my heel clipping the trapdoor.

It's so far down. The men peer up, their hats now in their hands, and Gert squints, shading her eyes and her lips are moving. *God don't hold you to your sins.*

The hangman drops the noose. The rope is heavy and coarse. I swallow, acid and saliva and stone.

A sharp flutter of black catches my eye. The chaplain flinches and ducks as the crow wings by and settles on a window ledge.

The stamping of the men turns to a single drumming beat.

"Lucy Blunt, have you any word to say to these people?" The hangman's voice has a lilt, the same as the guard who's sweet on Matron.

There. Matron's right in front of me, on the gallows, back to all who watch. Fingers threaded, eyes steady. Unwavering.

"This is it?" My voice cracks. "I'm not ready."

The sky is so blue.

Look at the sky, Lucy.

It's so blue.

Look.

ACKNOWLEDGMENTS

Mark Gottlieb: So many thanks for your invaluable advice, support, encouragement, wisdom, and all-around awesomeness. I am ever grateful to have you as an agent and look forward to many years and many books with you.

Alicia Clancy: Thank you for believing in this story. This book is stronger because of your editorial vision. I am so pleased to travel on this adventure with a fellow dark-sider. You are amazing to work with and a true superstar.

Laura Chasen: Your keen eye and precise advice were instrumental to Lucy's tale. I can't thank you enough, and hope we have the opportunity to work together again.

Nicole Pomeroy, Laura Whittemore, and Patty Ann Economos: Thank you for such attention to copyedit and proofreading detail. You have made the manuscript shine.

Gabe Dumpit, Ellie Knoll, and the Lake Union author relations team: Thank you for all the work you do to make an author's life easier.

The New Hampshire History Crew: Rebecca Stockbridge, New Hampshire State Library; Brian Buford, New Hampshire State Archives; Carrie Whittemore, Monadnock Center for History and Culture; Jay Shanks, local historian; Christopher Benedetto, historian; Joe Springsteen, researcher. Each of your mad skills, knowledge, and generosity of time and attention opened up antebellum New Hampshire to me. The rabbit hole was much smoother because of you. Thank you.

Thanks also to Historic Harrisville; New Hampshire Historical Society; Millyard Museum; Horatio Colony Museum; Historical Society of Cheshire County; Kevin Hartigan, Perkins School for the Blind; Old Sturbridge Village; Hancock Shaker Village; Kate Genet; Aleks Voinov; Ann Etter; Christopher Wakling; Maria McCann; Ron Hansen; Tucson Festival of Books Literary Awards; Regional Arts & Culture Council; Arvon Foundation; Women's Fiction Writers Association; and PDX Writers.

I could not have finished this novel without my talented, creative circle: Alida Thacher, Jennifer Springsteen, Thea Constantine, Gail Lehrman, and Gary Taylor. You are my blessed rocks. Thank you for sticking with the book, reading each chapter as I sent it, and commenting and questioning along the way. I am inspired by each of you—your talents make me strive to be a better writer. You are each held close in my heart, and my gratitude is immense.

Dana Blakemore: You listened without complaint to every strange idea, rolled along with every plot twist, let me obsess about all things 1850s, and still remain my number-one fan. I love you more.

To the readers: You make it all worth it. My gratitude is endless.

BOOK CLUB QUESTIONS

1. There are hints Lucy might not be a reliable narrator. What are some examples in her account of events that are unclear or perhaps twisted?
2. How does Lucy's past complicate her stay with the Burtons?
3. Do you find Eugenie a sympathetic character? Why or why not?
4. What is the state of Eugenie's marriage? How do the Burtons feel about each other?
5. How does class fit in to Lucy's predicament? Eugenie's? Rebecca's?
6. Lucy believes truth is pliable. Which serves her—the truth or the tale? Which hurts her?
7. What motive does Rebecca have for killing Eugenie? What motive does Lucy have?
8. Who killed Mary Dawson? Why does she haunt Lucy?
9. If Lucy ever had a "way out" from her current circumstances, *where* and *what* was it?
10. Is her judgment just?

ABOUT THE AUTHOR

Photo © 2016 Upswept Creative

Kim Taylor Blakemore is the author of the novels *The Companion*, *Bowery Girl*, and *Cissy Funk*. She has been honored with a Tucson Festival of Books Literary Award, a Willa Award for Best YA Fiction, and a Regional Arts & Culture Council grant. She teaches Craft of Fiction and Historical Fiction with PDX Writers in Portland, Oregon. Please visit her at www.kimtaylorblakemore.com.